THREE WEEKS TO SAY GOODBYE

THREE WEEKS TO SAY GOODBYE

C.J. BOX

CORVUS

First published in the United States of America in 2009 by
Minotaur Books, St Martin's Press, 175 Fifth Avenue,
New York, NY 10010

This edition first published in Great Britain in 2009 by
Corvus, an imprint of Grove Atlantic Ltd.

9 8 7 6 5 4 3 2 1

A CIP catalogue record for this book is available from
the British Library.

ISBN: 978-1-84887-291-2 (hardback)
ISBN: 978-1-84887-292-9 (trade paperback)

Printed in Great Britain by the MPG Books Group

Corvus
An imprint of Grove Atlantic Ltd
Ormond House
26-27 Boswell Street
London WC1N 3JZ

www.corvus-books.co.uk

To Marc and Jenny
. . . and Laurie, always

Acknowledgments

The author would like to thank those who provided background, suggestions, careful reading, and inspiration for this novel, including Allison Herron Lee, Ann Rittenberg, Laurie Box, Molly Box, Becky Box, and the wonderful team at St. Martin's Minotaur—Matthew Baldacci, Andrew Martin, Hector Dejean, and, especially, the peerless Jennifer Enderlin.

The bloodthirsty hate the upright,
and they seek the life of the righteous.
An unjust man is an abomination to the just,
and he who is upright
is an abomination to the wicked.

—Proverbs 29:10, 27

Denver

One

IT WAS SATURDAY MORNING, November 3, and the first thing I noticed when I entered my office was that my telephone message light was blinking. Since I'd left the building late the night before, it meant someone had called my extension during the night. Odd.

My name is Jack McGuane. I was thirty-four years old at the time. Melissa, my wife, was the same age. I assume you've heard my name, or seen my image on the news, although with everything going on in the world I can understand if you missed me the first time. Our story, in the big scheme of things, is a drop in the river.

I was a Travel Development Specialist for the Denver Metro Convention and Visitors Bureau, the city agency charged with bidding on and hosting conventions and encouraging tourism to Denver. Every city has one. I worked hard, often staying late and, if necessary, coming in on a Saturday. It's important to me that I work hard, even in a bureaucratic environment where it's not necessarily encouraged or rewarded. You see, I'm not the smartest guy in the world, or the best educated. My background doesn't suit me for the job. But my ace in the hole is that I work harder than anyone around me, even when I don't have to. I am the bane of an office filled with bureaucrats, and I'm proud of it. It's the only thing I've got.

Before doing anything, though, I punched the button to retrieve my voice mail.

"Jack, this is Julie Perala. At the agency . . ."

I stared at the speaker. Her voice was tight, cautious, not the confident and compassionate Julie Perala from the adoption agency Melissa and I had spent hours with while we went through the long process of adopting Angelina, our nine-month-old. My first thought was that we somehow owed them more money.

"Jack, I hate to call you at work on a Friday. I hope you get this and can call me back right away. I need to talk with you immediately—before Sunday, if possible."

She left the agency number and her cell-phone number, and I wrote them down.

Then: "Jack, I'm so sorry."

After a few beats of silence, as if she wanted to say more but wouldn't or couldn't, she hung up.

I sat back in my chair, then listened to the message again and checked the time stamp. It had arrived at 8:45 Friday evening.

I tried the agency number first, not surprised that it went straight to voice mail. Then I called her cell.

"Yes?"

"Julie, this is Jack McGuane."

"Oh."

"You said to call immediately. You've got me scared here with your message. What's going on?"

"You don't know?"

"How would I know? Know what?"

There was anger and panic in her voice.

"Martin Dearborn hasn't called you? He's your attorney, isn't he? Our lawyers were supposed to call him. Oh dear."

My heart sped up, and the receiver became slick in my hand. "Julie, I don't know *anything*. Dearborn never called. Please, what is this about?"

"God, I hate to be the one to tell you."

"Tell me what?"

A beat. "The biological father wants Angelina back."

I made her repeat it in case I hadn't heard correctly. She did.

"So what if he wants her back," I said. "We adopted her. She's our daughter now. Who cares what he wants?"

"You don't understand—it's complicated."

I pictured Melissa and Angelina at home having a lazy Saturday morning. "Of course we'll work this out," I said. "This is all some kind of big misunderstanding. It'll all be fine." Despite my words, my mouth tasted like metal.

Said Julie, "The birth father never signed away parental custody, Jack. The mother did, but the father didn't. It's a terrible situation. Your lawyer should have explained all of this to you. I don't want to be the one going over legalities because I'm not qualified. As I said, it's complicated . . ."

"This cannot be happening," I said.

"I'm so sorry."

"It doesn't make sense," I said. "She's been with us nine months. The birth mother *selected* us."

"I know. I was there."

"Tell me how to make this go away," I said, sitting up in my chair, leaning over the desk. "Do we pay off the kid, or what?"

Julie was silent for a long time.

"Julie, are you there?"

"I'm here."

"Meet me at your agency *now*."

"I can't."

"You can't or you won't?"

"I can't. I shouldn't even be talking with you. I should never have called. The lawyers and my executives said not to make direct contact, but I felt I had to."

"Why didn't you call us at home?"

"I got cold feet," she said. "You don't know how much I wished I could erase that message I left for you."

"I appreciate that," I said, "but you can't walk away. I need to understand what you're saying. You've got to work with me to make this kid go away. You owe us that."

I heard a series of staccato sounds and thought the connection was going bad. Then I realized she was crying.

Finally, she said, "There's a restaurant near here called Sunrise Sunset. On South Wadsworth. I can meet you there in an hour."

"I might be a little late. I've got to run home and get Melissa. She'll want to hear this. And on such short notice, we'll probably have Angelina with us."

"I was hoping . . ." Her voice trailed off.

"Hoping what? That I wouldn't bring them?"

"Yes. It makes it harder . . . I was hoping maybe you and I could meet alone."

I slammed the phone down. Stunned, I wrote down the address of the restaurant.

I SENSED LINDA VAN Gear's arrival before she leaned into my office. She had a presence that preceded her. It could also be called very strong perfume, which she seemed to push ahead in front of her, like a surging trio of small, leashed dogs. Linda was my boss.

She was an imposing, no-nonsense woman, a force of nature. Melissa once referred to Linda as "a caricature of a broad." Linda was brash, made-up, coiffed with a swept-back helmet of stiff hair like the overlapping armored plates of a prehistoric dinosaur. She looked like she wore suits with shoulder pads, but they were her shoulders. Her lips were red, red, red, and there was usually a lipstick line across the front of her teeth, which she moistened often with darts from a pointed tongue. Linda, like a lot of the people who worked international tourism marketing, had once had dreams of being an actress or at least some kind of indefinable celebrity, someone who judged amateurs on a reality singing show. Linda was not well liked by the women in our office or by many in the tourism industry, but I got along with her. I got a kick out of her because everything about her was out front in spades.

"Hello, darlin'," she said, sticking her head in the doorway, "I see you found the leads."

I hadn't even noticed them, but they were there: a bulging manila envelope filled with business cards that smelled of her perfume, cigarette smoke, and spilled wine.

"They're right here."

"Couple of hot ones in there," she said with mock enthusiasm. "They'll singe your fingers when you touch them. Let's meet on them in a half an hour." She squinted, looking me over, asked, "Are you okay?"

"No I'm not."

I didn't really want to get into details, but felt I needed to explain the situation to her in order to postpone the meeting.

She listened with glistening eyes. She loved this kind of thing, I realized. She loved *drama,* and I was providing it.

"Some boy wants custody of your baby?" she asked.

"Yes, but I'm going to fight it."

"The baby obsession skipped this broad," she said. "I guess I never really understood it." She shook her head. She had no children and had made it clear she never wanted any.

I nodded like I understood. Fragile ground, here.

She said, "Look, you know I'm leaving for Taiwan with the governor Monday. We've got to get together before then. Hell, I dragged my jet-lagged ass out of bed just to meet you here this morning. We *need* to meet."

"We will," I said. "Let me call you as soon as I talk to Julie Perala. That's all I ask."

"That's a lot," she said, clearly angry.

"I'll call," I said. "I'll even come meet you at your house if you want."

"Plan on it," she said, turning on her heel and clicking down the hallway, her shoes sounding like manic sticks on the rim of a drum in the empty hallway.

MELISSA WAS ON THE FLOOR with Angelina when I came in the door. Before I could speak, Melissa said, "What's wrong?"

"Julie Perala called. She says there's a problem with the adoption."

Melissa went white, and she looked from me to Angelina and back.

"She said the father wants her back."

"Back?" Melissa said, her voice rising in volume, "Back? *He's never even seen her!*"

I met Melissa when we were both students at Montana State University thirteen years before. She was a lean jade-eyed brunette—attractive, smart, athletic, earthy, self-confident—with high cheekbones and a full, expressive mouth that tended to betray whatever she was thinking. She *sparkled*. I was drawn to her immediately in a crazy, almost chemical way. I could sense when she entered a crowded room even before I could see her. She was taken at the time, though, involved in a long-term relationship with the star running back. They were a remarkably handsome couple, and I despised him for no reason other than she was his. Still, I pined for her. The thought of her kept me awake at night. When their breakup became news, I told my friend Cody, "I'm going to marry her." He said, "In your dreams," and I said, "Yes, in my dreams." He said, "You've got it bad," and urged me to forget about her and go out and get drunk and get laid. Instead, I asked her out and became Mr. Rebound. She thought I was solid and amusing. I found, to my delight, that I could make her laugh. All I ever wanted to do, all I still want to do all these years later, is make her happy. After we'd been married three years, she said she wanted children. That was the next step, the next easy, logical step. Or so we thought.

The look on her face now crushed me and angered me and made me want to pound someone.

I walked over and picked up Angelina, who squealed. Until this little girl entered our lives, I didn't know how much I could care. She was beautiful—dark-haired, cherubic. Her eyes were big and *wide open*—as if she were always in a state of delighted surprise. Hair that stuck straight up in spots when she woke up from a nap. Four pearly teeth, two top, two bottom. She had a wonderful laugh that started deep in her belly, then took over her entire body. Her laugh was infectious, and we'd start laughing, too, which made her laugh even harder, until she was limp. She laughed so hard we actually asked our pediatrician if there was a problem, and he just shook his head at us. Recently, she'd learned to say "Da" and "Ma." The way she looked at me, like I was the greatest and strongest creature on the planet, made me want to save and protect her from anything and anybody. She was my little girl, and like Melissa, she made me think differently about my place on earth. In her eyes, I was a god who as yet could do no wrong. I was a giant—her giant. I wanted to never disappoint her. And as the bearer of this news, I felt I had.

I THOUGHT I'D MISUNDERSTOOD the address or name of the meeting place as we entered because I couldn't locate Julie Perala at any of the tables or booths. I was lifting the cell to call her when I saw her wave from a private room in the back used for meetings and parties. I pocketed the phone.

Julie Perala was broad-faced and broad-hipped, with soft eyes and a comforting professional smile. There was something both compassionate and pragmatic about her, and we had liked her instantly when we met with her so many months before for our orientation. She seemed especially sensitive to our situation without being cloying, and was by far more knowledgeable about "placements" than anyone else we had met at other agencies. Nothing made her happier to be alive, she told us, than a placement where all three parties were perfectly served—the birth mother, the adoptive parents, and the child. She was to be trusted, and we trusted her. I also noticed, at times when she let her guard down, a ribald sense of humor. I had the feeling she'd be a hoot with a few drinks in her.

"Coffee?" she asked. "I've already had breakfast."

"No thanks," I said, pausing.

Melissa held Angelina tight to her and glared at Julie Perala with eyes I hoped would never be aimed at me.

"I know the manager," she said, answering a question I was about to ask, "and knew I could get this room in the back. Please close the door."

I did, and sat down as she was pouring coffee from a thermos carafe.

"I'm taking a real chance meeting with you," she said, not meeting my eyes, concentrating on pouring. "The agency would kill me if they knew. We've all been advised to communicate only through the lawyers now."

"But," I said, prompting her.

"But I like you and Melissa very much. You're good, normal people. I know you love Angelina. I felt I owed you a frank discussion."

"I appreciate that."

Melissa continued to glare.

Julie said, "If this comes back to bite me, well, I'll be very disappointed. But I hoped we could talk without lawyers around, at least this once."

"Go ahead," I said.

It took her a moment to form her words. "I can't tell you how bad I feel about this situation," she said. "This should never happen to a nice couple like you."

"I agree."

"We shouldn't have kept it a secret from you that Judge John Moreland contacted us three months ago," she said. "Our hope was we could settle it internally, and we offered to do exactly that. Our hope was you would never be troubled about it at all, that you wouldn't even know."

"Who is Judge Moreland?" I asked. "The biological father?"

"No, no. The biological father is his son, Garrett. Garrett is a senior at Cherry Creek High School. He's eighteen years old."

"Unbelievable," I said.

She shrugged and showed her palms to me. "I agree. But if we'd been able to resolve it internally, we wouldn't be here now. There wouldn't be a problem at all."

I said, "*Ninety-nine percent*. Remember when you used that figure when I asked about the birth father signing away his parental rights?"

Her face clouded. "I remember. And it's true. It really is. I've been involved in nearly a thousand placements in my life, and this is the first time this has ever happened. We just didn't think it could."

"Didn't you say you tried to find the birth father?" Melissa asked bitterly. "Didn't you say he'd agreed to sign the papers?"

She nodded.

"What happened?"

"We tracked him down in the Netherlands, where he was on vacation with his mother. He was staying with his mother's relatives, I guess. I didn't talk with him, but a coworker did. She explained the situation to him, and she said he was surprised. He agreed to sign away custody and he gave us a fax number where he could be reached. We sent the papers over."

"But he never signed them," I said.

"We dropped the ball," she said. "The woman who'd made contact left the agency. If any of us had had any inkling at all that he would refuse to sign, we would have kept you abreast of the situation. But as far as we knew, it was his wish not to be a parent. We can't coerce him, you know. We can't pressure. It has to be his decision."

My anger was building to the point that I had to look away from her.

"Legally, we covered our bases," she said sympathetically, almost apologetically to us. "We placed public notices for him and did everything we're required to do. Not having the signed papers isn't that unusual, because the family court judge always—and I mean always—awards full custody to the adoptive parents in a case like this. After all, we can't let a nonresponsive birth father hold up a placement, can we?"

"Did you contact Garrett's father?" I asked. "Is that how he got involved?"

"We normally don't contact the parents of the birth father. That's considered coercive."

"But you knew about him? You knew about John Moreland?"

"No."

"Interesting that his mother didn't know, since she was with him overseas when your agency contacted him. How could she *not* know?"

Julie shrugged. "It doesn't make sense to me, but a lot about this situation makes no sense. Maybe she knew but didn't want to tell her husband. Why—I don't know."

I said, "So this Judge Moreland entered the picture after Garrett told him?"

"As far as I know, yes."

"And that's when Moreland's lawyers contacted the agency?"

She looked down. "Yes. The letter came from them with less than ten days left in the public notice period. If they'd waited just two more weeks, custody would have been granted to you by the family court. It was bad timing for you."

"It sure was," I said sarcastically.

"If you and Melissa choose not to fight the Moreland claim, our agency will do everything in our power to make the situation right for you."

"Meaning what?" Melissa asked.

She took a quick breath and raised her eyes to meet Melissa's. "I've been a party to the meetings we've had with our executives and our lawyers. I know we would immediately refund all fees and arrange, free of charge, for a new placement. You would be moved to the top of the priority list for a new baby. And we'd offer a very large settlement to you and Melissa and our apologies. That's if we can keep this whole thing out of court and out of the news. I think you'd agree with me that the last thing anyone would want to do is discourage children's chances of future placements with loving families who might be scared out of adoption by this situa-tion."

"This can't be happening," Melissa said, as much to herself as to Julie Perala.

"Why didn't your lawyers contact our lawyer about these meet-ings?" I said. "Isn't that how it's supposed to work?"

"I thought they had," she said.

"We've heard nothing."

She shrugged. "I'm not a lawyer."

"Neither is ours, apparently," I said, spitting it out.

"You don't understand," Melissa said. "We can't lose our baby."

Julie started to speak, then bit her lip and looked away.

"We can't lose our baby," Melissa said again, but this time her voice was close to a shout.

"Judge Moreland is a powerful man," Julie said softly. "I get the impression he's used to getting what he wants."

"Tell me about him," I asked. "Tell me what kind of man I'm up against."

"He's a wealthy man," she said. "His wife has the fortune, from what I understand. Judges aren't paid that much, I guess. He owns lots of real estate. I'm telling you this because you mentioned something about buying off Garrett. I hate to say it, but I don't think you could. And the judge comes across as such a nice man. He's handsome, confident. He's the kind of man you instantly like, and you hope he likes you because you don't want to displease him, you know?"

I said, "Julie, when I think of you all having these meetings and talking about us it makes me ill."

She nodded, then looked away again. "We discussed what his options were. He was very concerned about doing things the right way so as not to hurt you and Melissa."

"How kind," Melissa said.

"Tell me, Julie," I said, "how do you live with yourself?"

She put her face in her hands and cried. I couldn't help it—I felt terrible for making her cry again. But I didn't take my words back.

Finally, she grabbed a napkin and wiped the tears from her eyes, smearing eyeliner down her cheek, making it look like a faded scar.

Melissa stood up with Angelina. "I've got to change her diaper," she said, and left the room. "We'll be back."

For a moment we just sat there not looking at each other.

"There's one thing you can help us with," I said.

"What?"

"If you were Melissa and me, would you fight this in court? Knowing what you know, do we have a prayer?"

She shook her head sadly, said, "The best you could hope for, I think, is some kind of joint custody that a judge would decree. But I don't think either of you would be happy with that. And if I were you, I'd pray to God your baby is raised by John and Kellie—that Garrett is kept as far away from the baby as possible."

I felt my skin crawl. "Why do you say that?"

She shook her head. "There's something wrong with that boy. He scares me. And it isn't anything I can quite put my finger on—there's just something wrong about him."

"Oh God," I said.

She pursed her lips and looked down at her hands. "It's like the temperature in the room goes down ten degrees when he enters. There's no warmth. He seems bloodless and cunning. I wouldn't trust him with a child—or anyone."

I felt myself tingling. I leaned forward, "I understand what you're saying, but do you have anything I can use? Have you heard anything about Garrett we can investigate to prove what a bad father he'd be?"

She was still, her hands mindlessly caressing her coffee mug on both sides. Thinking.

She said, "I think there's been some trouble at school," she said. "Once, when we were meeting with John, he got a call from someone at Garrett's high school, and he had to cut the meeting short. I don't know who called or what it was about, but the judge was quite upset."

"This happened within the last month?" I asked, trying not to show my anger that the Morelands and the agency had been meeting behind our backs in secret.

"Yes."

"Anything else?"

"One thing, but it's no more solid than the first. When we were looking over your placement application with them . . ."

I took in an angry breath, but she continued.

". . . the judge pointed out you owned a dog."

"Harry."

"The judge said they couldn't have pets because Garrett couldn't get along with them. I thought that was an odd choice of words. Not that he was allergic to them, or wouldn't take care of them or something, but that *he couldn't get along with them*. When he said it, I could see he wished he hadn't."

"Is that all?" I asked.

"Yes," she said. "And it all sounds so baseless when I say it."

"Thank you," I said. "At least it gives me something to go on. But it also makes me feel a little sick."

"Yes," she said, then she lifted her chin and looked at me. "I think the only answer is somehow to convince Garrett to sign the papers giving up his parental rights," she said.

She took a deep breath to compose herself, mumbling that she hated to cry in front of others.

"Maybe he needs some *strong* persuading," she said, letting an angry edge into her voice.

"Meaning?"

"Meaning," she said, leaning across the table, her eyes flashing, "if Angelina were my daughter, I'd hire a couple of mean-ass bikers or wranglers and have them scare the living shit out of Garrett so he's only more than happy to sign anything put in front of him. He needs the kind of persuading that makes him think his father's determination is the least of his concerns."

I sat back. *That* had come from left field, but obviously it was something she'd been thinking about.

"I'm speaking hypothetically, of course," she said. "Not as a representative of the agency or a placement professional."

"Of course," I said. "Could he be scared?"

She thought for a moment before whispering, "I think so."

ON THE WAY HOME, I said to Melissa, "You're taking this much more calmly than I thought possible."

"I'm not calm at all," she said. "I'm dead inside. But this does explain why we have a phone message from Judge Moreland. He says he's coming over tomorrow afternoon with his son."

"Jesus," I said.

"What should we do?"

"I'm going to go see Martin Dearborn," I said. "I'm going to his house. Don't call the judge back. In fact, keep the phone off the hook. I'll call you on your cell, so keep it with you. The judge may put off coming to our house if he isn't sure we got the message, and we don't respond."

She laughed—a chilling, uncharacteristic laugh I'd never heard before and never wanted to hear again. It was a false laugh filled with horror and defeat. She said, "You know how they say your life passes before your eyes before you die?"

"Yes."

"That's happening now."

MARTIN DEARBORN, OUR ATTORNEY for the adoption, was in his driveway wearing a gold-and-black Colorado Buffaloes sweater and loading seat cushions and blankets into the back of his Mercedes M-Class SUV when I drove up in my ten-year-old Jeep Cherokee. I remembered the CU alumni awards on the wall of his office and noted the CU license-plate frame. Dearborn was plump and sandy-haired and wore thick glasses that made his light brown eyes look bigger than they were. He had a large head and a deep bass voice and ham-sized hands. He squinted when I jammed my Jeep into park because he obviously didn't recognize the vehicle or the driver—at first.

When I jumped out, I saw something pass over his face that told me he knew why I was there but didn't want to admit it.

His wife, a too-thin woman with a pinched face, also decked out in Buffs colors, came out of the garage, saw me approaching, and said, "Who is *that?*"

Martin gestured for her to go back inside. He tried hard to blank his eyes and face as I came up the driveway, but he wasn't successful.

His wife theatrically looked at her wristwatch, and he said, "I know. We'll make it in time for kickoff."

She said, "It isn't kickoff I'm worried about. It's the preparty."

He said, "We'll make it, don't worry."

She stomped back into the garage.

"Jack," he said, "this can wait until office hours on Monday. My wife and I are . . ."

"You son of a bitch, how long were you going to wait to tell us?"

"Monday. During regular office hours. That's when we *work,* Jack."

"Monday's too late, and you know it."

"Look," he said, lowering his voice into his official lawyer tone, the one he used to impress Melissa and me, "I've been in the Springs on a big civil case. I wasn't able to return the calls to them during the day because we were in court."

I stepped close enough to him that he flinched. "You didn't have breaks? You don't have paralegals who could make the call on your behalf?"

He looked away.

"Damn, you look guilty," I said. "You've got to get us out of this, and I mean now. This guy and his son are coming to our house tomorrow."

His voice wasn't as low when he spoke. "I'd advise you to be civil. He's got the law on his side, I'm afraid."

I reached out and grabbed a handful of CU sweatshirt, then quickly let it go. I couldn't help myself. From the garage I heard Dearborn's wife say, "Honey, do I need to call the police?"

"No," he said. "It's okay."

I said, "So you know all about it, then. I'd advise *you* to pretend you're an attorney—our attorney. We need to go to court right now and do something. Isn't there a restraining order or something? Can't we prevent this from happening?"

"I'd have to research it," he said, uncomfortable.

18

"We don't have the time."

He turned to me, his face flushed. "Jack, he's a sitting federal judge. He's been appointed by the president and confirmed by the Senate. Don't you think he knows the law? Hell, he makes it."

"So that's it, then," I said.

"Our firm has cases scheduled before him next month, Jack. Big cases. Million-dollar cases with national implications. I've got a real conflict here."

I shook my head. I wanted to smash him. His wife was still in the garage, and I noticed she had a telephone, ready to call the police. She pointed to it with her other hand, and mouthed "9-1-1."

"Is he aware I'm your counsel?" Dearborn asked.

"No," I said, "because you haven't done a damned thing. How would he know?"

"You need to calm down," he said. "And I'm afraid you need to get a new attorney. I'm not your man for this case. He's best friends with the mayor and the governor, for Christ's sake. And his name has come up for the Tenth Circuit and higher."

"So what are you saying?"

"That he not only knows the law, he knows how to work the law. This is inside baseball, Jack. You never told me you were going up against Judge Moreland."

"I didn't know."

"I think you should calm down and look at this from his point of view."

"I think you're fired," I said, even though he'd resigned.

"Good."

"Nine-one-one," his wife said, holding up the phone like a totem.

I DROVE TO LINDA Van Gear's town house in an angry fog. I found her wearing sweats with her hair down, shuttling between a fish tank in the living room to the toilet in the bathroom carrying dead fish one at a time. Her town house was a shambles.

"This is what happens when you travel for a living and you ask your neighbor to feed your fish and he forgets and goes skiing '*because the powder was awesome, dude,*'" she said angrily. "You come back to a tank full of dead objects."

I told her my situation had grown much worse since I'd seen her last, and I needed to cancel my scheduled trip to World Tourism Bourse in Berlin in a week.

That stopped her cold, and she stood there with a pale and dripping angel fish in a little net.

"So you want to send someone else to WTB, then?"

"Yes."

"Whom do you suggest?"

Our department consisted of the two of us. I suggested Rita Greene-Bellardo, a new employee who served as executive assistant but seemed to have little to do.

"Pregnant," Linda said. "I just heard. She's gonna have her baby and take the maternity leave and quit. I heard her telling a girlfriend that was her plan. We can't depend on her to follow up."

I floated the name of Pete Maxfield, who headed the media-relations department. Pete sometimes worked with international journalists and might have some experience he could use at the show. Linda didn't like Pete, though.

"Honey," she said, "Pete is a hound dog. He'd spend the whole time drinking German beer and trying to get some deaf, dumb, and blind German girl to come to his room at the hotel, or he'd blow the entertainment budget on prostitutes. This is our biggest and most important market. We don't just send people for the sake of sending someone. The only choice we have is me, and you know it."

I did, but I didn't want to ask.

"I'll be in Taiwan," she said. "I can't be both places."

I knew where this was headed.

"You *need* to have that big meeting with Malcolm Harris," she said.

Malcolm Harris was the iconic UK owner of a travel company called AmeriCan Adventures—a play on America and Canada—which sent thousands of British tourists to North America on custom-designed package tours. AmeriCan was the number one tour operator to Denver and the Mountain West, and thus a very important client. Our marching orders were to treat him like a god, despite his reputation as being quarrelsome, cantankerous, and smug about his claims that he knew more about America than practically any American he'd ever met. He expected to be fawned over, wined and dined, and he was. Any requests he made were immediately first priority in our office and across destination promotion bureaus throughout the region. Linda was infamous for attaching herself to him like Velcro when she worked the European market, hanging on his every word, laughing at his asides, and beholding him with what was described by one of her detractors as "Nancy Reagan eyes."

She said, "As you know, he's thinking of establishing a U.S. reservations office and call center to handle his tours," she said. "We're talking hundreds of jobs. He's looking at three cities—New York, L.A., and Denver. We're the front-runner because of our location. If we got that office here, the mayor would love us because he could say our tourism efforts not only bring in tourists but jobs. I'm sure he's meeting with reps from L.A. and New York. If you just *don't show up* in Berlin to convince him to choose Denver, we may lose out on this."

There was an uncomfortable pause. I said, "Does the mayor know about this, then?"

"It was in my report to him last month. His chief of staff sent me an e-mail about it last week, asking if we'd landed AmeriCan yet."

I let her go on.

"Honey," she said finally, "do you realize that every time the city gets a budget hit, and they're looking for places to cut, someone always suggests international tourism promotion? We're the easy ones to dump because they think we have these glamorous jobs and jet all around the world. We're easy to dump, you know? Tab Jones has no love for us, but he sees us as a means for him to travel the world, so he's not given the department the ax. But every time there's a budget crunch, I go to the mat and fight for us. I show them facts and figures, and this time when we were on the chopping block I told them about the possibility AmeriCan might open up a company here. Tab and the mayor got all excited about that because tourists are ghosts, but a building and jobs are something he can take credit for. Are you hearing me?"

"Yes," I said.

"If you don't go, honey, we can kiss this department and your job goodbye. And I *need* this job."

"I do, too."

I wasn't kidding. Since Melissa had quit her job to stay home with our daughter, we were literally one paycheck away from not making our mortgage payment. The loan we had was one of those bad ones, one of the worst decisions we'd made. We had *no* cushion. If I lost my job, Jesus, I didn't know where we'd be. Especially given the situation we were in, possibly trying to prove in court what great parents we were. My job was *everything*.

She stepped back, sized me up, said, "So you understand me, then?"

"Yes," I said. "I'll be going to Germany and meeting with Malcolm Harris."

"Good man, Jack," she said. "I knew you'd come around. Let's get going on those leads now."

As I gathered up the work and stuffed it into my briefcase, Linda said, "Aren't there other babies out there?"

"Not an option," I said back with heat. "It's not like trading her in for a new model," thinking: *How can she not understand?*

She waved dismissively, "Well, good luck with the baby thing."

22

————

THE BABY THING.

We had tried everything to get pregnant. Melissa studied up on the medical literature, threw herself into reproductive studies with a single-minded will as only she can do, reading everything from the library, on the Internet, becoming as well versed in the subject as any doctor and better than most. Having sex became my second job. Melissa drew pink hearts on our wall calendar to chart our couplings. There were a lot of hearts. We had sex every morning for three weeks straight and every other evening in one magnificent stretch run. Once, when we were able to have lunch together downtown, she showed up with bare legs in a dress and told me over sandwiches that she wasn't wearing underwear and that she'd rented a dayroom in a hotel next door. I could barely eat. I was equally aroused and alarmed, pointing out to her (tepidly, I admit) that with my job at the CVB it was possible someone might recognize me and assume the tryst was something it was not. She laughed and shook it off, then led me outside by the hand. In the elevator on the way to our floor, she started disrobing. I got hard, and she squeezed me through my pants. She said, "So you're getting into it, then?"

But it was never about me not getting into it. I was. And I was, and am, wildly attracted to my wife. She's my *ideal*. That she seemed to think—deep down—that she no longer did it for me and for some reason that was why we couldn't conceive was as startling as it was desperate. I told her repeatedly she drove me wild. She said, "Then why can't we have a baby, Jack?"

THE DOCTOR'S NAME WAS KIMMEL. He was thin, athletic, and fastidious in appearance. When we finally sat down with him at the clinic to review the tests, he confirmed what she had already determined: It was me.

23

"Let me put it this way," the doctor said, turning slightly on his stool in my direction but not really facing me. "Imagine, if you will, that you are a machine gunner but not a good one. In fact, a lousy one. The worst one in the entire Corps."

Kimmel paused to let that sink in.

"So I'm shooting blanks," I said. "Thank you, Mr. Bedside Manner."

He nodded, first to me, then to Melissa.

I felt Melissa's eyes brush across the side of my face.

"There are alternatives, of course," Kimmel said. "In this day and age, there really isn't male infertility anymore. We can isolate a single sperm." He explained procedures, drugs, in vitro fertilization.

We were hopeful. We tried them all, one after the other. For years. Melissa had three miscarriages. Our marriage became tense and our time together frustrating. There were long, silent meals and times we would be in the same room for hours and not look at each other. She secretly blamed me, I secretly blamed her. Her emotions were raw and increasingly close to the surface. Sometimes I caught her looking at me as if she was assessing my manhood and character, and I'd lash back with something sarcastic and cruel that I immediately regretted. I suggested once that maybe if we didn't try so hard, maybe if we didn't make our entire life's mission to conceive a child, we could be happy again. She didn't speak to me for weeks after that. I thought she might even leave me.

Finally, she said, "Let's adopt."

We really didn't discuss it. I trusted her judgment, and adoption is a good thing. And I had my wife back, and the clouds that had been building for years in our lives broke up and sunlight poured through.

Julie Perala at the agency explained to us that there were three kinds of adoption: international, closed, and open. We chose open. But there were levels of openness as well, from meeting the birth mother (our preference) to agreeing on visitation with the birth mother and her family.

The birth mother was a fifteen-year-old named Brittany. She was pale, freckled, and slightly overweight even before the pregnancy. Every other word from her was "like," as in, "I'm, like, gaining weight," or "It's, like, a *drag* to get morning sickness." The reasons she gave the agency for choosing us included the fact that we were fairly young, childless, and we looked "calm" and "outdoorsy." We overlooked Brittany's arrogance at times. She knew she had what Melissa wanted. Brittany was fertile, and she assumed Melissa wasn't, so she took on a superior air. Once, though, when Melissa left the room, I leaned toward Brittany and said, "It isn't her. It's *me*."

Even though, frankly, with our unexplained infertility it was most likely both of us somehow. But I didn't tell Brittany that.

Terms regarding adoption are something we're both sensitive about now, especially Melissa. Often, the wrong thing is said in all innocence, but it can cut deeply. For example, Brittany is the birth mother, not the "real" mother or the "natural" mother or the "biological" mother. Melissa is Angelina's mother. Period. Brittany didn't "give her baby up for adoption," she placed the baby with adoptive parents. People have a natural instinct to pry. I try not to hold that against them when they ask, "Where did she get those dark eyes?" (since mine are blue and Melissa's are green) or "Her hair is so thick and dark!" when mine is reddish brown and Melissa's is light brown. We'd learned to answer, vaguely, "It runs in the family." We weren't lying. We just weren't saying *whose* family.

In retrospect, we could have asked more questions about the birth father. But we were assured by the agency and from Melissa's discussions with Brittany that the boy was no longer in the picture. Brittany wouldn't even say his name other than to call him "Sperm Boy" and say he refused to take her calls. She never mentioned that he was out of the country, which led us to believe she hadn't known where he was. He meant nothing to her, she told Melissa. She'd been drunk and in the backseat of Sperm Boy's nice car. One thing led to another.

Angelina turned six, seven, and eight months old. She was healthy, cheerful, loving. She began to form the words "Ma" and "Da." She loved Harry, our old black Lab and my last carryover from bachelorhood, who began to sleep under her crib to protect her. Everything was right with the world.

Then it wasn't.

THERE IS AN ABSOLUTE irredeemable beauty to pure routine, for if there wasn't, I'm not sure we could have gotten through that evening when I finally got home.

We ate, I'm sure.

We might have watched television.

I do remember halfheartedly playing with Angelina on the floor. She loved her Fisher-Price barn set. Angelina got all of the other animals as well as the farmer and his wife, and I was the cow and the cow only. Angelina's menagerie spent all of their time telling the cow what to do. The cow spent all of his (her?) time trying to make Angelina laugh. But my heart wasn't in it.

I also remember a disjointed, fierce "They'll never take her away" discussion Melissa and I had. We were in the midst of it when Melissa walked over to the telephone in the kitchen and hung it up on the receiver to check and see if there were any more messages. I watched her eyes widen and her mouth purse, and she pressed the speaker button.

The voice was male, mature, and sympathetic:

"Jack and Melissa, I hate to place this call. This is Judge John Moreland. I know you're aware of why I'm calling and believe me, this is just about as difficult for me as it is for you. No one ever in his or her life expects to be in a situation like this. For that I am deeply, *deeply* sorry. But I hope you appreciate the situation my family has found ourselves in as well. Angelina is our first granddaughter, and my son's child. I assume you are checking messages, even though you aren't picking up the phone. We will be at your house tomorrow at 11:00 A.M. Don't worry—we're coming simply to meet you and to talk. There's no reason to panic or overreact. It'll be a conversation among adults who find themselves in a bitterly tough situation through no fault of their own."

Melissa and I exchanged glances. I could see relief flood into her face, and her shoulders relaxed.

Then he said: "The county sheriff is aware of my visit tomorrow. I'm sorry I had to contact him, but I thought it best for all concerned—especially the baby—that our meeting be under the auspices of the authorities. Don't worry—he won't be with us. But he'll be available if the situation turns sour. Not that I expect it to. I admire and respect you both. And I think a reasonable solution to our dilemma is at hand. I hope you'll hear me out, and I hope you will welcome our visit.

"God bless and good night, and we'll see you tomorrow."
Click.

THAT NIGHT, as we lay in bed not sleeping, I slid out of the bed and padded over to the closet. On the top shelf of our closet, hidden by a ball of loose old clothing, was my grandfather's single-action Colt .45 Peacemaker revolver. The Gun that Won the West. I wish I could say he gave it to me in some kind of intergenerational ceremony loaded with symbolism and meaning, but the fact is I stole it while I helped my father move Grandpa from his house in White Sulfur Springs to a nursing home in Billings. He never knew it was missing and never asked about it at the time. Later, as he slipped deeper into dementia, the nurses said he called out for his weapon, but they had no intention of locating it for him.

The revolver was blunt and heavy, with a six-inch barrel. It was loaded with five ancient cartridges. The firing pin rested on an empty cylinder to prevent accidents. The handgrip was made of ash, polished smooth by years of handling. The cylinder was rubbed clean of blueing from being drawn and put back into a leather holster hundreds of times.

"What are you doing?" Melissa asked.

"Nothing," I said.

Two

On Sunday, Melissa looked both beautiful and scared. She had a smattering of freckles across her nose and cheeks I'd always found girl-like and attractive. Her hair was shoulder length and the cut sophisticated. She'd spent hours wondering what to wear, trying on outfit after outfit to find a combination that would give her confidence and strength. She'd agonized over whether to wear panty hose but decided against it. She'd chosen a simple white sleeveless top, a sweater, and beige skirt. Her legs looked long, firm, and tan. She wanted to look nice, but not too nice. Not so nice that the birth father would hold it against her, she said.

I wore jeans, a dress shirt that showed some wear, and a navy blazer. Nice but not too nice. Melissa had asked me to change from my old cowboy boots to loafers, saying she didn't want them to think me a redneck. When it comes to such matters, I learned long ago to defer. I think that deferring is one of the secrets to a happy marriage.

Angelina was in a white ruffled dress with red polka dots. She looked like a doll—jet-black hair, creamy skin, chubby cheeks, and those startling dark eyes. I loved it that our new baby loved me, and looked at me without a hint of what was going on around her, about her.

"Those bastards," I said, "putting us through this." My voice was harsh, and Angelina balled her fists and took a breath, ready to cry.

"No, it's okay, honey," I cooed. "It's okay." But it wasn't. Nevertheless, she relaxed. She believed me as I lied to her, which broke my heart. Melissa took her upstairs for her morning nap. I hoped that when she awoke our lives would be normal again, that she'd never have to learn about what almost happened.

OUTSIDE OUR HOME, a blue late-model Cadillac SUV slowed to a crawl on the street and swung into our driveway. I could see two people inside.

Garrett Moreland, son of the judge and supposed birth father of Angelina, got out first and looked at our house with an expression I can only describe as amused disdain.

GARRETT MORELAND WAS DARK, tall, chiseled, with raven-dark hair and striking eyes like brown glass marbles balanced on a whalebone shelf. Seeing Angelina's eyes mounted in this man-boy's face made my heart clench, and I could taste a spurt of something rotten in my mouth. Garrett had an abnormally long neck and prominent Adam's apple that bobbed up and down as his jaw muscles worked like taut cords while he surveyed the front of our home. His skin was pale white, his mouth a thin-lipped red cut that looked like a razor slash a second before it oozed blood. He was dressed like an eighteen-year-old forced to go to church—chinos, loafers, an open-collar button-down shirt and a slightly too-big blazer that

30

was probably his father's. As he stood there he bent slightly forward, rocking on the balls of his feet, with his hands held at his sides and the crown of his head bent so he was looking at the house from under his eyebrows and I thought, *He looks demonic.*

John Moreland was tall as well, and movie-star handsome. In his mid-to-late forties, he had a pleasant boyish face and longish brown hair combed in a long comma over his forehead. He looked like a hip Presbyterian minister, a man who was used to being noticed, a man supremely comfortable in his own skin; he was the deacon, the Rotary president, the former Peace Corps volunteer still remembered and worshipped back in the third-world village. His tan suit draped nicely, and he wore a cream-colored dress shirt. He was lightly tanned and had a mole on his cheek where a model would pencil a beauty mark. There was confidence in his attitude and walk, and a significant exchange of . . . *something* . . . as Moreland and Garrett Moreland glanced at each other before knocking on our door.

I heard Melissa come down the stairs.

"It's them," she said. "I saw them from upstairs."

I nodded.

"They're good-looking men," she said. "I can see why she went out with Garrett."

I looked at her, tried to remember the last time she'd made a comment like that.

"My heart sank when I saw them get out," she muttered under her breath. "I so wanted to hate them on sight."

"You don't?"

She shook her head quickly while she patted down her clothes and put on her game face. "I hate why they're here," she said. She took my face in her hands. "Remember what we talked about. Stay cool—control your temper. The last thing we want to do right now is to anger them—especially Garrett. We need him to sign the papers. Don't give him a reason to withhold his signature one second longer than necessary."

"Got it," I said.

"Are you sure?"

"I'm sure."

John Moreland smiled broadly when we opened the door. He had a disarming, sloppy smile, but he seemed nervous behind it. He carried a bulging white paper sack in one hand that he seemed to have forgotten he had. It hadn't occurred to me they would be nervous, too. The fact made me feel better.

We stepped aside and asked them to come in. Boy, we were gracious. Melissa asked if they wanted coffee. Moreland said he would like a cup. Garrett shook his head sullenly. I couldn't read him at first. He wouldn't meet my eyes, and his movements and attitude seemed designed to put distance between him and everyone else in the room.

"Please sit down," I said, gesturing toward the couch with the coffee table in front of it. I had moved two of our big chairs to the other side for Melissa and me. The chairs were slightly taller than the couch, and I wanted a scenario where Moreland and Garrett would need to sit closely together and look up at us. I'd learned this from business meetings. It gave us a psychological advantage.

Unfortunately, Moreland didn't bite on my seating arrangement, and acted as if he hadn't seen me point to the couch. He sat in one of the chairs. Garrett shambled over to the couch and sat down heavily with undisguised contempt for his father. Or me. Or something.

Melissa saw the situation the minute she came back from the kitchen. She could either sit in the chair in the dominant position or settle in next to Garrett. Her hesitation was obvious, and I filled it by taking the couch. She had cups on a tray I'd never seen before, which slightly annoyed me. Moreland took his coffee.

"I brought this for you, a little gift," he said, handing the bag to me. I looked inside and saw sticky pastries of some kind. I handed the bag to Melissa, and she looked inside, said "Thank you" to Moreland, and went back into the kitchen to put them on a plate, which she brought back out.

I broke the awkward silence by turning to Garrett, saying, "It's nice to meet you. You're a senior this year, right?" Showing I knew a little about him.

Garrett said, "Yeah, a senior," with a slight curl of his lip.

In social situations, Melissa always led the way. I turned to her and saw that despite the smile, her face had drained of blood. She was terrified to speak, to get to the matter at hand. I did my best to carry on, to maintain the slight edge I thought I'd gained by addressing Garrett.

There was some small talk about the weather (cooling), the traffic on the way to our subdivision (light since it was the weekend). Moreland had a deep sonorous voice with a homey Southern accent. I tried to place it and guessed either Tennessee or North Carolina. He had a way of looking directly at us when he talked that had the effect of putting me at ease. Garrett said nothing. Melissa either.

"The roads should be fine until the game tonight," I said. "Then it'll be bumper-to-bumper on I-25 for a while."

Moreland smiled knowingly and nodded. "We've got season tickets. I haven't missed the Broncos playing the Raiders in fifteen years. As far as I'm concerned, the Broncos can't beat them by enough." He looked at me empathetically, "Tell me you're not a Raiders fan and I've just insulted you."

"I'm not a Raiders fan," I said, wishing for a moment I was.

"Well," Moreland said, smiling, "we've certainly got that in common. I've learned since I came out here to go to school at CU in Boulder how special the Broncos are to those of us who live here. The Broncos are our touchstone, our way of establishing a common bond and interest. Even people who don't like football follow the Broncos, since a win means everyone will be in a fine mood to start the week and a loss means snarling drivers and grumpy service in the stores."

With that, control of the situation ebbed away from me and flowed to John Moreland.

I tried to take my cues from Melissa, but she wasn't helping me. Instead, she observed both Moreland and Garrett closely. Mostly Garrett. No doubt she was seeing similarities in his features to Angelina, or perhaps she was trying to imagine him as father material. I noticed Garrett stealing looks at her as well when he thought she wasn't paying attention. Long, predatory looks that took her in from her feet in sandals, up her bare legs, quickly over her hands in her lap to her breasts under the sleeveless white top and sweater. I tried hard not to let it bother me.

"I think we should get to it," I said, probably too abruptly. *Enough with the small talk. Enough with the staring at my wife.*

"Yes," Moreland said, almost sadly.

Even though no one really moved, it felt as if everyone's gears shifted, and the room suddenly became sterile. Melissa sat up straighter, as did Moreland. Only Garrett, who continued to lounge on the couch with his arm thrown over the backrest, continued observing something on the ceiling when he wasn't examining Melissa.

"We understand," I said, "you've contacted the adoption agency in regard to our daughter Angelina."

Moreland nodded.

"According to Mrs. Perala at the agency, Garrett doesn't want to sign the papers giving us full custody of Angelina. This came as an unbelievable shock to us. The agency said this was the first time this has ever happened to them. Of course, you can imagine this is something we never even thought possible, that someone could wait eighteen months, then step forward."

Garrett wouldn't meet my eyes. He alternated between studying the ceiling light fixtures and flicking glances at my wife. Moreland was still, but I could tell by a rapid pulsing in his temple he was becoming agitated.

"Mr. Moreland," I said, "we love Angelina, and she loves us. We are the only parents she's ever known. The birth mother selected us from several very deserving couples, and we've done everything we can to provide a loving house and family. Look around you. Melissa resigned from her job so she could stay home with the baby and provide full-time care. Melissa is Angelina's mother." I didn't say what should have come next, that I was her father. No reason at this point to alienate Garrett when I had the inkling he was on our side.

"We hope now that you and Garrett have met us and seen our home that you will consider signing the papers," I said.

I liked the way Moreland seemed to listen to me as I spoke, and noted that his eyes swept around the room when I mentioned our home.

I was encouraged when he said, "You have a very nice home, and I don't doubt your sincerity."

Then it came.

"*But . . .*"

In my peripheral vision, I could see Melissa squirm. Her hands tightened on the arms of her chair.

". . . we have a different view."

Moreland gestured toward Garrett. "My son made a very terrible mistake. I am ashamed of him. His mother, Kellie, is ashamed of him. He is ashamed of himself. This is a black mark on our family, this behavior. He had some bad friends at the time, and they encouraged this kind of thing. They are no longer his friends. That's why we sent him away for a while. We wanted him to get his head on straight, grow up into a man. But Garrett, and our family, can't avoid our responsibilities or the consequences of his stupid actions while he was younger. It is a situation we must deal with ourselves, within our family. We want to raise our child in our family."

I couldn't find words to speak. *Our child.*

"Mr. and Mrs. McGuane," Moreland said, leaning forward in the chair and looking from Melissa to me and back to Melissa, "I'm a federal judge, as I think you know. I'm known as a fair judge, and a tough one. I believe in accountability and being responsible for one's behavior. If there's one thing I want to pass along to my son, it's that there are consequences in life. It's vitally important that we bear responsibility. Garrett is responsible for the conception and birth of this baby.

"Please don't misunderstand what I'm saying," Moreland said in a conciliatory tone. "I have nothing against you or your wife. It is obvious you love the baby, and you've provided a wonderful home in a wonderful neighborhood. I am sorry this has to happen. I am truly, truly sorry. We didn't know about our granddaughter until I found the letters from the adoption agency in Garrett's room. He hadn't even opened them," he said, shooting a withering look at his son, who rolled his eyes. Then back to us: "Surely there are other babies?"

He sounded almost reasonable in his words if not his intent.

Come on, Melissa, I wanted to plead. *Say something here.* Instead, she studied Moreland with cold but curious intensity.

"Mr. Moreland," I said as softly as I could, "what you're asking is not possible. Angelina has been our daughter for nine months, and that doesn't include the seven months prior to that we were with the birth mother awaiting delivery. We've bonded as a family. I don't need to point out that during all of that time we never even knew Garrett, or you. If you had concerns, we would have reached out to you. To come here now is just unreasonable."

Moreland nodded in sympathy. He said, "I know this is going to be hard for you. I also know the financial outlay you've made."

I felt myself begin to squirm.

"I've done some research, Mr. and Mrs. McGuane. I know that it likely cost you over $25,000 to transact the adoption. I know Mrs. McGuane is no longer working outside the home, which is admirable. And Mr. McGuane, I know that a salary of $57,500 is not very much to maintain a house like this and a family. I'm sympathetic to both of you, but we know how deeply you are in debt, and that is not a pleasant place to be. I'm prepared to cover all of your costs, plus what it would take to adopt another child."

I felt violated by his knowledge. Our careful staging for the meeting was gone just like that. Poof. I shot a look at Melissa. Her face was an alabaster mask. Her eyes were pinched and hard, a look I'd never seen. A look that emboldened me and terrified me at the same time. I was amazed she had remained silent. I'm amazed I didn't leap across the table at him.

"It's not about money," I said. "It's much, much too late for that. Maybe if you'd come to us before Angelina was born . . ."

"I didn't know," Moreland said, his voice rising with anger, but not at us. He looked at his son with pure contempt. "Garrett was out of the country with his mother for several months. He never told us anything about it. If he had, we wouldn't be here now."

Melissa said to Garrett, "Where were you?" Her voice was leaden.

Garrett didn't seem to realize she was talking to him.

"He was in the Netherlands and England visiting relatives," Moreland answered for him. "Kellie's extended family and just being tourists. We learned of this," he gestured to us, "only two months ago."

In my peripheral vision, I saw Garrett roll his eyes.

"Did you know she was pregnant?" Melissa asked Garrett.

Garrett looked at Melissa with a half smile and shrugged in a way that said, "*Whatever.*"

I leaned forward in my chair until I had Moreland's attention, and said, "This is not about you. It's not about your son. It's not about us. This is about Angelina and what's best for her." Trying to drive a wedge between father and son.

Moreland paused a long time before saying, "It is about the baby, I agree. But the baby is part of my family, our family, despite my son's behavior. The baby is our blood and our responsibility, not yours. We must right this wrong."

It was later when I realized Moreland, the entire time he was in our home, never once said "Angelina." Always *the baby*.

I looked at Garrett. He was ignoring us, his eyes fixed on Melissa, who had caught him this time and stared back. The intensity of their gaze seemed to sizzle through the air. I couldn't stand it another second.

"Garrett," I said.

Nothing.

"*Garrett.*"

Slowly, he turned his head toward me. Contemptuous.

"I have to ask you a question."

He raised his eyebrows.

"Do you really want to be a father? Do you really want to change your life right now? Do you realize how much work it is to be a father, to care for and support a baby?"

Moreland spoke for him once again. "Kellie and I will raise the baby. She will be our granddaughter and our daughter. Garrett will go to college to become a lawyer or a doctor, and when he's married and has a home, he will take the child in with him."

"I asked Garrett," I said.

"He has nothing to say about it," Moreland said, heat in his voice. "We have discussed this in our family, and that is the way it will be."

Garrett watched me as his father spoke to read my reaction.

"So where is your wife in this?" Melissa asked Judge Moreland. "Why didn't she come with you?"

"She was too uncomfortable," Moreland said, tight-lipped.

"She doesn't want to meet us?" Melissa asked, bitterness in her voice.

Moreland flushed and looked at his shoes. "She's embarrassed."

It sounded like a lie.

He changed the subject, saying, "I'd like to see the baby."

Melissa said, "She's asleep."

"I won't wake her."

Melissa looked to me with horrified desperation.

"Maybe it would be best not to see her now," I said.

"I want to see her. I want to see what she looks like," he said firmly.

Standoff. And no one spoke for a full minute. My insides churned, and I realized the palms of my hands were icy cold and dry. The confidence I'd had when the meeting began was gone. It seemed as though the room we sat in had tilted slightly and become unfamiliar.

Melissa sighed. "I'll take you up there."

"Are you sure?" I asked. Were we conceding anything? I wasn't sure. Maybe Melissa thought if Moreland saw Angelina asleep in her crib, in her room, in our house, he would soften to our position. After all, the discussion so far had been abstract. Seeing the baby might help us.

"Sure," she said.

I turned to Garrett. "Do you want to go?"

Garrett shook his head. "That's okay," he said. "I'd like a Coke or something, though. Do you have a Coke?"

He didn't want to see her. That buoyed me. While Melissa led Moreland up the stairs, I went into the kitchen for the drink. Melissa kept a stash of Diet Coke in the back of the refrigerator. I filled an empty glass with ice from the icemaker and took the can and glass back into the living room. Garrett was standing at the mantel, looking at photos of our wedding, my parents on the ranch, Melissa's family at their reunion last summer at the Broadmoor in Colorado Springs, Angelina as an infant in Melissa's arms.

Over the baby monitor, I could hear the door to Angelina's room open.

I handed the can and the glass to Garrett. He took the can without a word. That he'd stayed downstairs gave me an opening.

"You don't really want to be a father, do you?"

"Not really."

"So it's your father?"

"He has ideas of his own."

"Can you talk him out of it?"

"I don't think so."

"Will you try?"

Garrett looked at me blankly. Something in his eyes disturbed me. It was as if he saw me as someone who couldn't possibly understand him, and I was not worth an explanation.

"Just sign the papers," I said. "There's nothing your parents can do if you sign them."

He smiled that half smile.

"I'll do what I can for you if you sign them," I said, having no idea what I could possibly do for him.

"My father is very rich," he said. "I don't need you."

"You might if you sign the papers," I said, trying to engage him man-to-man again. "Look, we've all made mistakes. None of us is perfect. Being a father changes your life, believe me. It's a good thing, but you need to be ready for it. There's a lot you need to give up. Your life is no longer your own. You lose your freedom. Plus, it's the right thing to do, and I think you know that."

He nodded while I spoke, and his eyes glistened. He was hearing me, and it seemed like he wanted to hear more. I got the strange feeling, though, that he wasn't offering me encouragement as much as egging me on.

Over the monitor, I heard Melissa say, "Don't touch her." Her tone startled me.

"I just want to turn her over and look at her face," Moreland said.

"I'll do it," Melissa said.

I could hear Angelina's covers rustle, and heard a murmur.

"There," Melissa said.

I realized both Garrett and I were staring at the monitor, straining to hear ever word, every sound.

"Ah," Moreland said. "She's beautiful. She looks like her father and me."

Silence from Melissa.

"See that little birthmark on her calf? I have that birthmark. It's a sign of being a Moreland."

"No!" Melissa said.

What was he doing?

He said, "I want to pick her up."

"I said no."

"Okay, okay," Moreland said. "I'll let her sleep. Can I take a photo of her at least? To show Kellie?"

"Please, I'd rather you didn't," Melissa said, sighing.

"Just a photo? Just one?"

Her silence was taken as acquiesence by both Moreland and me. I heard the click of a digital camera.

"I want to look at her for a few more moments."

Melissa said, "Just look. That's all."

I put the glass of ice on the coffee table and prepared to go upstairs. My hands were trembling and knotted into fists, and I felt myself on the verge of losing control. If he said anything more, took more photos, touched her . . .

"Please, Mrs. McGuane . . ." the judge said. "Don't make this harder than it already is."

Melissa said, "She's my baby, and you want to take her away from me."

"I understand how you must feel," he said gently.

I took a deep breath, tried to calm myself. It had been a long time since I'd been as angry. I wondered what I would have done up there. I thought again of the Colt .45. And I knew that Melissa and I had entered a whole new place, where everything was different.

I noticed Garrett watching me, a smirk on his face.

"What were you going to do?" he asked.

"Nothing," I said.

"I bet nothing."

"You don't want to see the baby, do you?" I asked.

"No," he said, with that lazy curl of his lip.

"Sign the papers," I said.

"You have a nice wife," Garrett said. "I like her."

His demeanor changed from the smirk back to stoic as Melissa and Moreland came down the stairs. His eyes were on Melissa, not his father.

"Maybe I'll come over and watch the Bronco game with you," Garrett said.

"What?" I was stunned once again.

"I should probably get to know you better," he said, his eyes still on Melissa. "We should hang out."

I didn't know how to react to that. I could tell by their faces that both Melissa and Moreland had missed the exchange.

Moreland stopped on the landing and shook Melissa's hand.

"Thank you," he said. "She's beautiful."

"She is," Melissa said, letting a tiny smile escape despite herself. "And she's ours," she added.

"Ah, we need to resolve this."

"No," Melissa said. "There's nothing to resolve."

Damn, I admired her for her toughness. Simply no.

Moreland turned to me. In response, I nodded toward Melissa as if to say, *It's out of my hands. The answer is no.*

"Come along, Garrett," Moreland said. And to us, "Thank you for the coffee. It was nice to meet you."

Garrett drained his Coke and handed the empty can to me,

letting Moreland walk by until he was out of earshot. He had an incredulous look on his face, as if he couldn't believe his sudden good fortune.

"What?" I asked.

The corners of his mouth tugged upwards and his pupils dilated and I could almost hear him say to himself, *I own you people now, don't I? You don't dare do anything or say anything that will make me mad, or I won't sign the papers.*

Then he smiled outright, and something danced behind his eyes. I felt a chill roll down my back.

"Son?" Moreland opened the front door and Garrett ambled out, shooting a look at me as he went by. "Later," he said.

Moreland said to Melissa, "I need to do some thinking. You are very impressive people. But . . ."

There it was again, that *but.*

"The circumstances of this issue are black-and-white. I've reviewed the case law, and met with lawyer friends well versed in family law. The birth mother signed away her parental rights, but the father—Garrett—didn't. Garrett should be the custodian of the baby, simple as that. No court would disagree. Regardless," he said, waving the legal argument aside though he'd made his point, "I still feel we can work together. You obviously have feelings for the baby, and you've acted in good faith. There may be some wiggle room we'd agree to. Maybe you could visit her occasionally and be a positive part of her life, like an aunt and uncle. But the fact is the baby is our blood, and she legally belongs to us. One can't diminish that fact. Blood is blood, the law is the law. Any judge can see we have the means to take excellent care of her and a wonderful home environment."

"What does that mean?" Melissa asked. "That we don't?"

"Of course you've done your best," Moreland said, not without sympathy.

"We love Angelina," Melissa said, a note of panic showing.

John Moreland nodded and pursed his lips.

"Think about having Garrett sign the papers," I said. "You say we can adopt another baby and Garrett needs to accept responsibility. Maybe *he* can visit her on occasion. Maybe Garrett can be the uncle."

I felt Melissa's eyes bore into me. She wanted nothing to do with either of them.

"Ah, compromise," Moreland said, toasting me without a glass as his way of acknowledging what I'd said. "That's not going to happen. I just hope we can resolve this among ourselves, without a protracted legal struggle you'd eventually lose. That would make it tougher and more emotionally draining on you and the baby. In fact, it could be cruel to her, since the outcome is certain, and your ability to pay lawyers is finite.

"Look," he said gently, "I know this is tough on you right now, and your head is probably spinning. But my offer still stands. There are other babies to adopt, and I can help make that happen. There are thousands of babies out there who could be nurtured and loved in a home like yours. My offer still stands to make things right for you.

"Let's talk about timing. While we have every right to demand the baby right here and now, that wouldn't be compassionate. And we want to avoid any scene of sheriff's cars rolling up to your house with lights on and having them forcibly return the child. So we'll give you three weeks to say goodbye—until the end of the month. That's a Sunday. That should give you enough time to get new adoption proceedings under way—with my help—and to say goodbye to the child. I've already notified the sheriff of the date, and he and his team are available. He won't come unless he has to, so please don't make him have to. That's the best we can do, I'm sorry. Three weeks."

Garrett stood there, his face stoic, giving no signal of what he was thinking.

"Well," Moreland said, "we had best be going. Go Broncos, I guess," he said. "At least we can agree on that, right?"

He closed the door behind him. Melissa joined me at the window. There didn't seem to be much oxygen in the room. We watched Garrett climb into the passenger seat, close the door, stare straight ahead. Moreland paused before reaching for the door handle to gaze at our house, as if making a decision that pained him. He looked remorseful, but at the same time he had a determined set to his face. My heart sank. I knew then he would never change his mind.

But he couldn't leave yet. My friend Cody had chosen that moment to pull up to our house in his police department Crown Victoria and unwittingly block the judge's car in the driveway. The judge stood there with his hands on his hips, glaring at him. Cody was oblivious. He swung out of his car and opened the trunk, his always-present cigarette dancing in his mouth. I could hear the loud twang of country music from the Crown Vic's radio. Cody grabbed the power drill he had borrowed months before and finally remembered to return as well as a twelve-pack of cheap beer and turned toward the house. That was when he saw the judge, and the judge saw him.

I couldn't hear their exchange of words, but it was obvious Cody was apologizing all over himself and backing up. He threw the drill and beer into the trunk and quickly backed up to let the judge and Garrett out.

Melissa saw none of it because her face was buried in my chest.

"This can't be happening," she cried.

"I know."

She looked at me fiercely. I've never seen such absolute manic conviction. "Swear to me, Jack, that you'll do everything you can to save our baby from them."

I nodded, squeezed her tighter.

"*Swear it to me!*"

"I swear," I said. "I promise." My stomach churned.

Cody let himself in the front door. His sandy-colored hair was uncombed, and he wore stained sweats. "Jesus Christ, I hope that judge didn't recognize me out there. I'm not supposed to use the car when I'm off duty to run errands. What was he doing here, anyway? Hey, what's wrong with you two? You look like you've seen a ghost."

From the other room, we heard Angelina stir over the baby monitor. We listened as the baby yawned, gurgled, sighed. We heard the crib squeak as she tried to pull herself up. She said, "Ma . . ."

Three

Two minutes into the first quarter of the Broncos game that evening, I heard the bass burbling of a car motor outside in my driveway. Melissa was upstairs bathing Angelina.

The doorbell rang.

There were three of them: Garrett, a young Hispanic covered in tattoos who looked like a gangster, and an emaciated red-haired Caucasian who was dressed in the same hip-hop style as the Hispanic. Garrett's bright yellow H3 Hummer was parked in the driveway, looking like the muscle-bound older uncle of my Jeep Cherokee.

Garrett said *hey* in an overly familiar way. Then: "I hope you don't mind that I brought my friends Luis and Stevie." They'd come, Garrett said, to hang out.

I said nothing.

"Problem?" he asked, wide-eyed and mocking. Stevie smirked.

Luis said, "Hey, *amigo,*" and nodded at me with a dead-eye stare.

Garrett and Luis sat on the same couch Garrett had occupied

earlier in the day. Stevie sat on the arm. Stevie's body language suggested he was subservient to them. The three boys watched the game in utter silence, not commenting on anything. I can't say they looked bored, because they were alert and didn't miss a thing. They both watched Melissa come downstairs and go into the kitchen and close the door. And I caught the "*See? What did I tell you?*" look Garrett gave Luis after she was gone.

Luis was shorter and darker than Garrett, with a blunt pug face that looked like it had been hammered in. He wore an oversized white T-shirt with an even larger open long-sleeved plaid shirt over it and massive cargo pants. He had close-cropped black hair and dull black eyes, and a tattoo on his neck below his jaw reading "Sur-13." Unlaced and oversized heavy boots with Vibram soles were splayed out in front of him. Stevie wore the same oversized clothing as well as a red bandana on his head. But his haircut, perfect teeth, and expensive new sneakers gave him away as a rich kid pretending to be a gangster. I could see Stevie as Garrett's friend. But Luis was the real deal and didn't seem to fit.

During a commercial for curing erectile dysfunction, I asked, "Garrett, is there anything you want to talk with me about?"

He looked at me sincerely, said, "Yes, there is."

I nodded, urging him on.

"I'd like a cold drink. Another one of those Cokes would be just fine. I'd bet my friends could use a cold drink, too."

"I'd like a beer, man," Luis said, grinning, showing gold teeth.

"Me too," Stevie said with a slight—and false—Mexican accent intonation.

I shook my head. Unbelievable.

"Maybe some snacks," Garrett said. "Chips and dip? Nachos? Don't you have snacks during a game?"

"We always have snacks," Luis said. "We like snacks during a game." Mocking me.

I cursed under my breath and went out to get soft drinks.

48

No beer for Luis or Stevie, though, and no damned snacks. Back in the living room, I could hear them chuckling. I had to close my eyes and take deep breaths to keep a handle on my anger.

DURING THE THIRD QUARTER, I asked Garrett if he'd thought about signing the papers.

"I haven't thought about it," Garrett said dismissively. "You need to talk to my father about that."

I detected an intransigent smirk on Luis's face when Garrett spoke.

"Does he always speak for you?"

"On this he does."

"Why?"

He locked eyes with me, and I felt a chill that made the hair on my arms rise.

"We have an agreement," he said.

Before I could ask what it was, Melissa came out of the kitchen to go upstairs to go to bed and Garrett's eyes and attention went with her.

Harry, our old Labrador, padded in from the kitchen. Garrett recoiled and sat back in the couch.

"He's harmless," I said, smiling. "Harry loves everybody."

"Can you please get him away?" Garrett asked me, his voice leaden.

"Sure," I said, puzzled. I am always surprised when someone doesn't like dogs. I put Harry out into the backyard. When I returned, the boys hadn't moved, although Garrett had a lingering look of what I can only describe as disgust on his face.

"Somebody allergic?" I asked.

"No," Garrett said in a way that signaled he no longer wanted to discuss the matter.

"He don't like dogs," Luis said. "Me, I got four. Fighting dogs, man. Nobody gives my dogs any shit."

"Do you mind if I use your bathroom?" Garrett asked.

"It's upstairs and to the left," I said, wondering if his plan was to sneak a peek at Melissa in Angelina's bedroom. But he was in and out quickly. As he came down the stairs, Luis said, "I'm next, man."

With Luis upstairs, I turned to Garrett. I ignored Stevie. "What do you want from us?" I asked. "Why did you bring your friends here?" I knew I was gripping the arms of the chair too hard.

"What, you don't like Mexicans?" Garrett asked innocently. "Does Luis make you nervous?"

"It's not that."

"Seemed like it to me. What do you think, Stevie?"

Stevie said, "Seemed like it to me, too."

Garrett smiled to me, "You remind me of my stepmom. She doesn't like Luis either."

"Your stepmom?"

"Yeah. My real mother died. Kellie's my stepmom."

"She's fine, too," Stevie said.

"We both know you gotta be nice to me," Garrett said, "or there's no way I sign the papers. You gotta be real nice. I know it's killing you, but hey."

"What kind of game are you playing?" I asked.

"No game," he said.

"Do you have any intention of signing?"

He shrugged. "I'm still thinking about it. It depends how nice you are to me and my friends. If you insult me or them, well, you won't get what you want."

I wanted to throw myself across the room and slam my fist into his mouth, but instead I gripped the arms of the chair tighter.

He looked up as Luis finally came down the stairs, his face oddly flushed.

"All through?" Garrett asked him.

"Yeah," he said. Then, to me, "There's something wrong with your toilet, man. You need to get that fixed."

"There's nothing wrong with . . ."

"We need to go," Garrett said, smiling at me. "I've got school tomorrow, you know?" To his friend, he said, "Ready, Luis?"

"Catch you later," Garrett said to me under his breath. They let themselves out. I heard the Hummer fire up. The three of them sat there for a few minutes in the dark with the motor running and a tricked-out muffler pounding out a deep beat. I shut the lights off inside to signal to them to leave and so I could watch them. I couldn't see them well, but it appeared by the way their heads bobbed that they were talking and laughing, which enraged me. Finally, the car backed out of the driveway and slowly, slowly, went down the street.

As their car rumbled away, Melissa cried out from upstairs, "Jack!"

Stained brown water pulsed out of the toilet bowl, flooding the carpet. The smell was horrific. A floating mass of feces bobbed in the water, breaking apart, pieces of it cascading over the rim.

"I'll call a plumber," I said.

"Call Cody," Melissa said, gagging. "Call Brian, too."

Four

I GREW UP ON a series of ranches in Montana. I remember each one clearly. What I mean is I remember the layout of each place, where the buildings were, the corrals, the hiding places. The ranches were near Ekalaka in eastern Montana, Billings, Great Falls, Townsend, Helena. My father was a ranch foreman, and he moved us around with his jobs. I wish I could say he moved up, but he didn't. Some ranches were better than others, but all seemed to have owners my dad couldn't get along with. He had his own ideas about cows, horses, and range management, and if the owner didn't completely agree with everything he wanted to do, my father would tell my mother that he and the owner "didn't see eye to eye" and my mother would sigh and they'd start asking around until he found another job. Once the new job was in the bag, he would angrily quit the old one, pack all of our possessions in the pickup and stock trailer, and we'd go off to the next ranch. My only constant was my parents, and as I grew older I became ashamed of them.

I've since reconsidered in part, and I feel guilty for being ashamed. They were simple people from another era and mind-set. They were the Joads. They worked hard and didn't even look up as the world passed them by. They rarely read books, and their conversation was about land, food, and weather. My dad didn't buy a color television set until he no longer had a choice. But in many ways they gave me gifts I just didn't recognize or appreciate at the time. They gave me perspective. I am the only person I know who grew up *outside*. I know hard work and suffering because that's what my family specialized in. When my coworkers complain about long hours or the amount of paper on their desks, I contrast it with calving time during a spring blizzard where if you don't get the newborn to the barn within minutes, it will freeze to death in midbawl.

I simply wasn't hardwired for ranch work. I fixed fence, branded, docked, vaccinated, fed hay out of wagons and pickups to starving cattle in the winter. But it just didn't take. I was never surly or disrespectful toward my dad and his occupation, just disinterested. He gave up on me early on as a future ranch foreman or competent hand. My mother withheld affection except for unexpected and oddly inappropriate moments. I remember once when I was walking down the dirt road to the school bus stop, and I realized she was running after me. I stopped and ducked, covering my head with my arms, expecting a beating and wondering what I'd done wrong. Instead, she smothered me in her arms, kissed the top of my head, said with tears in her eyes, *Oh, you're my world, you're my everything my wonderful, wonderful boy.* She was still kissing and hugging me when the bus pulled up filled with hooting rural kids hanging out of the windows. When I got home that night I asked her what had come over her, and she went pale and looked back at me with wide-eyed horror for bringing it up in front of my father. Only now do I understand the depth of parental love she revealed to me. I feel it myself when I look at Angelina and know that no matter what happens, I'll love her.

I used to take refuge in the theory that my mother secretly cheered for me to get away. Now that I have, I'm not so sure I was right about her secret wishes. Instead, I think she saw me as her surrogate for rebellion against her husband and her life in general. Not to say she was mean—she wasn't. But she was born with a dark cloud over her head that got darker as she aged. I've reconciled myself to that.

The only place we lasted more than two years was on the HS Bar between Townsend and Helena. The owner, whom I only met once, was a millionaire investor who lived in Connecticut. He was blustery, fast-talking, and abrasive. He showed up on the ranch in cowboy clothes that were inspired by *Bonanza* and looked more like a costume than real clothing. I didn't like him—he called me "Jake" instead of Jack—but due to his poor health, a bitter divorce, and problems with the SEC, we didn't see or hear much from him. Therefore, my dad said he was the best owner he'd ever worked for, and he got along with him. They saw "eye to eye," my dad said, meaning the owner never spoke to him. During those years, I took the bus into Helena High. I was a Bengal. On the way to town we picked up Cody Hoyt in East Helena, which was on the wrong side of the tracks. Cody and I became great friends. Later, we met Brian Eastman and the three of us clicked, probably because none of us really belonged to any other established group. Brian's father was a Presbyterian minister in Helena.

We hunted, fished, hiked, and chased girls together. Even early on, it was obvious Brian was destined for great things. All of the girls loved Brian. He was their best friend and confidant. Cody and I met girls through Brian because none of them ever seemed good enough for him. At least, that's what we thought at the time.

After high school, Brian and I went off to college. Brian to the University of Denver on a scholarship. I went to Montana State in Bozeman on financial aid and student loans that would hang over my head for ten years. When I took my twenty-year-old pickup to

Bozeman, I knew I would never return to the HS Bar or whatever ranch my parents were managing. Cody stayed around Helena and worked both construction and on ranches, pulling a six-month stint on the HS Bar working for my dad. He told me later that working for my dad convinced him to enroll in the police academy so he'd never have to work for such a mean old son of a bitch for the rest of his life.

I waited until Melissa and I were engaged before introducing her to my parents so as not to scare her off. My dad took a long look at her, turned to my mom, said, "She's too good for him." Melissa's parents, who lived in Billings at the time and were not yet divorced, felt the same way. With those hot winds of confidence filling our sails, we drove to Las Vegas with Brian and Cody in Brian's car, littering the highways with empty beer cans all the way to Nevada. While nursing screaming hangovers, my friends served as best men and witness to the wedding that took place at Chapel of the Dunes in Glitter Gulch.

I got my degree in journalism, which turned out to be practically worthless, and started as a reporter at the *Billings Gazette*. Mainly, I worked as an assistant in graphics making a dollar over minimum wage. We lived in a trailer out by MetraPark, within sight and smell of the livestock they brought in for auctions, sharing the place with two dogs who just showed up and stayed. Melissa landed better than I did, and went from assistant in reservations at a local hotel to assistant general manager to general manager within two years. When an opening came up at the Billings Convention and Visitor's Bureau, she convinced me to apply and used her connections to talk me up. Her reputation was so good the CVB board assumed her husband might be worthwhile, so they hired me. After a few years, I did stints in Bozeman and Casper, Wyoming, learning the travel industry. I started to feel like my father, moving about from place to place.

Brian stayed in Denver after graduation and was a highly successful real-estate developer who had quickly become prominent and high-profile within the community. He was also on the board of the Denver CVB, and suggested to Linda Van Gear, Vice President of Tourism, to hire me.

So we moved to the big city.

Cody bounced around in law enforcement from place to place as well, from small town to small town in Wyoming and Montana, then to Loveland, Colorado. His name began to pop up in the *Denver Post* and *Rocky Mountain News* in newspaper articles in connection with several high-profile crimes, including the kidnapping, rape, and murder of a college coed by an illegal Mexican immigrant. The article in the *News* referred to him as a "relentless investigator." He married and divorced twice. He eventually signed on with the Denver Police Department, and had recently been promoted to detective first class in the Criminal Investigations Division. Cody was the lead investigator who had arrested Aubrey Coates, the man known in the newspapers as the "Monster of Desolation Canyon."

We chose Denver like so many others. I meet very few people in Denver who are from Denver, or from Colorado. There is little sense of shared history or culture. Relationships and connections are as deep as the piddling South Platte River that trickles through the city.

"YOU COULD PROBABLY SWEAR out some kind of vandalism complaint and I'm sure they know it," Cody Hoyt said later that night. "It isn't whether you've got reason to press charges, it's whether you've got the guts to take them on and piss them off."

Cody came right over, as did Brian. Larry of LARRY'S 24/7 EMERGENCY PLUMBING was still upstairs.

Cody still wore the same sweats he'd had on earlier that day, and he hadn't shaved. He smelled of beer, cigarette smoke, and sweat, and he said he'd spent the evening watching the game at a cop bar near police headquarters on Cherokee Street after dropping off the drill earlier. As he grew older, Cody was looking more and more like his father, a notorious drinker and Vietnam War vet with a bulbous nose and kettle-sized potbelly who did odd jobs throughout the county from a ramshackle panel van. The semiautomatic pistol he had clipped to the waistband of his sweatpants gave me pause and created an air of seriousness and purpose our living room had been lacking, I thought.

Brian, on the other hand, wore chinos, tasseled loafers with no socks, and an untucked pale blue dress shirt. His hair was receding and had been reduced to a tight swoosh high on his forehead. He had penetrating hazel eyes. He'd lost even more weight from when I'd seen him last and was beginning to resemble a hanger for his fine clothes.

Melissa had asked if they wanted anything before settling down in a chair. Cody asked for a beer. Brian wanted ice water with "a little slice of lemon."

"I'm sure it was Luis," I said. "He was in the bathroom a long time. I'm not sure Garrett didn't put him up to it, though."

"Disgusting," Brian said. "*Animals.*"

"The 'Sur-13' tattoo you described," Cody said, "that's for Sureños 13—the local chapter of a nationwide gang. You see the gang graffiti all over the south side and downtown. We know all about them—they deal most of the meth in Colorado. I'll check out this Luis dude with the gang task force, see if they know him."

"Why would Luis be with Garrett," I asked, "and vice versa? Stevie is a white kid, too."

Cody said, "We're seeing it more and more. Rich white kids slumming with the Mexican gangsters. They want some of that power and cool to rub off on them. It's just like white rappers, trying to be something they're not. The Mexican gangs are the kings of Denver, just like every other city in the West and Southwest."

I asked, "What's in it for the gangsters?"

58

"Connections," Cody said. "Access to schools and neighbor-hoods where there are plenty of kids with disposable income. Plus, Luis is probably smart. He knows Garrett's dad is a federal judge. That connection could help him and his buddies somewhere down the road."

"Something else," I said. "The remote control for the television is missing. They must have taken it when I got them the drinks."

"That was nice of you," Cody said sarcastically.

"We were nice to them because we didn't want to start out as adversaries," Melissa said. "We hoped they'd see reason once they met us and saw the home we've established for Angelina . . ."

Brian and Cody nodded sympathetically.

Cody glanced down at his notes, said, "So did Garrett say anything you could consider threatening?"

"No."

"But he indicated you better be nice to him or he wouldn't sign the papers?"

"Yes."

"Melissa, did you hear that exchange?" Cody asked.

"No."

He turned back to me. "So it's your word against his."

I shook my head. "It wasn't just what they said, it was how they acted. Like they were sharing a big joke being here. They kept look-ing at each other like they'd burst out laughing anytime."

"It was really uncomfortable," Melissa said. "Garrett stares at me like I'm a piece of meat."

That agitated Brian, who leaned forward and gripped his knees with his hands. He was protective of Melissa and had been since our marriage. We were, he said, his surrogate family since he'd never have one of his own. He and Melissa talked on the telephone every few days. Long, aimless conversations punctuated by her laughter and her mock-outraged cries of "Brian!" when he said something catty or off-color. He had been there for her after the miscarriages, and he had a rapport with her I sometimes envied. She was still amazed that in all of those years growing up I hadn't realized he was gay, since she'd known the first time she met him. He was, Melissa said, her best friend. Brian's partner was an architect named Barry. They'd been together for several years and lived in a hip loft apartment in the heart of the city. Barry was hard to get to know, I thought. I found him stiff and standoffish, but he hit it off with Melissa right away. I didn't see Barry much.

Melissa once told me she always suspected Cody was conflicted in his feelings toward his old friend since Brian had become so successful—and more flamboyant in his personal life. I shrugged it off and attributed Cody's attitude to the cynicism so many cops held toward businessmen. Cody had grown up reciting the Honoré de Balzac line (even though he didn't know it was Honoré de Balzac), "Behind every great fortune there is a crime." I think he believed it. And he probably attributed it to both John Moreland *and* Brian.

Brian looked at me with anger. "Why did you just *let* them in?"

"I thought maybe Garrett wanted to talk," I said. "I hoped he'd offer to sign away custody. But he never even mentioned it until I brought it up."

"You can't prove they took the remote, though," Cody said.

"I know I had it when the game started," I said. "I went to the kitchen while they were here, and that's when I assume they took it."

"Why would they want a remote control they can't use?" Cody asked.

"A trophy," Brian said. "It's symbolic. It's like they are taking control away from you. Is anything else missing?"

Melissa and I looked around the living room. It was possible something else was gone, but I couldn't be sure. I still had the lingering feeling from our meeting earlier in the day that our house was unfamiliar to me.

Melissa's eyes paused on the mantel, and I saw the blood drain from her face. She quickly got up and went to the fireplace.

"The photo of Angelina and me in the hospital," she said.

"Garrett was looking at that earlier today," I said. "I saw him."

"Maybe he wanted a photo of his daughter," Brian said.

"His birth daughter," I corrected. Melissa was sensitive to terms.

"Or maybe," Cody said, "he wanted a photo of Melissa."

The thought made me clench my fists.

Larry the plumber cleared his throat while he came down the stairs. He was shaking his head and smiling. "All fixed," he said. "Happens all the time when you've got toddlers."

Melissa and I exchanged puzzled looks.

"I should start a museum collection of the things I've found in toilets," Larry said, standing on the landing and finishing up his invoice on a clipboard. "Barbie dolls, socks, shoes. One kid tried to flush a whole apple because he didn't want his mom to know he didn't eat it. Problem is, the only people interested in what we find in toilets is other plumbers."

"We don't have a toddler," Melissa said.

"You don't?" Larry said, looking up. "That's strange."

Then he saw Harry and he laughed. "Next to toddlers, it's the Labradors who drop things in toilets."

"What was it?" I asked.

"Your remote control," Larry said. "It was wedged down in there and it's ruined, I'm afraid. Unless you want me to clean it off and try to get it working again."

"That's okay," I said.

"It's still a mess up there," Larry said, handing me the bill. I tried not to gasp when I saw the amount—nearly $400.

"You pay dearly for twenty-four/seven emergency calls," Larry said, trying to sound breezy, "especially on game night after I've had a few cold Coors and gone to bed early."

As Larry left the house and climbed into his panel van in the driveway, Brian said, "The symbolism continues. He took your control and he and his buddy flushed it down the toilet and crapped on it. Exactly what kind of kid are you dealing with?"

CODY SAID, "LET'S COME up with a plan."

We were up until two in the morning. It took an hour for the four of us to strip the rugs and hose them down outside and to clean the bathroom floor. Brian wore a bandana over his nose and mouth, but we could hear him saying, over and over, "Animals." Before we started cleaning, Brian took photos of the mess with his digital camera and put the camera in his pocket.

Brian thought we needed a new attorney since I'd fired Dearborn. We needed a bulldog, Brian said, someone who would "go after the Morelands and drop a nuclear bomb on them."

"We can't afford someone like that," I said. "We're strapped as it is with the house, the adoption. We don't have Melissa's income anymore."

"I was wondering if that would come up," she said more heatedly than I could have anticipated.

Before I could explain myself, she said, "We can sell the house. I can go back to work. I've gotten calls from Marriott and Radisson . . ."

"I'll help you out," offered Brian. "Don't worry about money. In fact, let me be your advocate in this whole mess."

He leaned forward, his voice dropped an octave. His business voice. "Since I've been in Denver I've met a hell of a lot of people, and a bunch of them owe me favors. It's a big city, yes, and it's growing like crazy, but that's at the margins. At its core it's still a small town run by a cabal of old-timers, developers, and politicians. There are levers of power, and I know how to work them. I've been doing it for years. I know city councilmen and media people, and you know I'm familiar with the mayor's inner circle. If word gets out I'm fronting for you, this changes your problem into an *issue*. That's the last thing the powers that be want."

"Thank you, Brian," Melissa said, her eyes glistening with tears.

I didn't know what to say. No one in my life had ever said the words *Don't worry about money*.

"No," Cody said. "I don't think it's the best plan. Even with a loan and a new attorney . . ."

"I never said 'loan,' " Brian said sharply to Cody.

". . . you're still up against Judge John Moreland," Cody continued, dismissing Brian just as curtly. "Moreland is a judge, and he's connected in more ways than you can know. He can hire teams of lawyers to tie you up and drain you for years. Plus, any judge would determine he could provide real well for the baby while you two get deeper and deeper in debt."

"It's just not right," Brian said through clenched teeth.

"No, it ain't," Cody said, not without sympathy. "But the fact is Garrett didn't sign away custody, right? He may be a thieving, humping little scumbag, but he has the law on his side. And lots of luck finding a good lawyer who wants to take on a sitting judge. Particularly this sitting judge."

Melissa sighed, sat back. Her eyes were rimmed with red. There was a set to her mouth that indicated she was fighting back tears. "It's so unfair. We don't deserve this. We did everything right. I'll fight them to my last breath," she said, almost spitting the words out. "I'll do anything, say anything, to keep my daughter. If I need to act like I'm flirting with Garrett—I will."

I winced.

"Somehow," she said, "we've got to convince him to sign the papers. I can't believe he has any interest at all in Angelina. He doesn't want to be a father although I can't figure out what his game is. Maybe he's just using this situation to intimidate us."

"Sounds like he likes *you*," Brian said to her.

"We can't confront him," she said. "We've got to find a way to convince him to come around."

"This is headed the same direction Julie Perala suggested," I said.

She turned to me. "You can continue to be nice to him, can't you? At least pretend you don't hate him until we can figure out how to persuade him?"

"After what he did tonight?" I asked, gesturing upstairs. "He's not just calculating. He's evil. I looked into his eyes and got chills."

"That'll play well in court," Cody said, rolling his eyes. "Don't you know there is no such thing as evil in this day and age? In our politically correct city? Man, you've got to get out more."

Brian said to Cody, "Some of us call it tolerance and diversity, Cody. It's thought of as progress."

Cody blew out a stream of breath, said, "Progress, my ass."

"Please," Brian said, "let's deal with the issue at hand, okay?"

"It's not Garrett," Melissa said, ignoring them. "It's his father. If we could separate them, and I could just talk with Garrett . . ."

"No," I said. "I don't think it's a good idea."

She said, "Maybe if I talked with him or showed him how much care is required for an infant, it would scare him off. Maybe he needs to see some dirty diapers or throw-up on a bib and he'd realize he's in way over his head even if his parents are actually raising her."

"But he didn't want to see her," I said. "There's a reason for that. You're assuming he's reasonable. I didn't see any of that."

"You think he's *evil*," Cody sneered.

"Garrett doesn't want to confront the situation in real life," she said. "He wants to avoid her. Maybe if he actually saw her . . ."

"I don't know," Brian said, shaking his head.

I agreed.

Melissa took a moment to look at each of us in turn.

"Guys," she said, "we need to think of Angelina's best interests most of all here. If the worst possibly happens, she might end up with them. I'm not saying that should happen, but we can't just dismiss the possibility out of hand. John Moreland seemed pretty determined to me. And if the worst comes about, I don't want to poison Angelina's relationship with them."

There were several beats of silence. I was conflicted.

"You're amazing," Brian said to Melissa in a whisper.

She was. I was astonished she was mine.

But a cold fear worked its way through my insides. If the worst-possible scenario came true, if the Morelands somehow got Angelina, I knew it would destroy Melissa. And after all we'd gone through, it would destroy *us*.

"I won't let it happen," I said.

She looked at me and smiled sadly.

"I won't," I said.

"Jesus," Cody said, standing, "I need another beer."

"WHAT MORE DO WE KNOW about John Moreland?" Melissa asked rhetorically. "He's the key."

Cody shifted on the couch as if clearing the space around him before he spoke. Brian cut in.

"I've met him a few times. At society functions and charity events. I hate to say it, but he seems like an incredibly normal, nice guy. He's best buddies with the mayor, and he's really well connected to both U.S. senators, the attorney general, and even the president. What I've heard is he's on a fast-track to something bigger. U.S. circuit, maybe higher. He just exudes competence and confidence, you know?"

Melissa shook her head. "We know."

"He's married to Kellie," I said. "Garrett referred to Kellie as his stepmom. He said his real mother was dead."

Brian sat back, screwed up his face. "I've seen Kellie. She's a blond bombshell."

"I wonder where the Sureños 13 connection comes in?" Cody said.

"Anyway," Brian said, "I can start asking around in my circles. It's amazing what you can find out about people at a higher level, you know? At cocktail parties and charity events. Get these people a few drinks in them, and all sorts of deep dark secrets start coming out. It's no different than Helena, you guys—just bigger. Maybe I can find out that he's not so perfect after all, and we'll have a little ammunition to go after him."

Melissa and I nodded, knowing Brian was an excellent gossip who could dish with anyone on earth. Attractive married women—like Melissa, come to think of it—seemed compelled to spill secrets to him because his delight in hearing them was reward in itself.

"Be careful you don't ask the wrong people and have it come back on Jack and Melissa," Cody said, "or me. I work for the city, and occasionally I have to testify in Judge Moreland's court. I got to know him when he was a U.S. Attorney and I was working joint task forces."

Cody had complained to me over the years that he was frequently assigned to multi-agency task forces involving the feds, state investigators, and the Denver Police Department. He had a problem with the bureaucracy, procedure, and territoriality of the FBI, and clashed with them. But because Cody was good at his job and didn't care about making friends, he personally broke cases and let the feds take the credit as long as they left him alone. Cody had never played well with others.

"What's he like in court?" I asked Cody. "He described himself as tough and fair. And obviously he has a thing about accountability if he'd put his family and ours through this."

Cody nodded. "All judges describe themselves that way, so don't put too much stock in it. But I'd say Judge Moreland loves being a judge, maybe too much. He's a great judge to have if you've got a defendant he hates right out of the box because he'll throw the book at him. We kind of know which way the decision is going to go right off the bat by the procedural moves Moreland makes to get to the outcome he wants to get to. If he thinks the defendant is a scumbag, he'll make sure there's federal prison time. If for some reason he thinks we've got the wrong guy, there's nothing we can do to convince him otherwise.

"Judges are supposed to hear the arguments," Cody continued, "research the law, and make a judgment based on the facts presented. Moreland does that, but he prejudges the case, and most of us think he holds himself above the law. That's great if he agrees with us, but it sucks when he doesn't. But most of the time he's procop, and that's all we care about."

Cody said, "I'm testifying in his court tomorrow on the Coates case. You know, the Monster of Desolation Canyon. Maybe you ought to come to the courtroom and see the guy in action. Court's in session at one."

"Will I learn anything?" I asked.

"You'll learn what you're up against," Cody said in a way that gave me no confidence.

There were a few uncomfortable beats of silence. Brian broke it, saying, "Garrett is the one, Melissa. Garrett's got to have some kind of history if he comes off the way you two describe him. I mean, you say he exudes evil, and he shows up tonight with a gangbanger. Maybe if we found out more about Garrett, we could convince a court he's absolutely not father material, despite what Judge Daddy says."

Cody nodded. "Might be tough, though. If he's got a juvie record, it could be sealed."

"To a detective?" Brian asked, smiling wickedly. "To the star maverick detective who got fed up with working with the feds and finally arrested the Monster? I bet that detective has ways to take a look at the file."

I cautiously checked Cody out. I didn't want to pressure him.

"I'll make some discreet calls," he said. "But I've absolutely got to stay away from any kind of investigation of the judge himself. I've got to stay completely clean. Can you imagine what would happen to me and the department if word got out I was investigating a sitting judge on my own? Shit, I'd get sent back to Montana or worse."

Brian shuddered. The last place he ever wanted to go was home.

"Okay then," Brian said, a gleam in his eye, slapping his knees. "We have a plan and less than a month to implement it. I'll find out what I can about the judge, Cody will check on the kid. Jack and Melissa, you keep doing what you're doing. Hire a good lawyer and fight the bastards as long as you can. In the meanwhile, I think you should swear out a complaint against Garrett and Luis for that stunt they pulled here tonight."

Cody held up his hand. "If you do that, you can't implicate me in any way. And I think it's a stupid idea."

"Why?" Brian said, hurt.

Melissa jumped in. "We don't want to antagonize Garrett. Not yet. We want to try and win him over first."

Brian looked at me with a *what-can-you-do?* look.

WHEN BRIAN AND MELISSA went upstairs to look in on Angelina, Cody came out of the kitchen with another beer.

"You sure you want that?" I asked. "You've got to testify tomorrow, right?"

Cody shrugged and popped the top. "We're going to nail that Coates son of a bitch. We've got the Monster of Desolation Canyon dead to rights. I'm not worried, even though the feds are mad at me for breaking it. But I do hope the judge didn't recognize me in front of your house. If he knows we're friends . . ."

"What?"

He shrugged. "I'm not sure."

Cody took a long pull off the beer, and we sat in silence for a few moments. Then he leaned forward and spoke softly to me. "I know Brian means well, but . . . well, I can see him running his mouth to all his society friends. They'll eat this up. And if Judge

Moreland hears about a concerted effort to dig up dirt on him or his son, he might really lower the boom on you two—and maybe me."

"Meaning what?" I asked, a little angry.

"Maybe he takes back his offer to get you another baby. That's a pretty generous offer, Jack."

"Melissa would never consider it, Cody," I said. "Neither would I."

"Sometimes you've got to get the best deal you can, is all I'm saying. You know I've got a son of my own, right?"

"*What?*"

Cody wiped his mouth with his sleeve. "Yeah—the result of a little drunken tryst up in Fort Collins when I was working undercover. A barmaid name of Rae Ann. She's married now to her second husband, but I send her money for little Justin every month. On my salary it's a hit, but whatever."

"You never told us," I said.

He shrugged. "It happens. But that's not my point. My point is Justin and I are getting close now that he's turned six. Those first five years he was just a baby. He could have been any baby, to be honest. Now he's a real person, you know? He likes baseball and rocks. But for those first five years, he was just kind of a little fat . . . *thing*. Babies aren't people until they grow up, is what I've learned."

I shook my head. "I don't follow."

He killed the beer. "I guess I'm saying for a man, babies are babies. You could get another one, and she'd grow up to be a person. Hell, maybe you'd love her more than you love Angelina now. You just don't know. If you have the chance to get another baby, you and Melissa will raise a winner, is what I'm saying."

I saw a flash of red in front of my eyes. "Cody, I think it's late, and you're drunk. So shut up. Now."

He raised his hand, "I'm just saying . . ."

"I know what you're saying. Stop it. It's not an option."

"You might want to give it some thought, Jack."

"It's not an option."

He started to argue more when Melissa and Brian appeared on the stairs.

"Enough," I cautioned Cody.

"Okay," he said. "So, will I see you tomorrow?"

At that moment I didn't care if I ever saw Cody again.

"Call me," Brian said to Melissa as he hugged her goodbye.

"I will," she said. She was as exhausted as me, and showing it. Tears welled again in her eyes.

"Too bad we can't just call Uncle Jeter to take care of things." Cody laughed. "He'd love to drive down here and kick some ass."

I smiled at the thought. Jeter Hoyt was a legend when we were growing up in Helena. One of the reasons no one ever touched Cody, Brian, or me was because Jeter Hoyt was Cody's uncle, and stories about him were the kind told only in furtive whispers after the storyteller had glanced over his shoulder to see who was in the room.

When they were gone, Melissa said, "You have some good friends."

I said, "*We* have some good friends." I didn't tell her what Cody had said.

WE'D BEEN IN BED AN HOUR. Melissa had tucked the covers around Angelina and whispered something to her that didn't come over the monitor. Our daughter's sleeping breath provided the sound track in our room. I was sleeping fitfully.

AT 4:00 A.M. I heard the burbling sound of a motor cruising by on the street. I recognized it as Garrett's car.

I imagined him out there with Luis, looking at our house as they crawled by, the photo between them on the seat.

Monday, November 5

Twenty Days to Go

Five

ANGELINA WOKE US UP very early Monday morning, but in the most pleasant way possible.

"Listen to her," I said. "She's singing."

"It's not really a song," Melissa said. "She's just happy."

We listened to Angelina coo and say nonsense words over the monitor. Melissa's face, as she listened, was a picture of momentary serenity.

"Did you get any sleep?" I asked Melissa.

"Not much," she said.

"Me either."

THE COURTROOM OF JUDGE John Moreland in the Alfred A. Arraj United States Courthouse on 19th Street was spacious and blond–wood paneled and lit with recessed lighting that created an atmosphere of serious decorum. I got to the crowded courtroom and found a seat in the second-to-last row, just in time to see Detective Cody Hoyt take the stand. Large faded murals done in the Depression era depicting Colorado history—silver and gold miners, railroaders, Pikes Peak—lined the walls. The scenes reminded me that Colorado had a go-go, get-rich-quick beginning that was being replicated by the most recent wave of newcomers—like me—who came here not because of family ties or culture but because there was opportunity.

The acoustics inside the courtroom were amazing. Despite the size of the room and the number of spectators, I could hear the muffled clicking of the court reporter's fingers on her keyboard from her desk near the bench, the shuffle of paper as the Assistant U.S. Attorney reviewed her notes on a yellow legal pad, and the labored breathing of the defendant, Aubrey Coates, forty-three, accused of the kidnapping, sexual assault, and murder of Courtney Wingate, age five, who went missing from a playground area at the Desolation Canyon Campground where Coates was employed as a campground host. Because the campground was located within a national forest, the trial was taking place in federal court.

Although I'd spent some time in courtrooms in Billings as a journalist—I covered the infamous trial where the two Crow Indian brothers and their meth-addict girlfriends went on the weeklong crime spree across southern Montana and northern Wyoming and murdered a ranch couple along the way—Judge Moreland's courtroom had a slick sense of process about it that probably came from the no-nonsense, clipped way he moved things along. He didn't shout, or gesticulate, but when he spoke, everyone listened. He was charismatic and in total command. I couldn't keep my eyes off him in the way one can't keep one's eyes off a great actor—Denzel Washington, say—even when he isn't speaking or the focus of attention. I wasn't the only one so afflicted. If Moreland raised an eyebrow while a lawyer asked a question, that lawyer got the vapors, and the opposing attorneys acted smug. Of course, I observed him to see if

I could learn anything about him, to size him up, to find a weakness. If he saw me enter the room, he showed no sign of recognition. I was still buzzing from the events of the night before. There was a black ball of dread in my belly that seemed to be pushing upward into my lungs, leaving me short of breath.

I was seated next to a large and well-dressed black woman in a floral-print dress and with a fleshy wide face who seemed unrelated to the players. I continued to survey the courtroom. Cops, reporters I recognized from local television and cable news, plenty of observers attracted by the lurid nature of the case itself, including, I assumed, my new companion next to me. Then I found myself staring at the back of the head of Aubrey Coates himself, sitting at a table facing the judge.

"That there's the Monster," the woman next to me said, leaning my way. Her bare chocolate arm radiated heat as she pressed into me, and her breath smelled of mint and cigarettes. "He turns around and looks back every once in a while, seeing who is here," she whispered. "I think he likes the attention because he is a sick, sick man. When he looked at me I gave him one of these . . ." She instantly sat back with attitude and gave me a wicked dead-eye glare. "That look usually freezes folks where they walk. But he just kind of smiled at me."

I'd seen photos of Aubrey Coates in the newspaper. Of course, the photos were prior to his haircut and shave. Now he sat slumped, small, in an ill-fitting suit jacket. He had tufts of gray hair over large ears, and when he turned his head to whisper something to his lawyer, I saw a hawkish and heavily veined nose, protruding lips, and a pointy chin. When he turned back, his bald dome reflected the light from the walls in a checkerboard pattern on the side of his head. I thought of the nature of evil, how sometimes you could just see it and sense it.

"He did it," she said, nodding. "No doubt in my mind. And he did a lot more, too."

I held out my hand. "Jack."

"Olive," she said, her large hands enveloping mine. "Ask me any-thing. I know everybody in his room. This is what I do—observe trials."

"Do you know Coates's defense attorney?" I asked, looking at a rotund man sitting next to Coates with an easy smile and manner.

She nodded, and her eyes widened. "He's got the best—Bertram Ludik. I don't know how that little worm can afford him. I think if Charles Manson had hired Bertie Ludik, he'd be out there sticking forks into people to this day!"

"Come on," I said.

"You watch," she said. Then: "Luckily, Judge Moreland won't allow Bertie to be Bertie."

"That guy I know," I said, chinning toward Cody, who was ap-proaching the stand.

"Detective Hoyt," she whispered sympathetically. "I'd like to take that man home and hug him and tell him everything will be all right."

"Why?" I asked, perplexed.

"He's a troubled soul," she said. "Look at him. A great detective, but a troubled soul."

He's just hungover, I thought.

Cody was wearing a dark blue suit that gathered under his arms, a white shirt, and a solid but faded red tie. He looked courtroom savvy but disheveled at the same time. He shambled when he walked and raked his fingers back through his hair, messing it up. When he sat down in the witness chair, his eyes took in the room in a world-weary way that said "I'M A COP. JUST LET ME DO MY JOB." I nodded at him, but I'm not sure he saw me.

Judge Moreland said, "The witness is reminded he is still under oath."

"I understand, Your Honor."

"Miss Blair," Judge Moreland said to the Assistant U.S. Attorney, an attractive redhead who had been huddled in conference with the U.S. Attorney at the prosecution table, "you may continue to question the witness."

"Thank you, Your Honor," she said, standing, holding the legal pad at her side as she approached the podium. "I have just a few more questions."

Moreland gestured impatiently for her to begin.

"Detective Hoyt," she said, flipping back the pages on her pad, "you said Friday before the weekend recess that when you apprehended the defendant on the morning of June 8 last summer, he was in the process of destroying evidence . . ."

HERE'S WHAT I KNEW about Aubrey Coates, the Monster of Desolation Canyon.

Every summer, children vanish. Over the last decade children had gone missing while on vacation with their families in the Mountain West.

It happens quite a lot in the mountains. Often, the families are having picnics and reunions and suddenly someone realizes that one of the kids didn't show up for dinner. Sometimes the children got lost, sometimes they washed into rivers, sometimes they got mad at their siblings and "ran away," and sometimes they climbed into the wrong car. Most are found. I remember when my dad and I volunteered to search for a missing little boy who'd wandered away from a campsite near the Gates of the Mountains Wilderness north of Helena. We took horses, and I remember it as a great and serious adventure combing the trails and riverbanks calling out "Jarrod!" for two days. Until Jarrod was found less than a mile away from where he'd vanished and confessed he'd gotten turned around in the forest and fallen asleep. He admitted hiding from volunteer rescue people as they walked and rode by because they were strangers, and he had been taught not to talk to strangers—even those calling his name.

But in some isolated instances the children were never found. These children vanished from isolated locations in Colorado (Grand Junction, Pueblo, Trinidad), Utah (Wasatch, St. George), Wyoming (Rock Springs, Pinedale). Boys and girls, all under the age of twelve. In nearly every instance, the parents said the child was there one minute and gone the next. The places the children were last seen were playgrounds, near streams, on hiking trails. Then poof—they were gone.

In retrospect, when one looks at the instances of these particular missing children over the years, you can see a pattern, and the authorities are blamed for not seeing what should have been in plain sight. But that's unfair, as Cody explained to me. The children went missing in three states over ten years. The only "pattern" was that they vanished from campsites or in undeveloped areas. There were no calling cards left, no evidence of where the children were taken, and nothing left behind. All occurred in different jurisdictions, with different sets of law-enforcement personnel. The FBI was never called in because linkage wasn't discovered until after the fact. None of the parents were ever contacted for ransom or taunted. No one confessed or implicated others. And none of the bodies was ever found.

Aubrey Coates, who worked as a temporary replacement for campground hosts, was questioned on four different occasions because he had his trailer parked in the areas where the children went missing. In each instance, Coates answered all questions asked and was cooperative. More than once, Coates volunteered to help search for the missing children. He had no arrests, and his name didn't exist on any sexual-predator lists. National Forest Service staffing personnel in all three states knew him to be a kind of eccentric loner with his battered Airstream trailer that bristled with television and Internet satellite dishes and antennae, but he was considered experienced and reliable. Whenever a host got ill, or went on vacation, Coates was contacted to fill in. His job consisted of collecting overnight fees, keeping the campgrounds clean and neat, making sure campers didn't overstay their limits, and providing advice and assistance to campers in states where camping is part of the common cultural fabric. In twenty years of being a campground host, only two complaints had been filed against him. The complaints—parents in one instance felt he leered at their children, and someone accused him of being rude because he angrily refused to come outside his trailer ("What was he *doing* in there?") when a camping family wanted to borrow a tire pump— were minor and filed in two different states six years apart.

Coates covered his tracks very well. Three of the missing children were taken *after* the regular campground hosts had returned, so his name never came up.

Worst of all, Cody told me, was that the seven children prior to Courtney Wingate was an arbitrary number. The actual number of children Coates took could be ten, or twenty, or fifty. In the three decades across the West—years Coates has not accounted for—Cody said there were over seventy missing-children cases open from Nebraska to California. And dozens more in western Canada.

Why just seven? Because the police found photos of seven missing children on Aubrey Coates's laptop computer. If there had been others—and Cody thought Coates had been successful in destroying electronic records on a server located in the trailer as well as most of the laptop—Cody and the computer specialists brought in on the case couldn't find them.

After initially filing charges against Coates for the disappearance of all seven children in the hope Coates would bargain with them—lesser charges in exchange for a confession or the locations of the bodies— the federal prosecutor ran into a brick wall because Coates admitted nothing and proclaimed his innocence. After a few months, the charges were pared down to the disappearance of Courtney Wingate, who vanished most recently, in Desolation Canyon, where Coates had served as temporary campground host. Several digital photos of Courtney were found on Coates's laptop, and her parents identified him as lurking around their campsite the night before she disappeared.

As Cody and the prosecutor walked the jury through a Power-Point presentation of the photos found on Coates's computer—evidence Coates had been targeting the little girl for some time, including shots of her riding a big plastic three-wheeler and outside at an unidentifiable location with pine trees in the background—I found her parents behind the prosecutor's table. It was painful to imagine what they were going through. Crystal Wingate, Court-ney's mother, was thin, pinched, hard, with the wizened face of a woman who'd seen tough times, none tougher than this. Donnie Wingate, who worked construction, had a big mustache and mut-tonchops, and he looked very uncomfortable being indoors. He was so tense as the photos were shown that I could see cords in his neck popping out. Donnie looked big enough and capable enough to step over the rail barrier and snap Aubrey Coates's neck before the bailiff could stop him. I wished he would. He glared at the back of Coates's head as Cody explained the other photos he'd found on the laptop and the extensive—but sabotaged—array of electronics they'd discovered in Coates's trailer.

Cody testified for another hour and a half, much of it a sum-mary and recap of his all-day session on Friday. I was riveted. In un-ambiguous language and with a manner that had been honed doing exactly this in years of courtroom appearances, Cody let himself be led by Assistant U.S. Attorney Blair. The U.S. Attorney himself—tall, bald, athletic—looked on with obvious approval.

Cody built his case methodically from the initial missing child call from the Wingates to his suspicion when he arrived at the scene at the request of the county sheriff and first saw the campground tender's trailer with so much electronic capability.

He said, "Coates's trailer reminded me of one of those communi-cations units our military uses overseas. You know, the ones that can transmit audio and visual data to some commander all the way in Florida or Nevada, so they can give orders on the battlefield in real time. There were dishes and antennae all over the trailer, and a generator outside if his campground power source wasn't enough. So I asked myself why a man who wanted to be so connected to the Internet in such an immediate way would choose to be in an isolated campground when he could be in Denver, or any city. It started with that."

Without consulting his notes, Cody told the jury how, with that question in mind, he started his investigation of Aubrey Coates. The more he learned about Coates's habits and travels and the missing children that corresponded with his locations, the more he suspected Coates of taking Courtney. The records of Coates's satellite Internet provider showed patterns of massive activity, sometimes thousands of megabytes of data being uploaded and downloaded. Most of the activity took place from 2:00 A.M. to 6:00 A.M.

"The Internet activity fit the profile of someone involved in child pornography," Cody said. "And he was not only receiving streaming-video files and other high-density material, but he was transmitting it—uploading it—as well."

Aubrey Coates himself sat stock-still during Cody's damaging testimony. He didn't shake his head or roll his eyes but seemed to watch and listen carefully. It wasn't Coates who bothered me, though. Bertram Ludik seemed to behold Cody with amusement and barely disguised scorn. And as Cody built his case—convincingly, I thought, and so did Olive—the more agitated Ludik became. Once, when he sighed loudly, Judge Moreland shot a look in his direction that shut him up.

Blair read from her pad. "So when you entered the defendant's trailer on June 8 with the federal search warrant, what did you observe?"

Cody said, "We found the defendant in the process of destroying his electronic files. The video camera had been wiped clean, and the memory sticks for his still cameras were missing. He'd already burned a bunch of magazines in a trash barrel next to the trailer, material which through analysis was later identified as photos and magazines containing graphic child pornography. Obviously, he had somehow learned of the raid in advance, but we were still able to find enough evidence to arrest him."

Blair introduced the exhibits—charred photos and magazine pages in plastic envelopes. Members of the jury passed the evidence from one to the other. Several jurors looked visibly sickened by what they saw, and one lowered her glasses to the tip of her nose and glared at Coates with undisguised contempt.

"And the computers?" she asked, returning to her podium. "What did you find?"

"The photos of Courtney Wingate we showed to the jury," Cody said, "and photos of six other missing children."

When Cody said it, there were audible gasps in the courtroom. Heads of jurors swiveled toward Coates, who still sat impassively. It was a defining moment. How Donnie Wingate restrained himself is a mystery to me.

Blair concluded her questions but asked the judge for the right to follow up with Cody later, which the judge granted. As she walked to her table, there was a noticeable spring in her step. I think at that moment if the courtroom were polled—jury included—the vote would have been unanimous to find a rope and hang Aubrey Coates right there and then.

That is, until Bertram Ludik stood up, cleared his throat, shook his head sadly at Cody as if admonishing a child, and walked to the podium stiff-armed and stiff-legged, like a bear.

AT FIRST, I couldn't understand where Ludik was headed, and I didn't listen closely. Cody's testimony had taken everyone in the room up a roller coaster and plunged them down, me included. My mind wandered. Ludik's questions were procedural. When the search warrant was applied for, when it was granted. The exact time of the raid. How the items found inside Coates's trailer were cataloged. How many officers were present and the duties of each. Several times, Ludik messed up names of officers, and Cody had to correct him. Cody's patience with Ludik was impressive, I thought. He was gentle and professional, and I could see that the jurors liked him. Ludik seemed confused and disorganized. His questions bounced all over the place, and he paused after Cody's answers as if searching on his notepad for what to ask next to fill the time. When I looked to Olive with amusement, wondering what she had seen in the past of Bertram Ludik that so impressed her, she looked back and shrugged.

I looked at my watch, wondering how long it would go before Judge Moreland concluded the session for the day. I reconstructed my meeting with Julie Perala and the black ball of dread returned. My mind drifted back to yesterday.

I was jolted back to the courtroom when Blair bolted to her feet, saying, "Objection, Your Honor! Mr. Ludik's line of questioning is without foundation."

I looked to Olive. She had heard his question and was straining to hear more.

"What?" I asked her.

"Bertram asked Cody something about the laptop."

"Approach the bench," Judge Moreland said, clearly irritated with Ludik.

The discussion between the attorneys and the judge was heated. Judge Moreland covered his microphone with his hand while they argued. The U.S. Attorney heard enough from the table that he joined in the discussion. I had no idea, of course, what was being said.

Because Cody was in the witness box, he could obviously hear snippets of the argument. Although his face didn't change expression, it drained of color, and he seemed to be staring at something over our heads as if watching his life pass by. I recognized the look, and it scared me because I'd seen it before. When we were in high school together, Brian's father gathered the three of us, sat us down in his den, and asked which one of us had broken into his wet bar and taken two bottles of bourbon. I knew it wasn't me, and I guessed it wasn't Brian. Cody was the guilty party and looked it and finally confessed.

What, I wondered, was he guilty of now?

JUDGE MORELAND SENT the attorneys away. The U.S. Attorney looked furious and sat back down in a huff. Assistant U.S. Attorney Blair seemed tight as a bowstring, and she glared at Cody, her jaws clenched. Ludik, meanwhile, smiled at the jury as he walked back to the podium. I realized now Ludik's opening act of stumbling and disorganization had been a ruse, a way of getting Cody off his guard. His questions were now crisp, and his tone contemptuous.

"Detective Hoyt, I need you to clarify something for me."

Cody nodded. Then, before he could be reminded by the judge to speak so the reporter could hear him, said, "Yes."

"During the raid on my client's trailer, your report indicates 108 items of so-called evidence were taken."

"I believe that's correct," Cody said.

"I need better than your belief, Detective. You can check your notes or read the file. Don't worry, I can wait."

I knew Cody well enough to know he was angry, but he internalized it. It was the face and attitude he used to adopt when he played middle linebacker in high school, just before he fired through the offensive line and crushed somebody. He flipped through the pages of the case file until he found what he was looking for.

"Yes. There were 108 items of evidence."

"And these items of evidence were logged in at the Denver Police Department facility, correct?"

"Correct."

"But this was a joint federal and local task force. Why weren't the items taken to the federal facility, as per normal procedure in this kind of investigation?"

Cody cleared his throat and glared at Ludik. "Because the feds are nine-to-fivers. I *knew* our building would be open."

"So you not only arrested my client without informing or involving your federal partners, you took the so-called evidence to your friends downtown as well?"

"Yes I did," Cody said.

"Interesting. Now back to the evidence itself. At the DPD, each item is given a description and assigned a specific number, correct?"

"Correct."

"Each and every item. Each piece of charred paper from the trash barrel, everything."

"Correct."

"I've looked this list over many times, Detective, and I can't seem to find the description or number for the hard drive of the server in my client's trailer."

Cody looked up at Ludik.

"Did I miss something?" Ludik asked.

"No. There was no hard drive."

"What?"

"I said there was no hard drive. Coates destroyed it or hid it before we could have it analyzed."

Ludik rubbed his face. "Detective, I'm a Luddite when it comes to computers. My wife calls me 'Luddite Ludik' "—this caused some titters from the jury—"so please forgive me if I have to ask you to explain obvious things."

Judge Moreland, bless him, cut Ludik off at the pass. "Mr. Ludik, please get to the point or drop it," he said sternly.

"Yes, Your Honor. Sorry. Detective Hoyt, correct me if I'm wrong, but a hard drive is like the brains of a computer, correct? Where all of the files, all of the memories are kept?"

"Yes."

"Without the hard drive, a computer is nothing more than a nonfunctional piece of machinery, correct?"

"Yes."

"So without the hard drive of my client's server, there is no way to know what the computer was used for or where my client went in his midnight forays onto the Internet?"

"Correct."

"Same with the missing memory sticks for the digital cameras?"

"Yes."

"So all that you supposedly have to connect my client to the disappearance of poor Courtney are photos of her not on the missing hard drive from the computer supposedly used in the middle of the night or from the cameras found in his trailer, but from my client's laptop computer, correct?"

"Correct." Cody's voice was flat.

"And the photos of poor Courtney we saw earlier, they're from the laptop?"

"Yes."

"And the other photos of the missing children, they're from the laptop as well?"

"Yes."

"So did you find other things on the laptop connecting my client to child pornography? Like movies, or other disturbing photos?"

"No."

Blair was again on her feet. "Your Honor, this is going nowhere. Physical evidence of child pornography was found in the trash barrel outside the defendant's trailer!"

Ludik said to Moreland, "We don't dispute that, Your Honor. But no one has testified in this courtroom that they saw my client burning anything. There are no address labels on the magazines, and no subscription or postal records have been introduced that prove my client owned or used that material. For all we know, it could have been put in the barrel outside my client's trailer by someone else.

"Or," Ludik said, taking a theatrical step toward Cody in the witness box, "it could have even been placed there by a third party and burned just before the raid itself."

"OBJECTION!" This was from the U.S. Attorney himself, who until this moment had not been involved in the proceedings. "This is nothing but reckless speculation!"

"Get up here," Judge Moreland said angrily to the attorneys. "Now!"

The conference was brief and intense. Moreland was animated. He shook his finger at Ludik and told the U.S. Attorney loud enough for me to hear to "back off." I found myself admiring the way he ran the courtroom. And wondering what in the hell was happening.

When Ludik returned to the podium, he wasted no time.

"Detective Hoyt, back to the laptop. It is listed as 'Evidentiary Item #6' on the list, correct?"

Cody said, "Correct."

"Let me ask you something as an experienced detective and investigator. Did you find anything about the photos themselves to be unusual or odd?"

Cody hesitated. "I'm not sure what you're asking."

But I did. And it had occurred to me earlier when we saw them but didn't hit home until now. I felt sick inside. Olive, who suddenly got it as well, reached out and grasped my sleeve.

"The photos of the children," Ludik said. "In all of them, the children are at their homes or with their families. They are the kinds of photos all parents take of their kids. We all have these kinds of photos on our desks. Isn't that correct, Detective?"

"I'm not sure," Cody said.

"Get to the point," Judge Moreland said.

"I will do that now, Your Honor," Ludik said deferentially. But he hesitated and looked down, as if gathering strength, as if preparing himself to do something he really didn't want to do, but I recognized it as stage acting.

"Detective Hoyt," Ludik said, "before we go back to that, let me draw your attention once again to the list of evidence gathered at my client's trailer. Do you agree that there are 108 pieces of so-called evidence?"

"Yes."

"Now, please turn to another document in your file, Detective Hoyt. This is the check-in sheet from the evidence room at the Denver Police Department dated June 8. Can you find it?"

Cody took his time. Finally, he grunted.

"Look at it closely, Detective Hoyt. It's basically a copy of the other sheet, but there is a number on the right of each item of evidence where it's been officially received by the sergeant in charge of the room. As each piece of evidence is entered, the sergeant assigns it a specific inventory number and date, correct?"

Another grunt.

"As I read the document, Detective Hoyt, there is one piece of evidence not registered by the sergeant on June 8. It's *on* the list, but it isn't noted until June 12—four days later. Do you see the item, Detective Hoyt? I'm referring to evidentiary item number 6, the laptop. It appears that the laptop was collected from my client's trailer on June 8 but wasn't checked into the authorities until June 12. Is that what you see as well, Detective Hoyt?"

"Yes." Barely audible.

"And whose initials are those near the check-in entry on June 12, Detective Hoyt?"

"Mine."

"So did the sergeant in charge of the evidence room make a stupid error, or was there really a four-day gap between when the laptop was taken and when it was checked in?"

Cody fixed a dead-eye stare on Ludik.

"Detective Hoyt, did you answer the question?"

Cody mumbled something I couldn't hear. The whispering and murmuring in the courtroom among the spectators and the reporters drowned it out.

Judge Moreland called for quiet. When he had it, he turned to Cody, said, "Detective Hoyt, please answer the question."

"I had the laptop in my custody," Cody said.

"You did?" Ludik asked, false astonished. "Is that normal? Isn't that a breach of departmental regulations?"

Cody said, "I wanted to see what was on it. I was doing my job."

"Your job," Ludik repeated with sarcasm. "So you're a computer expert? You're qualified to root through a suspect's computer on your own for four days? Four days when real experts could have been going through it? And where were you doing this technical work—in your private Bat Cave?"

Blair was on her feet. "Judge, that's argumentative! He's harassing the witness."

Olive whispered, "The judge is letting Bertie get away with stuff I can't believe. He must be really mad at the detective, is all I can figure."

Uh-oh. I tried to make eye contact with Cody, but he wouldn't look up.

Cody glared at Ludik. His eyes burned red, his mouth was pinched tight.

Ludik apologized, then: "I'll rephrase, Your Honor. Detective Hoyt, where were you on the weekend of June 9 and 10 immediately following the raid in Desolation Canyon? And where were you Monday, June 11, when the Denver PD log shows that you didn't report for duty?"

Cody broke his glare from Ludik and looked to Blair and the U.S. Attorney, expecting something, help maybe. None came. The two of them were glaring at each other, obviously wondering who had missed this detail if it were true.

"Detective Hoyt?" the Judge prompted.

"Evergreen," Cody said. The town of Evergreen was in the mountains via I-70.

"In a hotel in Evergreen?" Ludik asked innocently.

"No," Cody answered.

"Where, then?"

"Where do you think I was?" Cody asked, baring his teeth at Ludik. "You seem to know everything, and you like drawing it out."

"You were in jail, weren't you, Detective Hoyt? Arrested for public intoxication Friday night, June 8. You were in the Evergreen town jail until Monday morning, weren't you?"

Cody said, "I was. I was celebrating our arrest of Aubrey Coates, and things got out of hand, I guess."

"You guess?"

"They got out of hand."

Olive whispered to me, "My God. *They didn't know!*"

Blair stood and asked for a recess. Moreland denied it.

Ludik shook his head sadly, as if it troubled him that the prosecution's case—all those hours of preparation, all those press conferences announcing the capture of the Monster, all of the witnesses leading up to this moment—were an unfortunate waste of time.

"So where was the laptop while you were in jail, Detective Hoyt?"

"In my car. Locked in the trunk."

"Are you sure? Could you somehow see your car out the window of the jail cell?"

"Your Honor!" Blair said, standing up, her voice high-pitched. "He's once again harassing the witness."

"It's a legitimate question," Judge Moreland answered, disappointment in Cody written across his face. He seemed the most letdown of all. "And one the witness will answer."

Not "Detective Hoyt," but *the witness.*

"Of course I couldn't see it," Cody said.

"So," Ludik said, "for two and a half days the crucial piece of evidence in this case—the piece of evidence the prosecution is counting on to send my client to prison for the rest of his life—was in the trunk of your car in a parking lot outside of a bar in Evergreen, Colorado?"

Cody tried to swallow, and it looked like it hurt. "No one tampered with it," he said.

"Oh? And how can you be sure?"

Cody looked away. "It wasn't tampered with," he said, without emotion.

Ludik moved in for the kill. "Detective Hoyt, let me follow up on a question that I brought up earlier—something that's been bothering me ever since I saw the evidence against my client. You say you're an expert in pedophiles and their behavior, that's why you targeted my client. But don't you find it strange that the photos he supposedly had on his laptop computer of the seven missing children were not pornographic or suggestive in any way? That they were candid shots taken mainly by their parents? That, in fact, the photos *were the same ones circulated by the various police departments in their missing persons alerts?*"

Blair, despite herself, let out a little gasp. The U.S. Attorney turned sidewise in his chair, away from Cody. Aubrey Coates slowly leaned back in his chair and looked over his shoulder at the Wingate family, as if saying, "*See?*"

"Detective Hoyt," Ludik asked, after the judge hit his gavel to once again quiet the room, "did you download those photos from your own police files onto my client's laptop?"

"No!" Cody nearly jumped from the witness stand. The bailiff took a step toward him, and the judge ordered Cody to sit down.

"Maybe Monday afternoon, after you were released from the Evergreen town jail and before you transferred custody of the laptop in question to the evidence room?" Ludik asked.

"I said no," Cody growled.

"But you can't honestly tell the jury that someone else might not have taken the laptop from your car and done it during the weekend?"

Cody shook his head.

"What, Detective Hoyt?"

"I can't say with certainty, but . . ."

"Detective Hoyt, can you recall an important case where the chain of custody of the key piece of evidence was broken quite so badly?" Ludik asked.

Cody sputtered. "We'll find that hard drive," he said. "And when we do, it won't matter. That man," Cody said, rising again, pointing at Aubrey Coates, who smiled back at him, "kidnapped and killed at least seven innocent children. You can't turn him loose to kill more!"

Judge Moreland, furious, said, "Detective, sit down and shut up, or you'll be arrested right here for contempt of my court." Turning to the jury, the judge said, "Please disregard what the witness just said. He was out of line, and what he said cannot be considered in your deliberations."

"No more questions at this time, Your Honor," Ludik said, flipping back the pages of his pad.

Judge Moreland said, "Miss Blair, redirect?"

Blair appeared stunned and angry. Her voice was weak. "We may have some more questions later, Your Honor. Right now . . . well, it's getting late in the day."

Moreland snapped, "I'll make the decisions to recess for the day, if you don't mind. I don't need your help to read the clock. Now, do you have any more questions for the witness?"

"Not at this time." Cowed.

"Bailiff," Judge Moreland said through gritted teeth, "please escort this witness off the stand."

As Cody was led through the courtroom with the bailiff at his shoulder, all eyes were on him. As he passed me our eyes met, and Cody angrily shook his head.

"Mother of God," Olive said. "I've never seen anything like that before."

I followed Cody out into the hallway. A few of his fellow cops were approaching him, trying to console him. He brushed them aside barking "Leave me alone!" and charged toward the glass doors. A couple of reporters shouted questions, which he ignored.

I caught the door as it closed and pushed it back open.

"Cody!"

He didn't turn around, just kept stomping down the stairs toward the street.

"Cody!"

On the sidewalk, he paused, and I caught up with him. I'd never seen him so furious. The skin of his face was pulled back, slitting his eyes and making his mouth a snarl.

"*That motherfucker!*" Cody hissed. "I'd like to go back in there and cap him!"

"Ludik?"

"No," Cody said, shaking me off as well. "Moreland. He fucked me. He just fucked me. And he fucked the families of all those kids."

"Cody," I said, as my friend knocked my hand off his sleeve. "It was Ludik . . ."

"You don't understand anything," Cody said. "You don't know how these things work. The judge could have steered it back my way or granted that recess so the prosecutors could regroup. He let it go when he could have stopped it. The prosecution was so stunned they couldn't think of anything to say. The judge can do anything he wants, and *he let it go on.*"

I found myself in the ridiculous circumstance of wanting to defend the man who was trying to take our baby away.

"Leave me alone!" Cody barked as I reached out for him again, and for a moment I thought he was going to cap *me.* I watched him walk into the street without even glancing at the oncoming cars, who braked so they wouldn't splatter my friend, the suddenly disgraced detective, across Bannock Street.

———————

IT WAS DARK and spitting hard little balls of snow when I arrived home. I'd called Melissa and started to tell her what had happened in the courtroom when she cut me off, saying, "It's all over the news. They say he's being suspended." She said Brian had been at our house most of the afternoon, and they'd been following the case for hours, switching from channel to channel. Cody's demolition had become a sensation.

I parked in the driveway next to Brian's Lexus and killed the motor. The falling snow sounded like sand as it bounced off the hood and roof of the Jeep. I sat for a moment, suddenly exhausted, very much confused.

I felt a hundred years old as I willed myself to open the door and get out. The snow stung my exposed face and hands. I was numb, and not paying attention to the rhythmic thumping of hip-hop music from the street and the sound of a motor that should have been familiar and should have warned me.

As I reached for the handle on our front door the hip-hop suddenly rose in volume. Later, I realized it was because the car had stopped at the curb, and the passenger rolled down his window and aimed the gun out.

The popping was muffled by the snow, and I was hit twice in the back. I turned on my heel and was struck in the face, hot liquid splashing into my open eyes, blinding me.

I could hear laughing over the roaring in my ears as the car sped away.

Six

PAINTBALLS. I'D BEEN SHOT four times with a paintball gun. The color of the paint: yellow. The people who shot me? Garrett or Luis or Stevie, I couldn't be sure.

Melissa called the police while I wiped paint off my face with a kitchen towel. It took several minutes for my heart to slow down, for the adrenaline that had coursed through me to dissipate. My hands shook as I wiped the paint from my eyes and ears. My terror faded and was replaced by anger.

The police officer who responded, who was in his midtwenties, Hispanic, with a wisp of a mustache and a belly straining at the buttons on his uniform shirt, wrote down my statement and took photos of the paint hits on the back of my coat. He shook his head while he did it, saying I wasn't the first.

"There were quite a few similar instances this past summer," he told us. "Kids compete by seeing how many citizens they can 'kill' in a given amount of time and tally it up. They get more points for a 'kill' in a good neighborhood, like this one. We've caught a few of them. Some are gangsta wannabes, but mostly they're just normal knuckleheads."

I bit my tongue, and Melissa and I exchanged glances.

He continued, "But you didn't actually see them, right? Or get a description of the vehicle or a license plate?"

"I was blinded by the paint," I said. "I told you that."

"We'll follow up and let you know if we find anything," the officer said in a tone that meant we would never see him or hear from him again.

WHILE WE ATE—Brian had fetched Chinese takeout—Brian slid his chair back and drew his cell phone out of his breast pocket. "I called Cody earlier and left a message for him to call or come by. He's not answering."

"I hope he doesn't do anything to hurt himself," I said, "or anyone else."

I rehashed the trial for them, and Melissa shook her head sadly. "Poor Cody," she said. "Do you think Ludik really thinks Cody set up the Monster?"

"Hard to say," I said. "But he injected enough doubt into the proceedings, I don't see how they'll get a conviction now. He even had me wondering if Cody or some of his fellow cops might have planted some of the evidence. Not that I don't think Coates is guilty of something—I'm sure he is. I just don't know if they've got enough evidence that isn't tainted to convict him."

Melissa shuddered. "If he goes free, no parent in Colorado will be able to sleep at night."

"And everyone will hate Detective Cody Hoyt," Brian said, not without a vicious little note of glee.

"I doubt Coates will be able to infiltrate himself again, though," I said, ignoring Brian. "Everybody will be on the lookout for the guy."

"Don't be so sure," Brian said. "If he is found innocent, there'll be nothing in his record. He might even be able to sue to get his job back. You can't prevent a man from getting a job because the cops may have set him up, you know."

"Cody didn't set him up, I'm sure," Melissa said, scoffing.

Brian steepled his fingers on the table and gazed over them at her. "Cody is capable of doing things you might not approve of," he said. "In fact, I would say it's possible they targeted this Coates guy and maybe did some things to make their case stronger. It wouldn't be the first time that's ever happened. And we know our Cody isn't pure as the driven snow."

"Brian!" Melissa said, angry.

"He isn't," Brian said. "I'm sorry, Melissa. But Cody takes pride in putting bad men in prison, and he doesn't mind cutting corners if he needs to. He's told me that. Once, he showed me what he called his 'throw-down' gun. It was a pistol with the serial numbers filed off he would have handy if he ever needed it."

Melissa shook her head and looked to me for support.

I shrugged. Cody, in confidence, had told me as much before.

Things happened on the street, on both sides, that were under the radar. Cody had told me about some of them. According to Cody, since Mayor Halladay had been elected and had started building housing for the homeless and declared Denver to be a Sanctuary City, we'd been flooded with the indigent and illegal workers, mainly undocumented Mexicans. The gangs preyed on the new populace and sold them drugs and protection. The police, according the Cody, did their best to keep a lid on the situation without calling attention to the sharp rise in crime. When Denver was named host for a major political party convention, word came down from the mayor's office to "get those people off the streets." An unofficial crackdown was under way. The level of tension between the newcomers, the gangs, the police, and the mayor's office was rising. The police, if Cody was an indication of the rest of the force, felt the mayor was "embracing diversity" on the one hand and issuing under-the-table orders to clear out the riffraff on the other. While acting on the mayor's wishes, individual officers knew that if a brutality accusation was made or an incident captured by a ubiquitous cell-phone camera of a cop pounding on a homeless man or a minority, the mayor would side with the alleged victim because Mayor Halladay was a champion of the downtrodden, according to his spokesmen. Brian had once been very close to Halladay, before he was mayor. They'd been involved in business ventures together, but they'd had a falling-out, and their relationship was no longer cordial.

"Cody might bend the rules," I said, "but he'd never set up an innocent man. And he'd only cross the line in this case if he thought he was punishing a monster who might do it again. That's why he was so mad at Moreland. It wasn't about Cody. It was about the fact that Coates might go free and hurt more kids."

"Speaking of Judge Moreland," Brian said, withdrawing a sheaf of papers from his jacket pocket, "Melissa and I have been doing some detective work of our own."

"Let's hear it," I said.

"I'm going to go put pajamas on Angelina," Melissa said. "I'll be back in a few minutes."

While she was gone, Brian said, "It's amazing what one can find out using Google and a few well-placed friends in the right offices. Plus, there are a couple of wonderful high-society gossips who love to dish."

With that, he outlined Moreland's professional and marital history:

"In 1980," Brian read, "John Moreland graduated from Ridgeview High School in Asheville, North Carolina. He was an outstanding student, first in his class. President of the debate team, quarterback, yadda-yadda. An only child, from what I could find. His parents are deceased."

"Really? He doesn't seem that old."

"He's forty-five. His parents died in a car accident when John was eighteen. I read the clippings. The police said John's dad must have fallen asleep while he was driving home and drove head-on into a tree. Both parents were killed on impact, and Mrs. Moreland was thrown thirty feet through the windshield. There was some speculation that someone might have forced them off the road, but no one was ever charged."

"Was Moreland a suspect?"

"My first thought. But he didn't appear to be. He was at home with his girlfriend, waiting for his parents to get there. His girlfriend's name was Dorrie Pence, and she confirmed his whereabouts. Remember that name, Dorrie Pence."

I nodded.

"I'm still looking into this," Brian said. "All I can get from the newspapers was it was a tragic accident. The whole community came to the funeral, and there were fund-raisers for Moreland, that kind of thing. I've got some real estate contacts in North Carolina, and I've put out some feelers to them to find out if they ever heard anything. In my experience, real-estate folks have their fingers into everything in the community—who might be moving, who might be divorcing and selling, that kind of thing. A lot of times they know more about what's going on than the local cops. I mean, I know more about what's going on in Denver than that doofus cop who was here, if you know what I mean."

"Go on," I said, seeing Brian was still clearly enjoying this.

"Okay, well, he came to Colorado right after he left North Carolina. He attended the University of Colorado on academic scholarships but he had plenty of life-insurance money from the deaths of his parents. He was never a poor college student, that's for sure. He graduated with a major in political science. Then off to Harvard Law School, where he graduated magna cum laude—of course. He was twenty-four, and he married his high-school sweetie, Dorrie Pence, in Denver."

"Ah," I said. "Dorrie provided the alibi, and he married her."

"Right-o," Brian said. "Garrett was born in 1989. No other

children. An only child, like his daddy. Anyway, Moreland was in private practice in Denver for the next few years. He was a very highly regarded criminal-defense attorney before switching over to civil litigation. He was named one of the ten best litigators in the nation, yadda-yadda. From what I can find out, he was one of those men who just shines at everything he does. He was appointed United States Attorney and held that position for the next five years. But here's where it gets interesting."

Melissa came back downstairs with Angelina in soft yellow pajamas with feet in them. She looked darling, and seemed to be mimicking Brian with her chatter. I took her and held her while Brian went on.

"In 2001, Dorrie dies tragically in a hiking accident in the mountains. John and Garrett were with her, and they were apparently hiking a trail in a canyon when the path gave way. She fell sixty feet and bashed her head in on some rocks. John and Garrett saw the whole thing, but they weren't able to save her. And it turns out she was six months pregnant at the time with their second child."

Melissa and I exchanged looks.

"Were they sure it was an accident?" I asked.

Brian nodded. "There's nothing in any of the news articles about it that suggested anything otherwise. In fact, Moreland is described as distraught and devastated. There isn't much about Garrett, but he would have been only twelve at the time. Big funeral, lots of city fathers and politicians in attendance. Yadda-yadda."

"So both his parents and his first wife die in accidents," I said. "How strange. How many people do we know who've died in accidents? I can't think of any."

"Your uncle Pete," Melissa said. "Didn't he die in a boat accident? Drown or something?"

"There's one," I said.

"Do we know anything about Dorrie?" Melissa asked. "Did anyone know her very well?"

"Not many," Brian said. "Judge Moreland was—and is—at all of the Denver society events and fund-raisers. I've seen him myself—he's a fixture. But apparently she didn't like the limelight, according to my gossips. She went back to the church big-time, apparently. She was a Catholic when they married, and she became very involved in the church here. Going to Mass every morning, that kind of involved. She was, well, very plain-looking from the wedding photo in the newspaper. John looked like some kind of movie star, and he married a homely girl on the heavy side. Later, she got *very* heavy. My best gossip described her as shy, overweight, and uncomfortable in a crowd. She and the judge were a mismatched pair."

Melissa snorted. "She sounds inconvenient to a man on the make."

"It gets better," Brian said. "John Moreland married ex-model and heir to a cosmetics fortune Kellie Southards almost twelve months to the day Dorrie died. It was a massive wedding. And that same year—2002—he was appointed to the United States District Court for the District of Colorado."

"One year seems a little quick to me," Melissa said, "for a man who was distraught and devastated."

"Interesting," I said, my mind racing. "But don't forget that all we're doing is speculating here. And we are talking about a judge who seems incredibly well liked and well connected. We might be jumping to conclusions."

"And now we get to Garrett," Brian said. "I'll let Melissa take it from here."

"GARRETT MORELAND SEEMS LIKE a very bright and a very troubled young man," Melissa said. "I don't think that information will come as any surprise to us. I also learned it is very difficult to get any background on a juvenile through official channels."

"How did you get what you got?" I asked, impressed.

"A friend of a friend I used to work with downtown is a counselor at Garrett's high school in Cherry Creek. We had coffee this afternoon while you were at the trial. At first, she was very coy about talking specifically about Garrett because she's not supposed to, you know. But when I told her the situation we're in"—she nodded toward Angelina in my arms—"she started telling me things. I'm sworn to secrecy, of course. But what she told me about Garrett makes me even more determined to fight them, Jack."

"Not that you were wavering before," I said.

"No. But I think we're dealing with a very sick boy."

"What did you find out?" I asked, chilled.

"Garrett had a reputation before he even got to high school," she said, digging the pad she used for grocery lists out of the diaper bag near her feet. "He wasn't an unknown quantity. There was an incident in middle school that made the rounds and she heard about it from a fellow counselor. Apparently, the middle-school counselor knew Garrett quite well because he'd talked to the boy after the death of his mother the year before. He said he thought the boy was hollow inside, and he couldn't get through to him to get him to grieve properly. Anyway, since Garrett knew the counselor, he went to see him one day to complain that his friends wouldn't have anything to do with him anymore and he wanted the school to punish them. He gave the counselor a list of four boys who should be punished."

I shook my head.

"The counselor asked why the friends should be punished, and Garrett told him they wouldn't walk to school with him anymore, that they ditched him whenever they could."

"Kid stuff," I said, remembering how casually cruel young teenagers could be.

Melissa said, "Next to each of the boys' names Garrett had written suggested punishments. He said two of the boys should be branded with a hot iron. He said one of them should be forced to wear girls' clothes for a month. And the last should be castrated."

102

Brian whistled.

"The counselor was alarmed and took the list to the vice principal. Keep in mind this was two years after the Columbine massacre, so school officials were ultrasensitive to anything that resembled a threat. But apparently the vice principal knew Garrett's father, and they agreed to handle the situation quietly. John Moreland and the vice principal gathered the four boys and Garrett together in a conference room and asked them to talk it out, to work out their problems. What it came down to was the four boys thought Garrett was weird and scary. Garrett was reprimanded for making the list, but he wasn't disciplined in any way. The counselor was furious at the outcome, and told his colleague—the woman I had coffee with—about it when Garrett moved on to high school.

"In high school," Melissa said, "there were disturbing writings. Garrett was—or is—interested in creative writing, and he wrote several fantastically violent plays and short stories. The counselor I had coffee with had read them and agreed with the English teacher that they crossed the line. Torture, beheadings, that kind of thing. He was very interested in criminal behavior. She talked to Garrett about this, but Garrett said he had the right of free speech, especially since he was an artist. He said he would get his father involved if the school tried to stop him from being an artist."

I said, "I thought these were the kinds of things that got kids bounced out of school these days," recounting stories I'd heard and read about students who were expelled for things like bringing a plastic butter knife to school in their lunch sacks.

"They do," Brian said, "but apparently it depends on who you are. And who your father is."

Melissa said, "The counselor said Garrett brought in books he'd found in the school library filled with violence and violent images, and movies he'd rented at Blockbuster which were just as graphic as what he'd written. He built a case that his work wasn't any worse than what anybody could get their hands on just about anywhere."

"A future criminal defense attorney," I said, thinking of Ludik's performance that day.

"So nothing was done with Garrett," Melissa said. "This empowered him, according to the counselor. And so did his money, which he flashed around the school constantly. He always has the best car, the best clothes, the best computer. He was the first kid at Cherry Creek to have an iPhone—that kind of thing. Other kids resent him for it, but they also want to be around him because he was always willing to pay for lunch, or give them rides, or buy them alcohol."

"This is where his gang connection comes in," Brian said.

Melissa nodded. "The counselor said when Garrett was a junior, he started showing up to basketball and football games with gang members from downtown. They were like his posse. Garrett played it up. The gang connections gave him power. So here was a kid who had both money and power in high school and nobody—including the teachers or the counselor—took him on. The school started having some serious drug problems that year as well, and the counselor suspected Garrett's gang pals of selling crystal meth and other drugs to students."

"A criminal-defense attorney and a gang kingpin," Brian said. "That's a deadly combination."

"Can we prove this?" I asked.

Melissa said, "In a court of law? Like in front of a judge if we could get a custody hearing to keep Angelina?"

"Yes," I said, feeling hopeful for the first time.

"There have to be quite a few students in that high school who would say the same things the counselor told me," she said.

Brian nodded, excited. "With the right bulldog lawyer and a parade of kids and teachers who know Garrett, I could see a judge ruling that you should keep Angelina for her own well-being and safety."

I wanted to believe him.

"Think about it, Jack," Brian said. "You've got a man whose parents and first wife died mysteriously and a son who comes across like Little Scarface. What court would rule they should get a baby girl because of a ridiculous technicality?"

"And maybe it doesn't even have to go that far," Melissa said. "Maybe we talk with Judge Moreland and tell him what we know. I'm sure he doesn't want this all aired in a courtroom. It might be enough to make him go away."

WE STAYED UP LATE after Angelina was put to bed and Brian kept us optimistic and hopeful. He was able to get Melissa to laugh at his jokes, and it was a wonderful sound to hear. It was as if days and nights of built-up terrors and fears were being released.

BRIAN WAS PULLING ON his coat to leave when there was a knock on the door. Melissa and Brian froze and looked at me. I glanced at the clock: 1:20.

A combination of fear and rage not far under the surface revealed itself. Were the boys back? If so, this time I wouldn't be humiliated. I ran upstairs and got the .45.

"Jack!" Melissa said, seeing the weapon in my fist.

"They may have paintball guns," I said, "but I have the real thing."

"Oooh," Brian said, shaking his head, "I don't know . . ."

But I'd already thrown open the front door, ready and willing to level the Colt at Garrett's or Luis's face.

Cody slumped against the threshold, his face flushed, his eyes watery. There was snow on his shoulders and head.

"Go ahead," he slurred, "shoot me."

I put the gun aside, and Brian and I helped him in. He could barely walk, and we steered him toward the couch. The smell of bourbon on him was strong. He sat down in a heap.

Melissa said, "Cody, you're covered in blood. Are you hurt?"

I hadn't even noticed, but now I saw it: dark floral patterns of blood on his pant legs and down the front of his coat. His knuckles were bloody, the skin peeled back.

"I'm just fucking dandy," Cody said, "but that kid out there in the Hummer with the paintball gun isn't doing so hot."

Seven

Like spring snowstorms in the Rockies, late-fall snowstorms often had a particular kind of all-encompassing intensity and volume that could make you slip out of your everyday life, look around, and say, "Do we have enough groceries in the house?"

But that night, when Cody showed up at our house drunk and bloody, the snow didn't divert attention from where we were but steered it back from our brief little respite of hope, and made everything more focused and harder-edged.

BRIAN WAS IN THE PASSENGER SEAT of my Jeep as we slowly circled the block looking for the kid or vehicle Cody described. The snow was falling in white-capped vertical waves of poker chip–sized flakes. The volume of snow muted outside sound and haloed the streetlights. It wasn't cold enough yet that the snow wouldn't melt, but it was falling so hard and so fast that it didn't get the chance. Cottony balls of it bunched on the hood of the car and rested on the tops of the blades of the wipers.

A few lights were on behind closed curtains in our neighbors' homes, and three or four porch lights. Falling snow, like fat summer miller moths, swirled in the glow one second and vanished the next as the neighborhood went black.

"Uh-oh," Brian said. "What happened?"

"Power's out," I said. "Maybe the storm took a line down."

"Wonderful. The hits just keep on coming."

"Jesus," I said. "What did Cody say before he passed out?"

"Something about nearly rear-ending a car that was coming down the street with its lights off," Brian said. "Then he saw who was inside and followed them."

"Did he say where?" I asked, my voice pinched with desperation. There weren't any unfamiliar cars on the curbs or in the driveways of my neighbors. Those that were there had at least six inches of snow on them, making the models hard to pick out in the dark.

"He was hard to understand," Brian said. "Bombed out of his mind. What I heard was that he pulled the car over and the boys in it tried to run away but he caught one of them. He's so out of it, though, that I can't even be sure he wasn't hallucinating."

"That blood on him wasn't a hallucination," I said.

"But we don't know if it happened here, is what I'm saying," Brian said. "I still think we should have called the cops, let *them* look for the boy and the car."

"And get Cody arrested," I said.

"Maybe he *needs* to be arrested."

"You heard Melissa."

Brian sighed. "By not calling them have we already broken the law?"

"I'm not sure," I said.

"But we know we *should*, right?"

"I guess so."

"But we aren't going to, are we?"

"No."

I CRAWLED THE JEEP down the length of my subdivision street and took a left at the next block, passing under a darkened street-light. In the dark and in the snow, my own neighborhood seemed unfamiliar. It was the same odd feeling I'd had on Sunday when Judge Moreland showed up at my home and somehow turned it into a place I didn't know or feel very comfortable in.

"There," Brian said, pointing through the windshield.

Halfway up the next block, Garrett's H3 Hummer was parked with a front tire on the sidewalk and the back end angled out toward the street. The headlights of my Jeep washed across the length of vehicle, revealing no one inside. I slowly drove on.

"I didn't see anyone inside," Brian said. "Where did they go?"

"Cody said one took off. But where's the other one?"

I didn't want to stop in the street and train my headlights on the Hummer in case any of my neighbors were looking out. In the dark, I wouldn't be able to see them, and they might recognize me or my Jeep. I wondered if anyone had noticed the H3—it was not exactly a model that would melt into the scenery—or called the police. For sure, I thought, someone had contacted the power company by now.

At the end of the block I flipped a U and cruised back.

"Not too fast," Brian said, "I'm looking."

"There he is," I said, pointing.

"Where?"

"*There* . . ."

The heap of clothing was about ten feet from the sidewalk on the lawn of an unfamiliar house. The pile of clothing was dark but substantial and flecked with snow. There was just a glimpse as we passed by, but I thought I saw a bloody face with the wisp of a mustache. A snow-covered FOR SALE sign with a local Realtor name was planted in the grass. Even though there was no power, the house looked absolutely still, and there was a good likelihood, I thought, that no one was inside.

"Luis," I said. "Not Garrett. Luis."

"Oh man, oh man," Brian said, grabbing my arm. "What are we going to do?"

"I'm not sure."

"Is he dead? If he isn't, he'll freeze soon enough."

"I know."

"And where's Garrett?"

I looked around, shaking my head. "Let me find a place to park. I've got to think."

"Jeez," Brian said, using an expression I hadn't heard from him since we'd been in high school. "If the lights come back on . . . if the cops show up . . . if Garrett comes back . . ."

"I *know!*"

I drove the length of the block again and turned around, nestling the tires of the Jeep against the curb and killing the lights and the engine. Garrett's Hummer was fifty yards up the street. Luis was motionless, looking like a dark sooty smudge against the snow. As my eyes adjusted with the headlights off, I could make out tracks in the snow from the driver's side of the vehicle leading up the street, into the shadows. Where Garrett had run.

"What if he's still alive?" Brian asked, nodding toward Luis, his voice high-pitched.

I wished I could drum up some sympathy, but all I knew of Luis was what he did in the bathroom of my home and the paintball attack. Plus, he was associated with the kid who wanted to take my daughter away from us. The very idea of him made me angry. In a prosperous city like Denver, which was booming economically and offering opportunities to anyone who sought them, Luis had opted to belong to a violent street gang that sold drugs. It wasn't like he didn't have choices. And I didn't mind right then if he went away. I didn't really mind if he died. But could I sit there and watch him die?

Yes.

But I didn't want Cody to be implicated.

As I reached down for my door handle I noticed a glow in the snowfall down the street. I paused. The falling snow started to light up yellow like shooting sparks. Headlights. A car coming.

"Slump down," I said, and we both slid forward in our seats.

"Man oh man," Brian whispered. "What do we say if it's the cops?"

"If they don't see us, we don't have to say anything," I said.

"I'm well-known in this town, Jack," Brian said. "I've got a lot of friends and a lot of enemies. If I get caught out here, there's no way it doesn't make the papers."

"I know. Don't forget who *I* work for."

"Yes, but . . ."

"But *what?*" I barked at Brian. "You're more important? You've got more money?"

"Honestly, yes on both counts," Brian said. "But I also won't be in a position to help you and Melissa."

Nice save, I thought.

I kept my head high enough that I could see through a slot beneath the top of the steering wheel and the dashboard. It suddenly occurred to me that the Jeep might be the only vehicle on the street not blanketed by snow, that we would be obvious. It was snowing harder. Flakes were sticking to the glass and beginning to cover the hood. Still, my Jeep was at least an inch behind in snow covering.

The approaching car appeared and swung behind the Hummer, keeping its headlights on. It was an older model low-rider four-door sedan, definitely not a police car. It was the kind of tricked-up American classic some Hispanics preferred. Three doors opened at the same time, and the dome light lit up. Garrett was in the passenger seat. The driver and occupant in the backseat were Hispanic, wearing oversized coats, trousers, big, tan, unlaced boots.

"Garrett and the gangsters," I whispered to Brian. "They've come back for Luis."

"Do they see us?"

"Not yet."

The .45 was on the seat next to my thigh, and I spider-crawled my hand across the upholstery until I found the smooth wooden grip. I cracked my window so I could hear them out there.

The driver and Garrett ran to where Luis lay and shouted at him to get up.

"Fucking get up, man . . ." the driver said, nudging Luis with his boot. "Get the fuck up, Bro . . ."

The gangster from the backseat stood next to the car, acting as lookout. He kept his hands in his pockets, and I instinctively thought he had a gun or two. He looked up the block and down, eyes brushing over my Jeep. His face was dead, impassive, a round pie tin with a soul patch and heavily lidded eyes.

Garrett and the driver tugged on Luis, eventually pulling him to his feet. They draped his arms around their shoulders and guided him toward the car. I thought I saw Luis's legs move under their own power, helping them, but I couldn't be sure. His head slumped on his coat as they got him to the car. When they lowered him into the backseat I could see blood on his face and clothes from the dome light. My impression was Luis was alive—barely.

I did see Garrett's face, though, and it was hideous, contorted with rage. He said something about a paint gun, and the lookout left the car and found it on the lawn and brought it back. It had been them, all right.

"Okay," Garrett said, slamming the back door and stepping away.

The driver swung into his car and the lookout jumped in next to him. Garrett started for his Hummer, keys in his hand.

As he reached for his door handle he suddenly froze and turned toward me, squinting.

"Oh no," I whispered.

"What?"

"I think he sees us." I lifted the .45 and put it on my lap. Suddenly, stupidly, I couldn't remember if the revolver was single-action or double-action. Did I have to cock it, or could I just pull the trigger? Christ . . .

The sedan made a slow turn in the snow and started down the street from the direction it had come. Its taillights looked pink in the falling snow.

Garrett still stood near the door of his H3. I could see his mind work, looking over his shoulder at his friends departing and again at my Jeep. His backup was gone, and he wasn't sure. I thought again of my car sitting there at the curb looking sleek and dark without nearly the amount of snow on it as the other vehicles up and down the street, sticking out like a sore thumb. Had Garrett paid any attention to what I drove? Had he seen the Jeep in my driveway?

He walked toward us in the dark down the middle of the street like a gunfighter. Twenty yards away. Reaching behind him for something tucked into his belt with one hand. With his other he flipped open his cell phone and raised it. I could see the glow of it shadow the handsome features of his face. Probably calling the sedan back, I thought.

I cocked the revolver, the cylinder turning, a fat bullet poised in the chamber. Aim for the thickest part of him, I remembered from deer and elk hunting in Montana, and if you need to, fire again and again.

Garrett was ten yards away but had slowed and was bending forward, trying to see into our car.

At that moment, the power was restored and the streetlights crackled and lit up. Porch lights blinked on up and down the block. Interior lamps lit up.

"It's Christmas," Brian whispered. Because we'd grown used to total darkness, the lights seemed more intense than they should have.

"For us it is," I said, as Garrett wheeled, jogged to his Hummer, and roared away.

Brian sat up and took a deep breath. I could feel my heart pounding, whumping in my chest.

"Would you have used that?" Brian asked, gesturing toward the .45.

"Yes."

"I'm glad you didn't," Brian said.

I wasn't so sure.

THE SNOW WAS STILL FALLING outside our bedroom window when I slipped into bed. I was tired, exhausted, and had taken three Advils to blunt the effects of an oncoming headache. Brian left as soon as we got back to the house, saying he hoped his hands would stop shaking so he could drive. Cody was downstairs snoring on the couch. Melissa had gotten his shoes and jacket off and covered him with a quilt.

I tried not to wake her, but of course she was not asleep.

"What happened out there?" she asked. I told her, leaving nothing out.

"I hate him," she said, referring to Luis, "but I wouldn't want anyone to freeze to death although I've read it's just like going to sleep. It isn't painful."

I wasn't sure how to respond.

"Will Garrett connect Cody to us?" she asked. "Does he know Cody is our friend? Will he blame us for what happened?"

"I don't know. I suppose it depends on whether Cody said anything to them or just started pounding on Luis."

"I'd bet he said something."

"We can ask him tomorrow—if he even remembers."

"Oh, Jack, it's gone from bad to worse."

I nodded even though she couldn't see me in the dark. She sidled over under the covers and put her warm palm on my chest.

"You showered again," she said. "Why?"

"I felt dirty, I guess."

"What time is it?"

"Almost three."

"Are you going to work tomorrow?"

"I've got to."

She put her head on my shoulder. Her hair smelled nice. "I wish you could just stay home. We could have a snow day—just our family."

"And Cody," I reminded her.

"And Cody." She laughed gently.

I glanced out the window. The snow had lightened considerably.

"We could just stay home and be a family," she said, repeating herself.

I kissed her on the mouth. She kissed back, but broke it off.

"Not that," she said, "not now. I just want to be held, that's all."

I held her.

We could hear Angelina stir and cry out over the baby monitor. Melissa was instantly alert, and she ducked under my arm and swung her bare legs out of bed.

"What?"

"She's having a bad dream," Melissa said, standing and pulling on her robe. "She's been having them since the Morelands showed up on Sunday. I don't know whether she's sensing something from me or what. I'm going to get her."

Melissa left, and I heard Angelina whimper and the sound broke my heart. Over the monitor, I could hear the springs of the crib mattress squeak as Melissa picked her up and cooed at her.

"I think I'll let her sleep with us for a while," Melissa whispered as she came back in the bedroom. I made room, and Melissa lowered Angelina between us. The baby was still sleeping. In the ambient light from the window she looked peaceful and content. Her long lashes were exquisite, and her little rosebud mouth formed a pleasant smile. Her breath was slight, little puffs of sweet air. I brushed her round warm cheek lightly with the backs of my fingers. So soft. She was just so *small*.

"Don't roll over and crush her," Melissa said.

I was always scared about that, and I edged farther away.

"We've got three weeks," she said. "And you'll be gone one of them."

"I'll be back sooner than that," I said. "I'll be back as soon as I have that meeting with Malcolm Harris."

"Still . . ."

"I'm more optimistic," I said, "after what you and Brian found out tonight. The judge and his son aren't so all-perfect and all-powerful after all."

"I was talking with Cody about that while you and Brian were out," Melissa said. "He might have just been out of it, but he wasn't very encouraging."

"What do you mean?" I asked, alarmed.

"I told him what we'd found out, and he just shook his head, and said, '*Third-party gossip shit. None of it would work in court.*'" She tried to imitate his particular sarcastic cadence of speech.

"But we're just getting started," I said. "We still need to prove everything."

"What if we can't?" she said. "Rumors are cheap. It's different when we try to *prove* these things."

"We don't have to prove that Moreland's parents and wife died mysteriously," I said.

"But it's nothing, really, when you think about it. The judge was never charged or even suspected of anything as far as we know. And Garrett just comes across as a moody teenager. What's so strange about that?"

"Cody said this?" I asked, getting angry.

"No," she said. "I was thinking about it. He's right. We don't have anything but a bunch of rumors. We can't go up against a powerful judge and his son with just a pack of stories. Somehow, we have to prove something—anything."

The minutes ticked by. The more I thought about it, the more I realized she was right. The last vestiges of the hope I'd had earlier skulked out of the room as if ashamed.

"Honey," I said, "there is no point getting a lawyer and going to court. We may find out something about them, but now Garrett has an attempted murder on *us*."

She sighed. "Maybe Brian can find out something more solid. He said he'd dig deeper."

It was as if she didn't hear what I'd just said.

She said, "And I can follow up on the school incidents, but all we've got right now is what a counselor says she heard from another counselor. If I were a judge I wouldn't even listen to us."

"I should have shot the son of a bitch," I said.

"Jack, don't say that. If you did, you'd get put into prison. This baby needs a father, and I need a husband."

Still . . .

"I HAD A STRANGE THOUGHT," Melissa said after a while. "Luis was somebody's baby. And Garrett was a baby once, too."

"It is a strange thought," I said.

"Jack, I love you," she said.

"I love you, too."

"What's going to happen now?" she said.

"I don't know."

"We've got to protect this child," she said.

"Yes."

"You were brave tonight."

I liked hearing that because I never thought of myself as

particularly brave. I wanted her to think of me as a man of courage, and I vowed not to give her a reason to think otherwise. I had never before that moment thought in those terms, although every man, I think, wonders what he'd do when it comes down to a fight-or-flight decision.

"I'm going to leave you two alone," I said, getting out of bed. "I'm still too wired to sleep. I'll be back. I'll try not to wake you up when I come in."

Melissa was already falling asleep, an arm stretched lightly over Angelina. At the doorway I stopped and looked back. My wife and my daughter in my bed, both breathing softly.

I KEPT THE LIGHTS OFF in the family room and turned on the television. Since our remote had been stolen and ruined, I'd learned where to power it up on the set itself. It was tuned to CNN. I was too lazy and disinterested to surf through more channels using the buttons on the set and I sat down in my chair. The light from the set flickered on Cody under the blanket on the couch. Periodically, he would make me jump with thunderous flatulence or a racking snort. I could smell old bourbon in the room, as if it were seeping through his skin. I smiled as I contrasted Angelina and Cody, and wondered what it was about age that made the odors so much worse.

Over the news anchor's shoulder on the screen were the graphics MONSTER OF DESOLATION CANYON and the booking photo of Aubrey Coates. They cut away to a local correspondent named Erin somebody doing a standup in front of the courthouse hours earlier as the snow began to fall.

"The case against Aubrey Coates was dealt a major blow today in the Denver courtroom of Judge John Moreland," the attractive dark-haired lady said, "when . . ."

I half watched, half listened. Cody was shown stomping out of the courtroom, snarling at the camera. I couldn't help but glance over at his broad back on the couch.

The segment ended as the reporter said, "I'd bet you a bag of donuts that unless the prosecutors have something powerful and un-expected up their sleeves, Aubrey Coates is going to walk. Back to you, Anderson."

Anderson said, "That was recorded earlier tonight. And Erin, a bag of glazed donuts will be just fine."

"*Motherfucker . . .*" Cody growled in his sleep, tossing about vio-lently.

Friday, November 9

Sixteen Days to Go

Eight

THREE DAYS PASSED. THERE was nothing in the papers about Luis. I had no idea if he was dead or alive. There were no police visits, no calls from Garrett or John Moreland. It was as if that night had never happened. I could say I felt relief with each passing day, but it wasn't like that at all. Instead, I felt the tension mounting, anticipating their next attack, wondering this time if it would be with real bullets. And never doubting that it would come.

While women can generally intuit the subtle feelings and motivations of other human interactions better than men, men instinctively know one thing: when they're at war. What shocked me was how smoothly I slipped from the bank into the full current.

ON FRIDAY, I went to the office early to tie up loose ends. I wasn't the only person at the bureau, despite the early hour. Jim Doogan, the mayor's chief of staff, flashed by in the hallway but made a point of pausing in front of my open door and looking in.

I waved hello.

"Let me get a cup of coffee," he said, and continued down the hall.

I smiled. Doogan couldn't even wave back until he had coffee.

Doogan was a curious man—he looked just like his name. Late fifties, Irish, beefy, red-faced with short-cropped red hair speckled with gray. He was a blunt object, so different from the mayor, who was young, thin, handsome if effete, so filled with energy one expected shooting sparks from his enthusiasm to start a fire in the wastebasket. But Doogan was necessary. Someone had to scare off sycophants and interest groups who wanted too much of the mayor's time. Someone had to run interference and fix things out of public view. Doogan was the man sent in to tell someone who'd met with the mayor and claimed Halladay had promised them something to tell them no, the mayor had simply *acknowledged* the problem. I'd always kind of liked Doogan. There was nothing slick about him. He reminded me of men in Montana—cattle buyers, country commissioners, who, when they bested you, would throw an arm around your shoulder and offer to buy you a beer.

Apparently, the mayor was having his monthly breakfast meeting with our bureau president, H. R. "Tab" Jones. Before being appointed to the bureau, Jones was the mayor's campaign manager and chief fund-raiser. Jones was tall, loud, slick, and from what I gathered from longtime staff, not as intolerable as past presidents. Jones came from banking and had no background in tourism promotion, which never stopped him. In staff meetings, he threw around hot business buzzwords and catchphrases—"metrics," "skill sets," "paradigm," "worldview"—but he often used them incorrectly. He urged us to "push the envelope" and "think outside the box." Behind his desk were dozens of current business and motivational books which, I noticed, had uncracked spines.

Doogan finally came back with a cup of coffee and entered my office, shutting the door behind him. He'd never done that before. I looked up and leaned back in my chair. His aftershave smelled sharp.

He shook his head and pursed his lips, as if what he was about to tell me saddened him.

"Brian Eastman?" he said simply. "Not a good idea."

And with that he was out the door before I could ask him how he knew so quickly, or more important, how the *mayor* knew.

LATER, LINDA LEANED INTO my office after an executive staff meeting, asked, "What on earth did you do to piss off the mayor?"

"What do you mean?"

She said Tab Jones told her Mayor Halladay specifically asked him about me.

"He asked if you were competent or some kind of loose cannon," she said. "The mayor asked if you could turn out to be a liability. Tab said he defended you and our department, but I think that's horseshit. I think he . . ." she delivered a devastatingly accurate imitation of Jones's best executive voice, *"expressed shock and concern and assured the mayor he'd look into it."* She reverted to her real voice. "Meaning, in all likelihood, your days could be numbered. Which leads me back to my first question: What on earth did you do to piss him off?"

I suddenly felt cold. I desperately needed this job.

"I didn't do anything to the mayor," I said. "But it's possible John Moreland said something to him." Wondering, did Garrett tell his father what happened Monday night? Or did he lie, make up some story about how he'd come to our house to see Angelina and was jumped by a maniac, his friend left to die in a vacant yard? Did our friendship with Cody, the disgraced cop, or Brian, who'd had a sour business relationship with the major before he was mayor, bring about this sudden interest in me? Were Brian's inquiries hitting soft spots? Or was it all Judge Moreland?

And I realized the Morelands didn't need bullets, or paintballs, to attack. Breakfast with the mayor accomplished the same purpose.

"Keep your nose clean," Linda said, studying me, the wheels spinning in her head. "I can't afford to lose you right now. I'm not sure we'd be able to hire a replacement, the way things are going with our budget. And even if we could, it could take months, and we don't have months. The trade-show season is upon us."

"I'll do my best," I said. "I always do."

She nodded, agreeing with me, but still with that look. The look of a racehorse owner assessing a promising colt who'd just come up lame.

MY FLIGHT TO BERLIN was to be Sunday, two days away, with arrival at Tegal at 7:05 A.M. Monday. The suitcase was nearly packed upstairs in our room, my briefcase heavy with my laptop, lead sheets, business cards, brochures, a six-pack of Coors beer for Malcolm Harris, who loved the stuff. I would be gone a week, returning the following Saturday. In my mind, I must admit, I was already halfway out the door.

I had tried to convince Melissa to take Angelina and stay with her mother in Seattle while I was gone, but she'd have none of it. Melissa was still smoldering about her parents' divorce and disliked her mother's new husband. Even given the circumstances, she didn't want to see her mother "hat in hand," as she put it.

CODY STAYED AT OUR HOUSE. He slept on the couch at night and watched television and helped around the house during the day. He's better at fixing things than I am, plus he had the time. He rehung a couple of sagging doors, fixed the toilet so it would stop running, and painted the kitchen. Melissa said he took breaks only to follow the Coates trial on TV and smoke cigarettes on the deck. He told her he couldn't remember what he said to Luis that night, but he had a feeling he "went all Dirty Harry on his ass." He asked if he could stay with us until the reporters camped out around his house gave up and went away, and we agreed. Melissa appreciated his help and companionship, and I liked the idea of his being there with his weapons and training and capacity for violence in case Garrett and his boys showed up again.

Saturday, November 10

Fifteen Days to Go

Nine

AFTER BRIAN HAD LEFT THE night of Cody's confrontation with Luis, we didn't see him for the rest of the week. He was in New York, Chicago, St. Louis, and the Bay Area on business. He kept in touch with Melissa by text messaging her from airports between flights. She kept the messages and showed them to me when I got home from work. I reviewed them over coffee Saturday morning.

LEARNING MORE AND MORE THINGS ABOUT THE JUDGE. CAN'T WAIT TO TELL YOU.

And,

TALKED TO ONE OF MY FRIENDS WHO DABBLES ON THE DARK SIDE. HE SAID THERE MIGHT BE SOME PHOTOS THAT WILL BRING THE JUDGE DOWN. I'LL FOLLOW UP. IT MAY COST US SOME CASH.

"Photos of *what?*" I asked.

"I texted him back," she said. "He hasn't replied."

She sighed. "You know how dramatic he can be. He won't just tell us, he'll want to show us."

Cody stood in the doorway in a paint-splattered T-shirt and a three-day growth of beard. He'd overheard.

"Let's take a drive downtown," he said to me.

"Do you mind?" I asked Melissa.

"No," she said, "as long as you'll bring dinner home and not drink too much. Remember, you've got an early-morning flight tomorrow."

As if I didn't know.

IN SEVERAL NATIONAL SURVEYS, Denver has been cited as the least-overweight large city in the country, usually neck and neck with Portland. Health and recreation is a religion. I know this because I sell it overseas. In contrast, Cody sucked on his cigarette with a kind of junkie intensity, sat back in the seat, closed his eyes, and slowly blew the smoke out. He smoked with such needy and obvious pleasure that he made me wish I was a smoker.

On workdays, there was traffic. Lots of traffic. On those days I compared the street we lived on out in the western suburbs to a tiny seasonal creek, like the one that used to flow through the ranch my father managed for a while near Great Falls. Like that creek, our street/creek trickled into a busier residential street (or stream, in my analogy) which poured into a tributary (C-470) of a great rushing river (Interstate 70 to I-25) toward downtown. Once I became a part of the river hurtling down the valley toward the high-rises, stadiums, and inner city, I became a different animal, a fish fearing for his life. Currents of traffic coursed across lanes while the entire river picked up speed and volume. Outlets (exits) lessened the pressure only temporarily, because inlets (entrance ramps) produced greater flows. I was a little fish in an ocean of them. At night, like a spawning salmon, I would navigate the powerful river of traffic back to my sandy creek bed of origin where Melissa and nine-month-old Angelina would be waiting for me, and all would be right with the world.

Saturday-morning traffic was sparse on Interstate 70 into the city, although the situation was different westbound into the mountains. Several ski areas were already open because of the early snow and the snow they'd made from machines, and I'd never seen so many Volvos, Land Rovers, and Subaru Outbacks with skis or boards on top in my life. I imagined the occupants inside to be listening to Dave Matthews if they were under forty and John Denver if they were over.

We took I-25 to the Speer Boulevard exit and plunged into downtown, past the gentrified lofts near Pepsi Center and Coors Field, empty except for the homeless on the 16th Street Mall.

We parked in a lot that cost five dollars in a still-seedy part of downtown the developers hadn't gotten to yet. Not that Cody paid. Instead, he badged the attendant as he strode past the booth. The attendant—tattooed, pierced, reeking of smoke—recoiled as if he were a vampire and Cody's shield was a crucifix. I followed my friend to Shelby's Bar and Grill on 18th. I knew it as a cop hangout.

The waitress knew him and bowed like a subject before her king, but with a smirk on her face to project her sarcasm. "Your throne is ready, sir," she said.

Cody grunted and sat down heavily in a dark booth. I took the other side.

"Hit you both?" the waitress asked Cody.

"Jameson's," he said to her. "Three of 'em."

To Cody, I said, "Three?"

When she went to the bar, Cody dug into his pocket for his pack of cigarettes, said, "I've got a guy coming in to meet with us. I hope he still shows up, given my current status with the department."

"About that," I said. "How is the trial going?"

"It's all over but the shouting," he said. "The defense rested without calling a witness. The jury's sequestered for the weekend, and Monday they'll all come in and set that bastard free."

I shook my head. "So there was nothing else on him?"

"We had enough," Cody said, lighting up. "We had more than enough." He inhaled and blew a long stream of smoke at the NO SMOKING sign above our booth. The ban was statewide.

"You want to ask me if I set him up," Cody said.

I didn't say yes, I didn't say no.

And he didn't answer.

Cody's cell phone burred, and he went through a comic ritual of patting all of his clothing with the cigarette dancing in his mouth before he found it in his breast pocket and pulled it out.

"Yeah, we're here," Cody said to the phone. "And I already ordered, so come on in."

He closed the phone and put it on the table so he wouldn't lose it again. "Jason Torkleson just came up to detectives last week," he said. "They assigned him to my squad. He's bright-eyed and bushy-tailed, like all of us were when we started. Before he could get bogged down with a caseload or get co-opted by the lieutenant, I asked him to research Garrett Moreland and Luis and Sur-13 and put together a background report."

The door opened and sunlight streamed into the dark room and a slender young man with pale skin and deep red hair came in grasping a manila folder. He was wearing a track suit, and he looked fit, as if he'd completed his morning workout shortly before the meeting.

"Is that him?" I asked.

Cody bent over and craned around the side of the high-backed booth and waved Torkleson over.

"Obviously, they're still talking to me," Cody mumbled.

After introductions, Torkleson sat down on my side so he could face Cody and present his findings to him. The file was on the table. The waitress delivered the three drinks, and Cody took his from her hand before she had the chance to set it down. He drank deeply, said "Aaaaugh," and slowly lowered it. I sipped mine. It burned nicely.

"Starting early, eh?" Torkleson said.

Cody sang a line from a Louis Jordan song, "*What's the use of getting sober, when you're gonna get drunk again . . .*" and laughed. I did, too. Cody had been growling that line for ten years.

"Maybe I'll pass," Torkleson said.

Cody's expression went dead, and he beheld Torkleson with heavy-lidded eyes. "What, you keeping in shape?"

"Actually, yes."

Cody said, "The word 'actually' is overused these days, and when it's used, it's not used correctly. You youngsters say 'actually' nearly as much as you use the word 'like' and 'basically.' They're all unnecessary words the way you use them. Both are incorrect usage, according to my Helena High English teacher Ms. Lesa Washenfelder. Right, Jack?"

I nodded solely so Cody would move on.

To Torkleson, Cody growled, "Now drink your fucking drink."

Torkleson sat back as if slapped. It took a beat, but he reached for his drink and sipped it gingerly, his eyes flinching at the taste.

The file just sat there.

"Aren't you going to look at it?" Torkleson asked.

"Later," Cody said. "Give me the gist."

Torkleson looked at me, then back to Cody.

"He's all right," Cody assured him. "Anything you tell me he can hear."

Torkleson tapped the folder. "I wish I had more in there, but there wasn't that much information available. Garrett Moreland is the son of Judge John Moreland, but I think you already knew that."

"We did," Cody said, working his fingers on the tabletop like a blackjack player wanting another hit from the dealer. "Give me more."

"Garrett's mother . . ."

"We know that, go on."

"There's no rap sheet and as far as I can tell no juvie record."

"Damn."

"The only thing I could link to Garrett was his name showed up a couple of times on cross tabs—he's listed as a known associate of a couple of gangbangers. I found that surprising."

"Go on."

"Sureño 13. I printed out all the info on them I could find in our files. *Sureños* is a Spanish word for Southerner . . ."

Cody held up his hand. "You don't need to go into all of that if it's in the file. I know all about Sur-13, from the fact that it was born in the California prison system and has now spread into all fifty states, that the thirteen refers to the thirteenth letter of the alphabet—M—which stands for Mexican Mafia. The gang identifies with the color blue, members have three tattooed dots on their knuckles, and as an organized crime gang they handle most of the meth and heroin in Colorado."

Torkleson nodded.

"What we're interested in is how a good Cherry Creek High School boy got mixed up with them, and why," Cody said.

"That I can't tell you," Torkleson said, tapping the file on the table. "What we do have are a half dozen photos of him—Garrett—with known members of Sur-13 going in and out of the Appaloosa Club down on Zuni Street. You know about the Appaloosa?"

Cody nodded. Even I had heard of the Appaloosa Club. The reason I knew about it was because it was on a block downtown the bureau made sure we steered journalists and other guests away from. Somehow, the area had been missed by the urban developers and probably would be in the near future. The buildings on it were dilapidated. Tattoo parlors, bars, and a couple of liquor stores with bars on the windows. In the middle of all of them was the Appaloosa, easily identified at night because the patrons had smashed most of the ancient red neon tubes above the door so it read P-OO. I'd heard from Cody that patrolling cops often took a detour around the club so as not to have bricks rained on their cruisers.

"There are some undercover shots of your boy inside the club, too. He looks like he belongs—he doesn't stand out like some of the adventurous white girls who show up there every now and then looking for trouble. But if Garrett is welcome and comfortable in the Appaloosa, we know he's in deep with these guys."

"That's it?" Cody said. "A few pictures?"

"I'm afraid so."

Cody sighed. I expected him to upbraid Torkleson, but he didn't. The new detective seemed to have gathered all he could within the department even though it gave us little we didn't already know.

"I wish I had more," Torkleson said, reading Cody's body language. "Juvie stuff is hard to get without a warrant, even though I have a few buddies downtown. My impression is there was really nothing to get—that Garrett has kept himself clean. And the other name you gave me, 'Luis,' well, you can just throw that section in the file away."

Cody honed in on that. "What do you mean?"

Torkleson said, "If the subject you wanted intel on is Pablo 'Luis' Cadena, known associate of Garrett Moreland and vice versa, well, he's no more. His body was found a couple of days ago in the South Platte. He'd been stomped and beaten. The coroner said he was dead before he was dumped."

I stared at Cody, willing him to look back. But he didn't. I realized Cody didn't want to give any hint of alarm away to Torkleson, and Cody's face was a mask. Under the table, I felt the nudge of a boot—Cody telling me to look away from him and keep my mouth shut. I did.

"Any suspects?" Cody asked.

Torkleson shook his head. "Nothing. Cadena had a sheet as long as your arm. The homicide's being categorized as 'gang-related' and was handed over to the task force."

"I hadn't heard anything about it," Cody said.

"You haven't been in," Torkleson said, looking away to spare each of them the embarrassment. "And it's not exactly front-page news when a gangbanger is found dead these days."

Cody finished his drink and signaled for another. He seemed not to have heard what Torkleson said. "So," Cody said, "what's the word on me in the department these days?"

Torkleson used the question as a reason to push back and stand up to leave. "Actually, basically, to the brass you're like dead meat, buddy."

AS WE WALKED BACK to my Jeep two drinks (for Cody) later and Torkleson long gone, Cody said he'd personally protect Melissa and Angelina while I was away.

"Are you up for that?" I asked.

He shot a hurt look at me.

"I don't mean the drinking," I said defensively. "I meant whether or not your schedule allowed it."

"I don't *have* a fucking schedule until my hearing," Cody said.

We got into the car and shut the doors. I was overwhelmed and could feel my chest constrict.

"Aren't you going to start the motor?" Cody asked.

"We got away with it," I said.

Cody looked straight ahead.

"Cody . . ."

He turned on me. "I heard you. And Jack, this isn't something we will ever talk about again. *Ever.* What's done is done. Tell me you didn't tell Melissa what happened."

"Not all of it," I lied.

"Good. Don't."

Then: "Who are we kidding here? You tell her everything, don't you?"

"Yes."

He sighed heavily. "You may want to rethink that," he said.

WE DIDN'T TALK FOR TEN MINUTES while I drove home. Cody was smoldering, thinking, and smoking.

"This deal with Luis tells me a lot," he said, finally. "It should tell you a lot as well. That Garrett decided to dump Luis's body and make it look like a neighborhood hit—it's interesting. Especially considering what he *could* have done, like either calling the cops that night or going to the press with it. But what this tells me is Garrett didn't want it out that he was cruising your street with Luis."

I shook my head, not following.

"If Garrett reported the beating, the question would be asked why he was there in the first place. Angelina would have had to come up, and that would have sucked Judge Moreland into the story. Either Garrett didn't want his dad involved—or to know he was there—or the good judge didn't want it known. So instead, they covered it up the way they did."

"I don't get it."

"I don't either entirely," Cody said. "But what this tells us is there is a lot more going on than we know. There's a reason—or reasons—they would risk dumping Luis's body rather than have the spotlight turned on them right now. Which makes me wonder what in the hell they don't want found out, especially since they claim to be on the right and legal side of this adoption business."

I said, "Maybe Garrett and Moreland aren't talking. Maybe they're operating independently of each other."

Cody shook his head. "I can't buy that. I'd bet money they're communicating, coordinating their moves."

I thought about that.

He said, "What this also means is they've chosen to go below the radar, just as we have. We are no longer operating above the surface. Which means we're really in dangerous fucking territory."

We cruised back downtown into the old warehouse and industrial section. There were no pedestrians on the sidewalks and few vehicles. This was the area where Jack Kerouac and Neal Cassady used to hang out in the 1950s when Kerouac was "researching" the beat travelogue that would become *On the Road*. The construction cranes that hovered over LoDo like praying mantises had not yet perched here, but it was only a matter of time. The old tobacco, wool, and dry-goods warehouses would soon be condos and retail stores.

"I realize what you're doing, and I appreciate it," I said, finally. "You'll never know how much I appreciate it. You're going above and beyond."

"I know," he said, his eyes half-lidded. "But you're my best friend. If I can't help you out, what good am I? You and me and Brian—we've got to watch out for each other. We're just Montana boys in the big city even though Brian pretends he isn't."

The sentiment touched me and surprised me.

"Is this the drink talking?"

"Partially."

"Well, I appreciate it anyway."

He snorted.

"Damn, you're cynical."

He took a deep drag on his cigarette. "You have no idea," he said.

ON THE WAY BACK to my house, Cody leaned back and put his head on the headrest and closed his eyes.

"One more thing," he said.

"What?"

"Remember when I told you I wouldn't go after the judge? That I couldn't go after him?"

"Yes."

Cody flicked his fingers as if tossing aside something small and dead. "Forget that. That ended in the courtroom. I'm going to war with that motherfucker."

Then he slipped off into sleep and his head bobbed while I drove. I thought, *This man will watch over Melissa and Angelina?*

WHEN WE GOT BACK to my house, Cody's head popped up, and he seemed perfectly sober and lucid.

"I guess I conked out," he said without a slur.

"Would you like some dinner?" I forgot I was supposed to pick up something. "We can order a pizza."

"Naw, I'm fine. I've got to sneak down to my place and get some clothes."

"Should I tell Melissa you'll be here all next week?"

"Tell her whatever you want. Just make sure she's okay with that."

"Cody . . ."

He waved me away. "Don't worry," he said.

I walked him to his car.

"You'll be back in a week, right?" he asked.

I said yes.

"By the time I see you next, I will have talked with my uncle Jeter," Cody said.

I froze.

"Don't worry. I'm just making sure he's still around and available if we need him."

"Don't you know someone around here who could do the job?" I asked, uncomfortable with the fact that I'd acquiesced, that this all just seemed so inevitable. That I'd said "the job" like some kind of low-rent mobster.

"I know people," he said. "But for something like this, I can only trust blood relations. I can't risk somebody talking, and neither can you."

"Jeez," I said, "I don't know."

"I'm just checking on availability," he said. "That's as far as I'll go. If you want to talk to Jeter, you'll have to make that decision yourself."

I nodded.

Cody grinned at me, then held out his hand. "Have a good trip," he said. "And don't worry about anything. She'll be safer with me around than she is with you, for God's sake."

I think he meant it to be a joke.

LATE THAT NIGHT, Brian called. He said, "Get Melissa on the phone—you've both got to hear this."

"Where are you?" I asked while Melissa scrambled to the other room to grab the extension.

"San Diego. Seventy-two degrees constantly. I don't even know why they have weathermen."

Melissa picked up, and Brian launched, speaking in his rat-a-tat-tat manner, "I talked to a friend of a friend who went to high school in Asheville with John Moreland. He didn't paint a happy picture of our boy growing up. Apparently, John was the unwanted son of his wild-about-town teenage mother, who gave the child to her older sister and her husband, the Morelands. Just *gave* John to them. Apparently it wasn't all that unusual down there. So John grows up in this tight-assed, repressive household where his 'mother' is actually his aunt and his 'father' is his uncle. They go to court and get John's name changed to Moreland—I don't know what it was before and it doesn't matter. Anyway, John hates his parents. He doesn't say a lot about them in high school, other than they '*try to keep him down,*' whatever that means, but my friend's friend thinks it has to do with

142

his ambition. Maybe they wouldn't sign scholarship or financial aid applications, something like that, but I'm just speculating. But when they pass on as a result of that car wreck, well, our boy not only gets two insurance-policy payoffs, but the whole world of financial aid must have opened up to him. That's how he could afford to leave and go to CU. And he just washed his hands of his upbringing, from what I understand. Never went back to North Carolina for reunions or anything like that. Never went back to visit the graves of his parents, according to my source.

"So," Brian said, "we're dealing with one cold bastard."

"But he had an alibi the night of the crash," I said. "You told us that."

"And he brought his alibi with him to Colorado," Brian said. "Later, he married her. And later, she died, too."

Berlin

Monday, November 12

Thirteen Days to Go

Ten

TEGAL AIRPORT WAS AS it always was—too small, bustling, confusing, metallic, and round. Gray-white morning light seeped through windows that seemed dirty but weren't—it was the quality of the light itself—and I waited for my luggage at a squeaking, lurching, stop-start-stop carousel in a crowd so dense there was no way not to touch shoulders with others and be jostled. I was still lost in the familiar fuzzy twilight of jet lag. I had the feeling of being alone in my head, looking out through dry and bloodshot eyes. My skin felt gritty. I needed a place where I could regroup and shower.

Arriving passengers were a mix of Euros from the east and west on business, North Africans in flowing robes, large extended families of Turks. The crowd was veined with distinct groups of four or five who were no doubt arriving to attend WTB, as I was. Jamaicans, Thais, Argentines, Cubans—all sticking together, waiting not only for their luggage but their display booths, boxes of tourism brochures printed in German, and in the case of the Cubans their cigar-making gear so they could hand-roll smokes for select German tour operators. Everybody in the world sought the well-heeled and determined German travel market. We all wanted these people who got five to six weeks of mandated vacation time, who thought of travel as a right and not a privilege, who many times knew more about us and our geography and culture than we knew ourselves.

It was easy to pick out the Americans, with our open and animated faces, our loud talking as if no one else could understand English, our inadvertent and instinctive élan that so annoys others. A contingent from Las Vegas, including tanned men with dark, slicked-back hair and showgirls who, without their costumes and feathers, were simply too tall, pale, and thin, looked like a Mafia excursion to Tahoe or Atlantic City that had taken the wrong airplane.

As I checked my wristwatch to see how long we'd been waiting for our luggage, I thought I heard my name called out and raised my head. I recognized no faces and decided it was simply a similar-sounding word barked out in another language. Then, in an English accent, "Jack! Are you lost, my boy?"

Malcolm Harris of AmeriCan Adventures, wearing a tailored English suit with his trench coat folded over his forearm, clapped me on the shoulder from behind.

"I almost didn't recognize you," I said, trying to snap out of my dreamlike state so as to be as sharp as possible for the most important tour operator to our area. "The last time I saw you, you were wearing jeans and a cowboy hat and sitting on a horse." I remembered how much he'd loved playing cowboy on a dude ranch.

Malcolm Harris was pale, with thin black hair and a twitchy smile that slid back to reveal two rows of bad teeth. His suit hid his paunch. His sharp nose was discolored with the red and blue road map of a serious drinker and there was a strand of sweat beads along the top of his upper lip.

Harris tipped his head back and laughed. "I wish I were back out in Colorado now instead of this bloody place."

"Me too," I said.

"So, when did you get in?"

They always ask "So, when did you get in?" even though it was obvious I had just arrived.

I said, "I'm just hoping my luggage got here with me."

Then I recalled Linda Van Gear's first maxim of tourism marketing: *It is always about them. It is never about you.*

"It's good to see you," I said. "You're looking very good. Do you have a booth at the show?"

"It's good to be seen," he said as an aside. "No, I never get a booth here. You think I want to talk to bloody Germans?" He whispered that last part, but not quietly enough, I thought. "No, I'm here because it's the best place to see all of you and get some business done. All of you all in one place—it's brilliant, even though I despise Berlin. And the whole bloody Fatherland, for that matter. They have no sense of humor here, and that's just to start with."

I quickly looked around to see if we were being overheard. I locked eyes with a green-uniformed *Polizei* who looked back at me, dead-eyed.

"Where are you staying?" he asked.

"The Savoy. On Fassenstraße."

He nodded with recognition. "Fine place. I know it. English ownership. Still have that great cigar bar?"

"I think so."

"Brilliant. How about I meet you there tonight, and we go to dinner afterwards. Your treat." And he laughed.

"Perfect," I said enthusiastically, thinking I would rather put a bullet in my head—or at least get some sleep.

"Seven o'clock then," he said, patting my shoulder again. "I was hoping I'd see you. I have a lot of questions for you—important concerns. All on the QT, of course."

I nodded as if I knew what he was talking about.

The carousel belt groaned, and luggage appeared. The crowds

rushed the apparatus, as if their items would appear sooner as a result of their aggression.

"I've got to get out of this hellhole," Harris said, sneering at the crowd and patting the carry-on he'd brought with him from London. "See you at seven, then."

I reached out to shake his hand goodbye, but he'd already shouldered his way through a family of Turks toward the exit. The *Polizei* who'd overheard his remarks watched him the entire way, burning eyeholes into the back of his suit jacket.

THERE WERE SKIFFS OF dirty snow in the shadows between buildings and along the River Spree as my cream-colored Mercedes taxi—something I still got a thrill from, a Mercedes taxi—sliced through the traffic of midmorning. The skies were leaden. Through breaks in the trees, I could see sky cranes in the east bobbing their heads like prehistoric ocean birds.

I looked at my wristwatch again. It was 2:30 A.M. at home. I couldn't wait to call. I envisioned Melissa and Angelina sleeping in their beds, and Cody tossing and turning on the couch. And—it came out of nowhere—Garrett Moreland sitting in his Hummer down the block, watching my house in the dark.

I straightened up and shook my head, trying to shed the image.

The taxi driver was observing me in his rearview, and when I locked eyes with him, he looked away.

THE HOTEL WAS FILLED with WTB people from countries all over the world. My room wasn't ready, so I stored my luggage and shoved my hands in my pockets and went for a woe-is-me walk along the Kurfürstendamm, the main shopping street in Berlin, known as the Ku'Damm and pronounced "Koo-Dahm." High-end stores, restaurants, bustle. I couldn't believe there were still peddlers selling pieces of the Wall, whose last authentic remnants disappeared nearly twenty years before, as well as ersatz East German caps and "*Stasi*" binoculars made in Asia. Jet-black-skinned Africans sold jewelry and knockoffs on blankets that could be gathered up in two seconds' notice if a *Polizei* strolled down the block. There were women shopping in furs and carrying bags, and the smell of ciga-rette smoke hung in the cold damp air. The smell reminded me of Cody.

Something I couldn't explain nagged at me. I blamed the jet lag for my inability to determine what it was, but it was like a pebble in my shoe I couldn't locate and discard.

Berlin still had a sort of prewar men-in-hats-women-with-shoulder-pads feel to it, although every year, it seemed, there were fewer Germans and more North Africans, Turks, and Arabs on the streets.

I walked as far as the big department store, the KaDaWe, before crossing the street and working my way back. Unlike home, where we'd been watching every penny for months since we'd adopted our baby, I was on the bureau expense account now. My wallet was flush with euros, and my CVB credit card was primed and ready. I couldn't go crazy, but I could eat an early lunch of white sausages with a beer in sight of the Broken Tooth, a bombed-out church the Berliners had chosen not to reconstruct after WWII.

As I sat and ate and drank I tried to figure out what was bother-ing me about my walk, what I'd seen that had set me on edge. Fi-nally, as I sat back and waited for the bored waiter to bring me back my change and the hated receipt, I realized it wasn't what I'd seen on the street but what I *hadn't* seen that was eating at me.

Children. There were no children. Obviously, the older kids would be in school. But in the entirety of my walk I hadn't come upon a sin-gle stroller or young mother with a baby. It was as if it were a street, a city, filled only with adults. I thought how strange, how horrible it would be to live in a world without children. Until that moment, the notion had never even occurred to me. Here in Berlin, because of the choices they'd made for whatever reason, there were no little ones to punctuate the day with noise and harmless chaos. Instead, there was a sense of quiet and antiseptic order.

As I folded my receipt into my wallet, I withdrew a photo of Angelina taken a few months ago. In it, she was beaming and reaching out for the camera to try and gum the lens.

Even though it was just a photo, she was the only child in sight, and they were trying to take her away from us, to turn our house— our lives—into cold and quiet Berlin.

· DESPITE WHAT LINDA VAN GEAR had said about my job being in danger, I decided I would rebook a flight home the next day after my meeting with Harris. I feared for my wife and my daughter, and I already missed them. Linda would be angry, but if I returned with the AmeriCan deal in hand, she'd get over it.

When I got back to the hotel I had a message from Malcolm Harris. He needed to postpone our dinner meeting until the end of the week. Something had come up, and he needed to return to London for several days.

I balled up the message and threw it across the hotel lobby.

Eleven

For the next four days, I was in hell. Waiting for Malcolm Harris to return to Berlin was torture. I was in bad humor—annoyed with cloying tour operators and journalists and the kissy-kissy greetings of Europeans (one cheek or two, two cheeks or three—it was maddening) and cigarette smoke and crowds. Our Colorado shell-scheme looked good from the outside but was held together with wires and tape and everything about my job and my life right then felt as false and cheap and ready to collapse as our booth.

I talked to Melissa every night and things were fine but the tension was building because we both thought something could explode again at any moment. She wanted me home. I wanted to be home. Garrett could show up at our house. Luis's friends might come calling. Cody could go on a bender. Moreland might decide three weeks was too long to wait.

I obsessively checked my watch during the show and in the hotel room at night, trying to chart what Melissa and Angelina would be doing eight hours behind me. The only highlight of those days was when Melissa put Angelina on the phone. I talked to her and heard silence back for several beats before she squealed "Da?" with absolute wonder that made me laugh out loud with joy.

ON THE NIGHT I was finally to meet with Harris, Melissa didn't answer the phone.

It was 10 A.M. in Denver, and no one was home. I felt something hot and sour rise up in my throat, and fought to keep it down. I didn't have enough information to panic.

I didn't leave a message, but went through the whole procedure again to call her cell. Again, straight to voice mail. What was going on?

Cody, I thought. So I went through the long procedure again, talking to long-distance operators, giving my phone card number . . . to find out his phone was off, too.

I was running out of time. Despite that, I called home again and got voice mail.

"Honey," I said, "what the hell is going on? I've been trying to reach you and Cody. Call me at my hotel and leave a message. I'm going to a business dinner but I'll call as soon as I get back. I want to make sure everything is okay. Love to you and Angelina. *You need to keep your phone on.*"

I SMOKED A CUBAN cigar for pure defense purposes—everybody else in the dark, cramped bar was smoking—in the Habana Haus off the hotel lobby and waited for Harris to arrive. He was a half hour late. Smoking the cigar and drinking a Berliner Kindle lager gave me something to do while I fretted, running scenarios through my mind explaining why Melissa didn't answer. I ran the gamut: Melissa and Cody were having a wonderful time together and decided to go shopping and take Angelina to the zoo and both had simply forgotten to turn their cell phones on; Melissa had taken Angelina to the pediatrician for a long-scheduled checkup she'd no doubt informed me of but I'd forgotten and she and Cody had obeyed the NO CELL PHONES sign in the waiting room (although it didn't make sense that Cody, for once, would obey a regulation); the power went out, rendering both the landline telephone and the cell towers useless.

Then the not-so-innocent explanations. Cody and Melissa had been arrested by the Denver PD in association with the beating and death of one Luis Cadena, and Melissa was being questioned in a spare room by detectives; Judge John Moreland and son Garrett had decided a month was too long and had shown up with a phalanx of cops to forcibly remove Baby Angelina and a fight had ensued, leading to the arrest of both Cody and Melissa; the two of them declared their long-smoldering love for one another and had bundled Angelina into the Honda and headed for Vegas.

SEVERAL HEADS TURNED when Malcolm Harris pushed through the heavily curtained entrance. He was recognized. At the travel show, he was a prize. Returning home with his business card impressed bosses. That he strode over toward me surprised a couple of the old female tourism warhorses from Florida, and one, a hatchet-faced woman who had likely once sold cars, was out of her chair with a quick movement that belied her bulk and started tugging at his sleeve. I noticed a little weave in his walk, probably because he'd been drinking already. Harris's face went cold when she hugged him, but he smiled gamely and hugged her in return with the enthusiasm of a twelve-year-old boy embracing a hated aunt, and she hung on his every word, which consisted of, "So, when did you get in?"

And she began to tell him, not only about her flight but about her luggage that hadn't yet arrived and her new condo and that she'd divorced and had been sick but was feeling much better now and she'd even lost sixteen pounds.

I rescued him by standing and clamping onto the back of his shoulder and pointing toward my watch with urgency.

"Are we late?" he asked, mock-surprised. "People have been buying me drinks all afternoon, and I've lost track of the time."

"I'm afraid so," I said. To the woman, I said, "I'm sorry, but they started serving at seven thirty." I lied, of course, having no idea who *they* were.

As Harris extricated himself, she followed him, poking her business card at him until he took it, pocketed it, and handed her one of his own, which instantly soothed her. She retreated to her table with the prize card as if she'd counted coup with her war club, waggling her eyebrows at her companions.

"God, thank you," he said when we were on the street. It was cold and damp, which felt good after the smoky closeness of the Habana Haus.

"You're welcome," I said, still brandishing the cigar.

"Florida people," he said, shaking his head. "They can be so obnoxious. It's as if they don't realize there is anything else in the world, you know, but Florida. Unfortunately for them, Florida is so over. But some of these marketing women will do anything for UK business, you know. That's where we got the phrase, '*Been there, done that, fucked the rep.*'"

I laughed politely. The lights of the Ku'Damm were ahead.

"Are we going the right direction?" I asked. "I don't know where we're going to dinner."

"Your treat," he said, reminding me. "This is the right way. First another drink, then dinner."

"Great," I said, not meaning it and tossing the cigar aside. Thinking, *Let's get this over with so I can get the hell home.*

THE RESTAURANT WAS A twenty-minute walk. Harris prided himself on having discovered it a few years before, and said it had the best schnitzel in Berlin.

"They make it the old way," he said, rubbing his hands together, "You can hear them pounding the veal with mallets in the back to tenderize it. They pound it *hard* with mallets."

The place was called Der Tiefe Brunnen, and it was located on Rankestraße. It was dark and old, lit by candles, looking very much like "The Deep Well" of its name. Black-and-white photos of un-known (to me) celebrities covered the walls. A cloud of cigarette smoke hung low in the room, but through it men and women eyed us from booths as we took our table up front near the bar. The owner, a severe man in muttonchop sideburns, greeted Harris in German. Harris shook the man's hand and pointed me out, obvi-ously telling the owner I was new to the place and would be paying the bill. A tray of schnapps shots was sent over immediately, brought by a woman dressed to showcase her massive breasts. She wore a see-through spandex support bra under a filmy shirt. Her hair was dyed German Red, a crimson/purple color not found in nature except for buckbrush in October when the leaves turned color. When she bent over the table to dispense the glasses, I was afraid her breasts would swing out of the confines of her shirt and hit me in the face like a pleasant one-two punch. The place re-minded me of something prewar, or at least pre–falling of the Wall, a throwback to the fatalistic island mentality of Berlin before that structure came down.

"I've already ordered for the both of us," Harris said, sitting down. "Schnitzel Cordon Bleu. And more beer, of course. This isn't like most places—it takes ten minutes to pour a proper beer, which is as it should be. But everything is worth the wait in here, believe me.

"Just listen to that," he said, smiling. There was indeed pounding going on in the kitchen behind the bar. The blows were so powerful that silver and glassware on the table jumped. "*That's* how you tenderize veal—the old-fashioned way."

Something about the way he said it hit me wrong.

He excused himself to find the toilet, he said, and on the way he had an animated conversation with the proprietor that I didn't track. The two of them laughed, and Harris followed the man through the back of the bar into his office. They closed the door. The proprietor returned to his place at the bar, but Harris remained in the office a long time. Maybe he was using a private bathroom? I checked out the photos on the walls and fought back exhaustion and sipped beer. I was sure I could lean back in my booth right there and sleep. Instead, I checked my wristwatch.

Nine o'clock in Berlin, one o'clock in Denver. I hoped Melissa and Cody were back from wherever they'd been, or at least had turned their phones on.

When Harris returned to our booth, his face was slightly flushed even in the candlelight, and the droplets of sweat had returned along his upper lip.

"Fritz let me use his computer to check my e-mail," he said, sliding back into the booth and taking a long pull from his beer. "It has to do with some urgent matters in London—the reason I had to postpone our dinner the other night. A minor crisis, it seems. The authorities are making my life miserable."

"Really?" I said. I hoped he wasn't going to tell me the relocation was off after all this time waiting for him.

"Nothing to worry about," he said, apparently reading my eyes. "Nothing I can't deal with. But you must know that in Europe, it's 1984. Big Brother is always watching, and they seem to be watching those of us who dare to be different."

I assumed he meant the entrepreneurs.

He called to Fritz, "Another round, my friend!"

As Fritz poured and rested the beers so the foam could subside, Harris leaned in to me and spoke sotto voce, "This is what I hate about Europe, Jack, the creeping fascism of the politically correct. It's everywhere, but most of it comes from the EU in Brussels in the form of edicts. They want to control what we eat and how we measure it, what we say and think, how we live, those bastards. They want to control bloody *everything.* And what Brussels doesn't decree, our own government takes care of."

Harris was getting animated, and his voice was rising. I had no idea what he was talking about, but I needed to act interested and hope—pray—he would state his intentions in regard to the reservations center.

"Is it really that bad?" I asked, surprised at his vehemence.

"Yes! In England these days, the worst thing you can be is a proper Englishman. Believe me, I know of what I speak, Jack. I wish I could say it's a cauldron, and it's going to blow up soon, that we're going to rise up and take our country back. But the sad thing is, I don't think we've got the balls anymore. I think we'll just sit there tut-tutting while the government assumes all control."

The waitress with the breasts brought our veal. It was tender, all right. In fact, it was fantastic—huge palm-sized pieces of meat breaded with crispy crust that was still sizzling and the whole thing covered with ham and cheese. I should not have been so hungry, but I was. I noticed a bit of a slur in his words. This was going to be one of those nights.

"You've probably heard I'm considering moving my headquarters," Harris said through a mouthful of veal. "I need to find a place where I can breathe again."

Finally.

"I have."

"I'm strongly considering Colorado," he said, watching me carefully for my reaction.

"That would be fantastic," I said, putting down my fork to shake his hand. "We'd love to have you."

He shook his head as if to say, *Of course you would.*

"It's a great place," I said. "The sun shines over three hundred days a year. We've got the mountains and the skiing, as well as a great airport and a mayor who really encourages international business . . ."

He interrupted, "I know all that. You don't need to sell it to me. I'm very familiar with the state and the powers that be. I've been in touch with several of them, although not yet officially."

The beer arrived, and he took a long draught before continuing. He didn't wipe the foam away from his upper lip, which I found distracting.

"It's a great place to raise a family," I offered. "The schools are pretty good, and there is lots of recreation. Here," I said. "Let me show you . . ." and reached back for my wallet for my photo of Angelina.

The look on his face was anticipatory. Most people will feign interest, but Harris was sincere. He smiled broadly at the photo of our daughter. "A new one, eh?" he said. "Recent?"

"A couple of weeks ago," I said. "She's almost walking now."

"She is still an angel, just like her name," Harris said, handing the photo back. I was confused.

"You probably get so many photos shoved at you that it's easy to lose track of which kid is which," I said.

"What are you talking about?" he asked.

"I don't remember showing you a picture of her before," I said.

"Of course you did," he said.

I shook my head. "I just can't remember it, I guess."

"Have another beer," he said, and laughed roughly. He seemed to be studying me all of a sudden.

160

When did I show him a photo before? I wanted to know. But I remembered, *This isn't about you.*

As discreetly as I could, I settled back into the booth and reached for my beer. Unaccountably, I seethed with a sudden rage. I had no idea where it came from, or why it was so intense. All Harris had done was contradict me, show that he had a better memory than I did. But big shot or not, it would have been very easy that moment to smash my fist into his face, to wipe the foam off his lip with my knuckles. I could feel an explosion just beneath the surface, anger that wildly outmatched the transgression itself. Maybe the past week was catching up to me, I thought, coming to a head. All this miserable waiting while my family was vulnerable thousands of miles away. I was ready to unload everything on a British tour operator who brought thousands of tourists and millions of dollars into my city and who might soon be moving his business there.

"Looks like you could use another one of those," he said, nodding toward my beer glass.

"That's okay," I said, tight-lipped.

"Meaning you'd like another one," he said, his face animated again. "Me too. Fritz!"

He paused. "Are you all right? You look pale."

"I'm okay. Just tired."

"Buck up, man. This is the world of international tourism. You've got to hit the ground running."

I agreed. I was grateful he was drunk enough—or self-absorbed enough, or both—to not pick up on my anger a moment before.

"You know"—he laughed—"you Americans seem to think your government is taking away your civil liberties, but you don't know what you're talking about. There aren't bureaucrats looking over your shoulder as you live your life, telling you how to speak and think and whom to associate with—taking your freedom away. My friends in Colorado say that compared to what I'm used to, I'll be bulletproof! That's the term they use, *bulletproof*. I love that."

"Really? Who says that?" I asked.

"Oh no," he said coyly, "I won't reveal my sources."

Suddenly, he was silent. He studied his empty and greasy plate. I didn't realize until that moment how drunk he was, and how he'd apparently ventured into territory he now wished he hadn't.

The restaurant was emptying out, which was good. I didn't want Harris—or me—to engage with anyone in any way, especially in the belligerent mood he was in. I called for the bill, always a frustratingly long experience. Fritz delivered it (finally) in person, and Harris raved about how good the food was, and I agreed.

Fritz leaned down conspiratorially, said to Harris, "Do you need to check your e-mail again?"

Harris laughed, squeezed Fritz on his arm, said, "I've seen enough for tonight."

Which I thought an odd choice of words at the time.

MY HEAD WAS SPINNING when I sat down on my bed. I had four messages. I fumbled through the codes and prompts, cursing the phone, the hotel, the German language, and Malcolm Harris for the condition I was in.

The first message was from Melissa.

"Oh Jack, I'm sorry I missed you. I'm so sorry. You won't be-lieve who I met today—Kellie Moreland! Call me right away!"

The second and third messages were the same.

By the fourth, she was angry.

"Jack, are you even there? Are you checking your messages? I know it's two in the morning, so don't even call." She paused, then: "My God, I need to talk to you right away. I met Kellie Moreland today—Brian arranged it. And guess what? Are you sitting down? She doesn't know anything about Angelina!"

In the Air / Denver / Wyoming

Friday, November 16

Nine Days to Go

Twelve

J ET LAG WORKS BOTH ways.

On the flight home, in the cocoon of the 747-400 with the lights dimmed, I couldn't sleep. I was preoccupied that Melissa—with help from Brian—had "run into" Kellie Moreland at a society fund-raiser at a local library and posed the question about Angelina only to be met with a blank stare.

"Angelina who?" Kellie had asked.

Which meant a lot of things. Either Kellie was stupid—Melissa swore she wasn't—or Judge Moreland was making a play with his son on their own for reasons that were unknown to us. When Melissa asked Kellie about Garrett, she said Kellie shrank back as if slapped, as if the mere mention of her stepson's name filled her with horror. As Melissa followed her, trying to engage her, Kellie walked away faster through the crowd until she was running. Melissa ran, too, until Kellie called for security, and my wife was stopped by two men who asked what her problem was.

"What my *problem* was," Melissa said, over and over that night on the telephone. "How could I explain what my *problem* was?"

Brian was back in Denver and fully engaged in our *problem*. And according to Melissa, he was waiting for the photos he'd referred to earlier.

"Once we have them," Melissa said, "Brian says the whole thing blows up. According to Brian, we'll have Judge Moreland and Garrett by the balls." She growled that last bit, and I'd never heard her do that before. The day at the fund-raiser and the encounter with Kellie had charged her up, given her hope again. If Kellie had no idea her husband and son where trying to gain custody of a baby, then something was seriously wrong with this picture, Melissa said. The judge was hiding something from his wife. And if he was hiding something, he couldn't be as cocksure about his position and his leverage as he'd led us to believe.

WHEN I LANDED AT DIA, I could barely wait for my luggage. On the other side of the frosted glass would be my wife and daughter and either Cody or Brian or both. The marble floors were gleaming and new. Despite the late hour, there was space, light, no cigarette smoke. So American. So not Berlin. My world.

Brian was with her, looking sharp. But the downcast of his eyes clued me in immediately that something was wrong. Melissa's face was puffy and red, her mouth downturned. Angelina saw me from her stroller and started clapping, though, oblivious to what was affecting Brian and Melissa.

"Harry," Melissa said, as I hugged her. She whispered in my ear. "Harry's dead."

The news made me go cold. "Harry?"

"Harry!" Angelina said, mimicking me and clapping her pudgy hands. "Harry dog!"

Brian tugged at my arm so we could distance ourselves from Melissa and Angelina in her stroller.

"The cops said someone threw raw hamburger into your back-yard laced with rat poison and fishhooks," Brian said. "We found Harry coughing up blood on the back deck, but by the time we got him to the vet it was too late. The vet said there were a dozen hooks imbedded in his throat."

"When did this happen?" I asked, numb.

Brian looked at his wristwatch. "Five hours ago, I guess. We left the vet an hour ago to meet you, but it was over long before then. Melissa gave the okay to put him down because it was only a matter of time before he died."

"So," I said, "I was somewhere over Michigan when my dog died."

"I guess so."

Hot tears filled my eyes. I angrily wiped them away. I'm not a crier and was surprised by my reaction, but the news had hit me like a hammerblow.

"We know who did it," Brian said. "Remember how Garrett reacted to your dog?"

"Harry never hurt anyone," I said. "He wasn't capable of hurting anyone."

"Garrett got you back," Brian said. "And I don't think he's done with you."

"Jesus," I said, "this is so . . . depraved." I wiped at my face, not wanting Angelina to see me—or Melissa. I couldn't believe I was crying, especially because I hadn't cried after all of the things that had happened to us. But Harry? What had Harry done to anyone?

"I know how tough this is," Brian said, putting his arm around my shoulder. "But when we get home, Cody is ready to drive to Montana. I know you're tired, but are you up for that?"

"All of us?" I asked.

Brian said, "All but me. I can't afford to risk being out of town if my source calls with the photos. He could call anytime," he said, brandishing his cell phone. "Besides, Jeter Hoyt and I never really got along."

He whispered when he said the name Jeter Hoyt.

I said, "Are you going to tell me what these photos are? I'd like to know."

Brian shook his head. "I'm not positive myself—I'm leery of asking too many questions. My contact is jittery as it is. All I know is that he swears these photos will bring down the judge, or at least dissuade him from going forward with this thing with your daughter."

"And you're sure he's right?"

Brian said, "How can one ever be sure of anything? But I've told him I won't pay unless I've seen the photos and he's right. And believe me, brother, we're talking big bucks. So I don't want to be in the middle of nowhere when he calls."

I nodded.

"So, are you ready to go?" Brian asked.

"Right now?"

"Right now."

"Let's hit the road."

"Do you want to pay your respects to Harry so you have some closure?"

That hit me wrong. I guess it was the unreasonable but fashionable sensitivity of the question.

"I hate that word, 'closure,'" I snapped, shrugging off Brian's arm. "Like it's just a procedure, then we're all right. It's midnight. Do we break in to the vet clinic so I can cry, or what? Will that give me *closure?*"

Brian shrugged. "Sorry, Jack. Just trying to help."

"I know you are," I said. "I don't mean to take it out on you."

I paused for Melissa to catch up. She looked at me for some kind of guidance I didn't feel capable of providing. "I guess we're going to Montana," I said. "Are you up for that?"

She said, "I've been packing our stuff all day. Before this thing happened with Harry, I was getting us ready. Everything is in your Jeep. I guess we might as well go."

I turned her toward me and hugged her. I could tell by the way she went limp on my shoulder that she was exhausted. I buried my face in her hair. I loved the smell of her.

"God, I missed you," I said.

I squatted down and kissed Angelina. "You, too," I said.

As we walked out of the airport I thought about Harry. I wanted vengeance. I wanted blood.

WE PULSED NORTH through Wyoming in my Jeep in the dark, passing through Casper at four in the morning. Cody drove and I sat in the passenger seat. Melissa was in the backseat with Angelina in her car seat. There were no city lights, no southbound traffic. I slipped in and out of consciousness. When I slept, I slept hard and awoke groggy. It comforted me that Cody seemed alert, serious, and sober. I was very pleased to be *taking action*.

DAWN CAME SPLASHING across the Bighorn Mountains north of Sheridan, Wyoming, near the Montana border, the morning sunlight so intense Melissa pulled a blanket up over Angelina's sleeping face. We'd stopped for gas and coffee in Ranchester, and the smell of coffee filled the Jeep. The morning was cold and crisp. Spiderwebs of creeping frost headquartered in each corner of the windshield.

"Maybe we can get breakfast in Billings," Cody said.

"He speaks," Melissa said from the backseat.

"I've been thinking," Cody said.

"He thinks," I said, chiding him.

169

Cody didn't smile. Instead, he reached down and turned the defroster fan up a notch. The frost retreated.

He said, "We've got, what, nine days now before Judge Moreland's deadline? Before he said he'd come and take the baby away?"

"Yes," Melissa said.

"Not much time," Cody said, shaking his head.

"But that means nothing anymore," Melissa said. "We've got the photos coming anytime now. And this . . ." She indicated us, the Jeep, our purpose.

Cody cleared his throat and spoke softly so as not to awake Angelina. "I just want to be clear, so we're all on the same page. Every mile we drive takes us farther across the line. And the farther we get, the less likely you'll be able to use any legal options, like getting the baby awarded to your custody in court if it comes to that. That's because you're now tainted. We've left the land of the innocent and willingly entered the underworld. You understand that, right?"

I exchanged looks with Melissa, expecting at least some fear in her eyes. There was none.

"We understand that," I said, for both of us.

"Okay, then. So what we're trying to do here is hit the judge through his son. We want to scare Garrett into signing away custody."

After a few beats, I said, "Yes."

Cody nodded. "And you realize that whenever you choose to scare someone into doing something, there can be unintended consequences." He paused, then said, "It's not an exact science, being a criminal."

"Cody!" Melissa said from the backseat.

"I just want to make sure we all understand each other," Cody said. "It's better to use plain language."

"We're not the criminals," Melissa said. "We're not the people trying to take babies away from their parents!"

"The law is on his side," Cody said patiently. "I don't agree with it. There's a lot about the law I don't agree with. We've got Aubrey

Coates out on the street, for one thing. But the law is on Judge Moreland's side."

Melissa said, "But his wife doesn't even know about Angelina, so something really weird is going on. And his son, Garrett, killed our dog, not to mention what he and his friend did to Jack and in our house!"

Cody talked to her via the rearview mirror. "Melissa, his wife not knowing is not a crime. It's strange, yes. But it's not a crime. And we think we know who killed Harry, but we haven't proved it."

"What about Luis?" I said.

Cody smiled bitterly. "I'm the one who kicked the shit out of Luis. For what? For cruising through your neighborhood. Who is the criminal in this instance?"

"Garrett dumped him. That's a crime."

"And how do we know that?" Cody asked. "How do we know Luis didn't dump himself? I mean, Garrett could claim Luis wanted out of the car, that he didn't know how badly Luis was injured, that Luis just didn't want to go to the hospital. So Luis wanders off by himself in the dark and stumbles into the South Platte. How is Garrett liable for that?"

I said nothing.

"Why are you *doing* this?" Melissa asked, tears in her eyes.

"I want to make sure we all realize what we're doing," Cody said. "That's all."

"We realize," I said.

"Do you?" Cody asked.

"When Brian gets his hands on those photos, it might all go away," Melissa said. "Maybe this is as far as we need to go."

"You trust Brian and his photos?" Cody asked into the rearview. There was a pinch of sarcasm in the question and a dollop of pity. "Think about it. What are these photos supposed to show? Judge Moreland in bed with a girl? With a boy? What if they're doctored? What if the judge sees them as what they could be—amateur

C. J. BOX

blackmail? Then where are you? And where is Brian when this happens? I'd guess he'd be long gone on one of his business trips.

"I'm just saying," Cody said. "Speculating, because that's what us cops do."

Melissa said, "I don't like your attitude about Brian."

Cody shrugged. "Jesus, this is why I *should* be suspended from the Denver PD, I guess: I can't keep my mouth shut."

"Why are you doing this?" Melissa asked again. I reached back for her hand, but she'd withdrawn, crossing her arms across her breasts.

"Because," Cody said, "once we unleash Jeter Hoyt, we don't know what the hell will happen."

I asked Cody to pull over, which he did, and I climbed into the backseat with Melissa. She was stiff at first, but finally let me hold her.

"We're doing the right thing," I whispered into her hair. "It'll be all right."

"I've got one more question for you," Cody said. He took our silence as assent. "If you had it all to do over again, would you still adopt?"

"Yes," we said simultaneously.

"Good," Cody said. "Good for you." His voice started trailing away. "Children need to be wanted . . ."

I noticed that as I'd held her, she'd slipped one of her hands out from beneath the blanket and she was holding the edge of Angelina's car seat in a white-knuckled death grip.

Montana

Saturday, November 17

Eight Days to Go

Thirteen

LINCOLN, MONTANA, POPULATION ELEVEN hundred, was a hamlet in the Helena National Forest on the bank of the Blackfoot River. The little community made the news in the 1990s when Theodore Kaczynski, known as the Unabomber, was arrested there in his hovel of a cabin, which was later shipped whole over Stemple Pass to the capital city of Helena fifty-nine miles to the southeast. It was a tough and sloppy little town that looked as if it had been dropped into the trees from a helicopter, and some of the buildings didn't land well.

It was also the home of Jeter Hoyt.

We arrived at 3:00 P.M. on Saturday. Fourteen hours. It was like driving across most of Western Europe, and all we'd done was cross one state and enter another.

Cody parked at a bar. Apparently, his cell-phone charge was depleted because it had spent seven or eight hours searching vainly for a signal to grab on to, so he'd need to use the phone inside. I got out with him, said, "You were a little rough back there."

He lit a cigarette. "I get like that when I'm not smoking or drinking," he said. "When all I've got is reality staring me in the fucking face."

"Thanks for driving, though," I said.

"My pleasure."

"What if your uncle isn't around?"

"Always a possibility," Cody said. "It's the tail end of hunting season. Remember hunting season?" he asked, his expression wistful.

"I do. But you talked to him a while ago, right?"

Cody nodded. "I told him we might be coming up. He didn't say he'd be here or not. He just grunted at me."

While Cody went inside, I leaned against the Cherokee with my hands in my pockets. There was snow on the tops of the peaks to the south and the Scapegoat Wilderness Area to the north. I could see a skiff of snow in the shadows of the pines behind the bar. Little mountain towns like this were especially unattractive during two periods of the year: now, when there was just enough early snow to muddy the ground but not enough to freeze and cover it, and again in the spring, when the snow melted and revealed all the garbage that had been tossed aside. But as if to offset the appearance, this is when a town like Lincoln smelled best, a heady mix of pine trees, the forest floor, woodsmoke. As I breathed it in, it reminded me of home, wherever that was.

I turned to see that Angelina was awake and grinning at me through the window. Melissa held her tightly. That smile filled me with such unabashed joy that I knew I was doing the right thing. I rapped at the window so she'd open it.

"Smell that," I said.

"It smells, um, woody," she said.

"If only these little places had jobs for international tourism specialists," I said, reaching inside the Jeep so Angelina could grab my finger. "What a great place to live, to raise little kids."

"Where her neighbor could be the Unabomber," Melissa said, and we both laughed. Angelina squealed with delight simply because her parents were laughing. We hadn't done enough of that lately, I decided.

Cody came out of the bar with a Coors Light in his hand and a cigarette.

"Some old high-school buddies in there," he said. "D'you remember the Browning brothers or Chad Kerr? They asked about you and Brian."

"They did?"

"Yeah," Cody said. "So much for coming up here incognito, eh? I forgot how everybody knows everybody's business in Montana."

"What about Uncle Jeter?"

"He's waiting for us out at his place. He said he'd disarm the trip wires so we could drive right up to his house."

"*What?*"

"I'm *joking*," Cody said, tossing his cigarette aside into the mud.

UNCLE JETER'S CABIN WAS tucked away in an alcove of pine and aspen trees and accessed via an ascending two-track road with potholes filled to the top with chocolate-milk-colored water. Cody said, "I *think* I still remember how to get there . . ."

We passed under an ancient sagging lodgepole-pine archway that was dark gray with moisture and crawling with bright green and white lichen. On one support pole was a tiny wood-burned sign that said HOYT OUTFITTING SERVICES. On the other was a rusted metallic sign that said NO WHINERS. Inside the archway, Uncle Jeter's cabin was shambling and low-slung, looking like a scene from 1880 except for the satellite dish mounted on a pole and aimed at a southern gap of cloudy sky to the south. I saw two four-wheel-drive vehicles—a Dodge Power Wagon from the 1960s and a new-model but beat-up Ford pickup—parked butt end first in an open garage. A cross pole high in the trees supported the hanging carcasses of an elk and what looked like a heavily muscled man.

I started to point when Cody said, "Bear. Skinned bears look like if you hung a linebacker. It always creeped me out. Melissa, if I were you, I'd not let Angelina see that."

"Luckily," Melissa said from the back, "she's looking out the other window at the horses." Three horses, two mules, and a couple of goats watched us from a corral.

"Quite a place," Melissa said, deadpan.

"About what I'd always expected," I said.

Uncle Jeter greeted us at the front door with a cheese plate: dozens of overlarge squares of Velveeta hastily cut up on a chipped dinner plate with Ritz crackers piled up in a couple of columns and colored toothpicks bunched together by a rubber band. It struck me as incongruous and sweet that this man, after receiving Cody's call, set about chopping little squares of cheese with a hunting knife for a snack.

Uncle Jeter was tall but not as tall as I remembered him, broad but not as wide as I recalled. In fact, he looked distressingly normal, except for the long beard striped with gray and the ponytail that fanned down half of his back. His eyes were the same, though—light blue-gray and piercing, set in hollows that were slightly red-tinged. His nose was large and beaky, complicated with hairlike blue veins. His hands were outsize and looked like mitts. He wore a heavy flannel shirt and a wool Filson vest so old it was shiny, tight Wranglers, and lace-up outfitter boots with heels for riding.

It was dark inside, the walls covered with tanned bear and elk hides. The antlers of mounted deer and elk served as gun racks for a dozen long rifles and shotguns. The place smelled of smoke, grease, and gun-cleaning solvent. Melissa, Angelina, and I sat on an ancient leather couch with three-quarter wagon wheels on the ends for armrests. Melissa had a tough time keeping our daughter on the couch and not scrambling to the floor. Jeter set the cheese plate sat next to a six-pack of Molson beer on a coffee table.

"I'm sorry," Uncle Jeter said in a gravelly voice to Melissa and Angelina as we entered. "This ain't no place for a lady and a baby."

"It's fine," Melissa said, flashing a tight-mouthed smile.

"No," he said, "no it ain't. Is there anything I can get the little one? Some milk or something?"

Melissa gestured to her overlarge baby bag, and said, "Not necessary—we came prepared."

To our surprise, Angelina seemed to be charming him. She'd give him her silly demure look, bat her eyelashes, then cover her face with her hands. It wouldn't be long before she'd spread her fingers and gaze at him through them, then giggle. I noticed that he had a tough time devoting his attention fully to Cody, who outlined our problem. Despite what Cody had said to us in the car, he didn't indicate any doubt at all as he told his uncle Hoyt how Garrett and Luis had fouled our house and shot me with paintballs, how Garrett said he owned us now. When Cody told him about Harry, I saw Hoyt's eyes turn hard.

When Cody was done, Uncle Jeter sat back and raked his fingers through his beard.

"So," he said, "you've got a boy who needs scared, and you came to me to do it. Why?"

Cody deferred to me.

"Because you scared *us*."

"That was twenty years ago, Jack."

Cody leaned forward and handed his uncle the envelope of reports and photos Torkleson had given us. Jeter took it and fanned through the photos of Garrett, while Cody said, "Because you're not known in Denver, Uncle Jeter. You've got no priors down there. I know how things work with the police—where they'd look if something went bad. They wouldn't look to Lincoln, Montana, unless you did something stupid like dropped your wallet."

Or if the Browning Brothers and Chad Kerr in Lincoln were questioned, I thought.

Uncle Jeter shot him a look that made me fear for Cody.

"Not that I'm saying something like that would happen," Cody said, backtracking. "Or even that Garrett would go to the police. The point is for him *not* to go to the police. The point is for you to persuade him to sign his custody rights away."

Hoyt raked his beard again, as if considering all of the odds. "I ain't done too many things like this in the last few years," he said. "I might be a little rusty. But you say this Garrett likes to associate with Mexicans, that it makes him feel like a big shot?"

Cody nodded. "Specifically, a gang called Sur-13."

Uncle Jeter turned to Melissa. "I'm sorry, ma'am, would you want to take a few minutes and show the baby the horses outside? I got some horses and two fine mules out there. And a goat, a good goat. He don't bite. Do you think that little angel might want to see them?"

Melissa looked at me, and I nodded.

As soon as the front door shut, Uncle Jeter said, "I got a problem with this illegal immigration. I got a big problem with the way them Mexicans are taking over our cities and flying the Mexican flag and all. A big problem, you understand me?"

Cody nodded.

Jeter said, "I called my bank in Helena a couple of weeks ago because they fouled up a deposit I made from a hunting client. They don't know what to do with cash anymore, it makes their eyes get all buggy. Well, when I called them, I got this recorded message that said press one for English and two for *Espanõl*. This was Helena, Montana, fellows! I got so goddamned mad I drove down there and took all my money out. When the bank manager asked why I was doing it, I said, 'Press one for English and two for *Espanõl*, you little prick!'

"As I was leaving town I drove by the hospital, and I saw these Mexicans lined up—lined up!—outside the emergency ward. They was carrying their little sick kids and just waiting in line because I guess the doctors have to treat them no matter what. I thought, whose country is this, anyway? What's wrong with our so-called leaders that sit by while we get infiltrated by our so-called neighbor from the south. Now I hear that some wannabe Mexican and his Mexican gang friends want that little angel out there." He glared at us and stabbed a long finger toward the front door. "It ain't right!"

Uncle Jeter was on such a frightening roll I didn't want to tell him the problem was the judge.

"Taking down a couple fucking Mexicans don't bother me at all," Uncle Jeter said. "Getting this Mexican wannabe to sign a piece of paper sounds like a piece of cake."

To demonstrate, he stood up swiftly—much quicker than I thought him capable of—and put an imaginary Garrett in a headlock and fashioned his other hand into a pistol and cocked his thumb back.

"Remember that scene in *The Godfather*?" Jeter asked us.

"*Either your name goes on that agreement,*" Jeter said in a fake Mexican accent to imaginary Garrett, "*or your brains, senõr!*"

He continued to talk to imaginary Garrett, and his playacting was intense, unnerving, as if Garrett were truly in his hands.

Jeter snarled, "And if you think you can sign this paper, then run off and tell your daddy or the cops that you were coerced, you got another think coming, little *senõr*. 'Cause if that happens I'm coming back for you and I'm feeding your nuts to my goats. And that's just for starters, little *senõr!*"

He looked up. "Think that'd do it?"

"Maybe a little more subtle," Cody said.

"We've got eight days," I said.

Uncle Jeter nodded, let the imaginary Garrett drop to the floor, and took a breath to cool down. "Compensation?" he asked.

"You'll be working that out with Brian Eastman," I said. "He's handling the money."

"Brian Eastman?" Jeter asked, rubbing his chin beneath his beard, "Your old pal? Son of the minister?"

"Yes."

"He was queer, wasn't he?"

I sighed, "Yes. And he's helping us out with expenses. He's done well in Denver."

"I bet he has," Jeter said, sneering. "But fag money is as good as any, I guess."

I bit my tongue and glanced at Cody, who was rolling his eyes and shaking his head, embarrassed.

Jeter said, "Give me a day or two to get my poop in a group. There's supposed to be a hell of a storm coming first of next week, so I need to get out of here shortly, I guess. I can be in Denver by Tuesday or Wednesday latest. I ain't seen that city in years. I hear it's grown like crazy."

"It has," Cody said.

He turned to his nephew. "You regret leaving Montana and moving to a place like that?"

Cody nodded. "Lately I have."

Jeter nodded back. "Yeah, I can't see why anyone would want to leave Montana. Makes no sense to me. In my experience all cities are the fucking same—filled with undesirables."

I slapped my knees, stood up, and said, "Cody, a minute outside?"

After he'd shut the door, Cody said, "Second thoughts?"

"Yes. He's older and crazier than I remember. I don't think we can control him or count on him to stop what he's started."

Cody slowly nodded his head. "I agree. He's not the same guy we remember."

"Look, can you just tell him I got cold feet at the last minute, and we can get the hell out of here?"

Melissa walked up to us holding Angelina. She'd overheard. "He does seem unstable," she said.

Cody barked a short laugh. "He's always been unstable. It's hard to find a stable hit man these days. But yes, he's gotten worse. I guess I didn't realize how damned *old* he was."

Cody put his hands on our shoulders. "Look, you two get in the car. I'll go in and tell him you're reconsidering your options."

AS WE DROVE THROUGH LINCOLN, I asked, "How'd he take it?"

"He's hard to read," Cody said. "I think he's disappointed. He was really getting worked up there."

"It was the right choice," Melissa said from the backseat. "I just wish we had a ready option. Maybe Brian has one if we ask him."

Cody snorted. Then: "I wish the old fart had given me that envelope back."

Fourteen

H ER VOICE WAS HESITANT. Who called on Saturday evening except telemarketers or someone complaining that there were cows on the road? "Hello?"

"Hi, mom."

"Jack!" Her voice was a mixture of excitement and trepidation. I called so rarely that when I did it must be bad news, I knew she was thinking. That tone unnerved me, sent me back in time.

"We're driving through Helena and I've got Melissa and your granddaughter with me. We'll be coming down through Townsend and thought maybe we'd stop by."

"*Oh my!* Why didn't you let us know you were coming?"

"I'm sorry. Don't worry about dinner or anything, and I mean that. We just thought you might want to see your granddaughter. Is Dad around?"

"Oh my, yes! He's outside doing something with the tractor. I was just starting dinner, and, oh, you've got me flustered. I don't know what to say. Why didn't you let us know sooner?"

"It's a long story," I said, feeling my face flush. "Look, if this isn't a convenient time . . ." I could feel Melissa's eyes on me from the backseat. How was it that even after seventeen years in the outside world, I instantly reverted back to my sullen high-school-senior self, when I had left the ranch—and them—for good? How quickly I was ready to call it off and go on down the road.

"No, no! You must come by! I was just so surprised you called. I was just opening a package of steaks and the phone rang and it was you. No, come by. When will you be here?"

"About forty-five minutes."

"Oh my!"

"Look, Mom . . ."

"Goodness. I'll open another package of steaks. Is it just you and Melissa and the baby?"

"Cody, too."

"Cody! Cody Hoyt?"

"Yes."

"*Oh my!* I'll go tell your father. Forty-five minutes, now more like forty, I suppose."

"Mom, we can grab something to eat. We can take you out to dinner. You don't have to fix anything. Really!"

"Don't be ridiculous," she said, a little angry I'd even suggested it.

I closed the cell and looked back at Melissa. "There, are you happy now?"

"Aren't you glad you called?" she said, smiling.

"I'm not sure. Mom's in a dither."

Cody said, "This is a good thing to establish some cover since everybody and their dog knows we're up here. If need be, we can always say you decided to visit your folks with Angelina for the last time. That makes perfect sense. And I drove because I don't have anything else to do." Then, sourly: "I just hope your old man doesn't put me to work fixing fence or some damn thing."

AS WE CLEARED EAST Helena en route to Townsend, and I saw Canyon Ferry Lake to the left—a few more houses on the banks than I remembered, but not many—I felt a twang of recognition.

"Hasn't changed much," Cody said, as if reading my thoughts.

"No."

"Not like Denver, where there's a new subdivision every few days," he said. "It's frozen in time here. I used to not like that, but now I do."

My anxiety grew. I was getting more nervous than I had been earlier in the day on the way to meet with Uncle Jeter.

"Maybe we should have gotten fast food in Helena," I said.

"Your mother would be furious," Melissa said. "Showing up and not eating? What are you thinking?"

Cody said, "Saturday night is steak night if I remember. Steak and baked potatoes. Every Saturday night. I wonder if that's changed?"

"It hasn't as far as I know," I said. "She said something about opening up another package of steaks."

"Good steaks, too," Cody said, nodding. "I can still remember the drill. Pork chops on Monday, spaghetti on Tuesday, hamburgers on Wednesday, cabbage rolls Thursday, pot roast Friday, steaks on Saturday, fried chicken on Sunday."

I nodded.

"Did it ever change?" Melissa asked.

"Never," I said. "If she tried something new, Dad would just sit at the table and just stare at his plate and pout."

"I really liked the cabbage rolls," Cody said. "Maybe next time we drive up here to hire a hit man we can come on Thursday."

"Cody!" Melissa said. "Stop that. What if Angelina starts using those words?"

Cody grinned as he slowed down and clicked the turn single, and we were soon on the gravel road that led to the ranch.

THE HOME RANCH LOOKED almost exactly as I'd left it. A few new things—a bigger gas tank, a larger Quonset for the equipment—but basically the same buildings, the same layout. A few inches of snow lay in the hayfields, and the Big Belt Mountains rose dark blue and snowy to the east. Between the ranch and the mountains, the foothills shimmered with the intense gold light of dusk, the kind that makes snow look like molten lava. I saw a small herd of mule deer hanging around the windmill and tin stock tank. A few hundred bald-faced Angus were bunched in the east meadow, massed and no doubt awaiting the cattle truck.

We swung into the ranch yard. Through Cody's window I got a glimpse of Dad in the Quonset working under a trouble light, tractor parts and tools scattered around his feet. On my side, Mom's face was framed in the kitchen window, looking out anxiously, and as soon as she saw us, she vanished and reappeared at the front door wearing the same apron she'd had on eighteen years before, the one with the blue ducks.

"Melissa!" she called out. "Bring that little darling in here!"

"She means Angelina," Cody deadpanned, "not you."

Mom gave me a quick cheek kiss and punched Cody affectionately in the arm to say hello, but both gestures were done en route to Angelina, who she scooped up in her arms. Angelina squealed happily, and Mom turned and took her in the house. Melissa followed with one of the diaper bags and gave me an amused over-the-shoulder look before going inside.

Cody and I walked over to the Quonset. Cows bawled in the

meadow, punctuating the otherwise complete silence. I had forgotten about silence.

Although they'd been to the wedding and to Denver to see Angelina when we brought her home, I hadn't been back. I didn't want to come back and feel like I was feeling now. I didn't know what to expect, but my heart was thumping, and my hands felt cold.

Dad stepped back from the tractor and wiped his hands on a rag with very little white left on it and watched us approach. His face had filled out some recently, and his lenses were so thick they distorted his eyes bigger. He looked old, which shocked me.

"Couldn't cut it in the big city, huh?" he said. "Coming back begging for your old jobs back, you two?"

My belly clenched, but Cody realized he was kidding and said, "Naw, Walt. We just want our wages. We don't want to have to *work* for 'em."

"Nothing's changed in that regard," Dad said, before breaking into a grin. "Good to see you, Jack," he said, reaching out. *My God,* I thought, *is he going to kiss me?* And he did! After a rough one-handed hug, he kissed me on the cheek before letting me go. I was left with a whisker burn and a lingering smell of engine oil in my nose. "You boys mind helping me put away these tools before we go in and eat?" he asked.

"See what I told you?" Cody joked.

"Hurry up," Dad said. "I want to go in the house and see my good-looking daughter-in-law and especially my granddaughter!"

"It's not like you haven't seen her, Dad," I said, gathering up from the floor scarred wrenches that were as familiar to me as my own fingers and toes.

"Yeah, but that's when you first brought her home. When she was just a little pink thing. I haven't seen her since she became a person."

"I'm sorry we just showed up without any warning," I said. "This was kind of a last-second trip."

He shrugged. "I'm just glad you're here. Besides, after dinner I got some fence that needs fixed." Again, I thought he was serious. Again, he was joking. What had happened to him?

"You sure you don't mind us crashing dinner?"

"As long as we've got enough steaks we're okay," he said, gesturing to the hundreds of bawling cattle out in the meadow. "I think we'll be okay."

DINNER WAS PLEASANT. No, it was more than pleasant. I was *joyous*. Angelina, as she had with Jeter Hoyt, spent most of the time trying to get Dad's attention. In turn, he doted on her, fed her, made funny faces that made her laugh. I looked at Melissa, and Melissa shook her head, as surprised with this new turn in both of them as I was.

Cody declined the offer of a beer with dinner since he was driving, which I thought admirable because I knew he wanted one.

Through a mouthful of steak, Dad said the ranch had sold, the result of a divorce settlement with the old owner. It was bought quickly by a hedge fund manager in New York City.

"This new bird, I don't know," he said, gesturing with his fork, "I'm not sure we're gonna see eye to eye."

"Give him a chance, Walter," Mom said. "We've been here a long time. I'm not sure I'm up to moving again."

"Hell, I'll give him a chance," Dad said, grumbling. "As long as he doesn't say the word 'bison' again in my presence, we might get along. There are too many goddamn buffalo in Montana as it is, and too many Ted Turners."

For the first time, I thought about what my parents would do when they finally left the ranch. Did they have retirement savings? Medical insurance? These were things that had never been discussed in my presence. Where would they live? I thought about the marriage they had, which, despite its flaws, had lasted forty years. Just the two of them, out here twenty miles from the nearest town on an expanse of land so big and raw it could have easily swallowed them up. *God,* I thought, *they're tough.*

The topic turned to Judge Moreland and Garrett. Melissa told the story but left out the most unpleasant details. Even with that, it was too much for Mom to handle, and she simply shook her head as if it were another of those big-city things she'd just never understand.

"Tell them to screw themselves, I like this one," Dad said, reaching over and mussing Angelina's hair, which resulted in a belly laugh that was contagious. "Keep her."

As if that were the end of the subject.

Angelina tried to reciprocate and stretched her arm out at him. Surprisingly, he bent forward and dipped his head so she could tousle his white hair.

"Yup," he said, sitting back while she laughed. "Keep *this* one."

"ARE YOU SURE YOU CAN'T STAY?" Mom begged. "Jack and Melissa can stay in Jack's old room. Cody can have the spare or the bunkhouse if he'd prefer. Jack's old crib is up in the attic for Angelina."

Looking past the fact that they'd kept my crib all these years, I explained that I had to go to work Monday, that I'd just returned from overseas the night before and had follow-up to do.

"I've never understood your job," Dad said. "What—you go to foreign countries and hand out maps? You get paid for that?"

Actually, I'd explained my job to him three or four times over the years. His eyes glazed over each time.

"Why don't you stay?" she said again.

He said, "I'm sure they can spare you for one day, for Christ's sake."

"I'm sorry," I said.

His face darkened, and I braced for it; *you sure are sorry* or something similar and cutting. He was still Walter McGuane in there. But he caught himself, held it in, let it pass. "I wish you weren't going to take this little one away from me," he said instead, tickling her, making her laugh.

"Isn't there supposed to be a big storm coming down from the north?" Melissa said. "I'm sure you wouldn't want us to be snowed in here." She was good at saying reasonable things.

"Hell," he said, "I wouldn't mind."

WHILE MELISSA AND MY MOTHER cleaned up dishes, Dad said he wanted to show me something out in the barn. He didn't. As we walked outside in the last gasp of dusk in the cold, he didn't look at me as he said, "I've realized something since you left this place, Jack. I was hard on you. I guess I didn't know how to be a father. My old man was a bastard, and he's the one supposed to teach you those things."

"You did okay," I said, a lump in my throat. All I remembered of my grandfather was a tall man with a full black beard that smelled of cigarette smoke and eyes that weren't kind.

"Naw. But that don't mean you shouldn't know how to be a son. Call your mother more. Hell, invite her to Denver. That little girl in there is her only grandchild. I'll survive if she comes down to see you. I know how to cook a steak."

We walked to the Quonset, crunching gravel. So much to say. "I'll do that, Dad. But didn't you hear what Melissa was saying about Angelina?"

"I did."

"We may not get to keep her."

"Bullshit. Fight it."

"We are."

"Good," he said. "And if you ever get the time from your busy damned job passing out maps of Denver, come back and stay a little while. I got fence to fix."

I laughed.

"I'm proud you done so well on your own," he said. "I was telling a cattle buyer about you just yesterday morning. He acted all interested, but you know you can't trust those bastards. But I am proud of you."

IN THE CAR, the lights of Bozeman looking like the last vestige of civilization in the pure dark of a cloudy, moonless night, Cody said, "We'll never figure 'em out, Jack. They are what they are. My old man's a drunk. I didn't fall very far from that fucking tree. This is a good place, Montana. I hope to come back someday."

"It is a good place," I said. "Or is it just because it isn't Denver right now?"

"Maybe for you. I just hope I can figure out a way to make it back."

Why did he say that as if he never would?

I WAS SLEEPING when Melissa's cell phone burred. I sat up, had no idea at all where we were in Wyoming. It was midnight.

"It's Brian," she said from the backseat, looking at the display.

She listened, mostly, saying, "That's great," and "You be careful, Brian."

She closed the phone, said, "Brian's meeting the guy with the photos tonight someplace downtown. By the time we get back, we'll have them."

"Everything's working," I said. "I'm glad we canceled that thing with Jeter."

"We'll see," Cody cautioned. "Brian could just as easily be on a wild-goose chase. That would be very Brian-like."

WE WERE APPROACHING CASPER at two in the morning when Melissa's phone rang again. She said "Brian again," and answered. A few seconds went by when she gasped, and said, "Who *are* you?"

"Give it to me," I said, and she quickly handed the phone over, as eager to get rid of it as I was to get it.

I could hear city noises and the sound of someone laughing in the background.

"Who is this?" I asked. "What are you doing with Brian's phone?"

"Brian?" the voice said. A young voice, Hispanic accent. "*Brian? We kicked his ass.*"

Again the laugh in the background, and a phrase I'd heard before. My entire body went cold.

We fucking own you, man.

"Brian," the caller said before punching off, "is one dead faggot."

"Oh no," I said. "Someone called us on Brian's phone, and I think I heard Garrett in the background."

"Shit," Cody spit, and floored it.

Denver

Sunday, November 18
Seven Days to Go

Fifteen

W E HURTLED DOWN I-25, reaching speeds of 110 miles per hour, with Cody barking out the names of detectives he used to work with. I'd locate the numbers on his cell and speed-dial them and hand the phone over when someone answered. We woke up a lot of detectives. All were groggy from sleep. Cody asked whether the detective was aware of a homicide or attempted homicide in downtown Denver.

"Okay, thanks, man," Cody said three times in a row. "Sorry to wake you up," and handed the phone back to me to place the next call.

"Nothing?" I said. "Could it be a joke? A way of screwing with us?"

"That was Brian's phone they used," Melissa observed. "How would they have gotten it?"

"She's right," he said. "Goddammit, who was on shift? They won't tell me anything if I call the desk. I've got to find who might have worked it and talk to them personally. Jack, scroll down through the numbers. I can think of two other guys who might know some-thing."

I found both numbers and called each in turn and switched on the speaker feature of the cell so Cody could talk and speed at the same time. It scared me when he held the phone to his ear and drove at the same time because he was incapable of talking without ges-turing as well. The first detective didn't pick up, the second asked Cody if he was drunk to be calling at this hour.

"I'm fine," he said. "I need to know who was on shift tonight."

"The FNG—fucking new guy. Who else would be on mid-nights?"

"Torkleson?"

I felt a little trill of recognition.

"Yeah."

"Do you know his cell number?"

"It's fucking four in the morning, Cody. I don't know anything except that I want to go back to sleep. He's the FNG. I'm not sure I wrote his number down."

"Please, Dan, I really need to know it."

"Are you even working? Aren't you suspended?"

"Yeah."

"What the hell are you doing, Cody?"

"Checking on a friend. Please, Dan."

Dan sighed, and grumbled, "Hold on."

I was afraid we'd drive out of cell-phone range before Dan found the number. Wyoming was notorious for huge expanses where there was no signal. Luckily, it was also notorious for its lack of state troopers on the highway. Finally, Dan came back and gave Cody the number.

"Can I go back to sleep now?" Dan asked.

"Sure. Thanks. Good night."

To us, he asked, "Got it?"

"I do," Melissa said, and tore out the page of her check register that she'd used to write down the number.

I punched the numbers in, keeping the speaker on.

"Yeah?" the detective answered, no doubt leery of the late-night call.

"Jason, it's Cody Hoyt."

"Shit, I didn't recognize the number, and it's four in the morning. What can I do you for?"

"I need to know if you worked an incident tonight. The subject's a friend of mine named Brian Eastman. Tall, thin, Caucasian, midthirties. Probably somewhere downtown."

After a pause, Torkleson said, "He's a friend of yours?"

"Yeah."

"Oh man, I'm sorry to hear that, I really am. We took the call an hour ago—some drunk found a body in an alley. We just sent him to the trauma center at Denver General."

Melissa gasped in the backseat and buried her face in her hands.

"How bad?" Cody asked.

"Real fucking bad," Torkleson said.

"What happened?"

"Well, it looked like somebody tried to kick his face off. The paramedics weren't even sure at first if he was still alive, man. I've seen some beatings, but this one was really, really bad. I hate to tell you this considering he's a friend of yours and all."

"And I hate to hear it," Cody said softly.

Melissa began to cry.

"Hey, who's that with you?" Torkleson asked.

"My girlfriend," Cody said absently, obviously not wanting to explain our circumstances.

"Hey, I'm not sure your girlfriend wants to hear this."

"It's okay," Cody said. "Tell me, did you find anything on him?"

Torkleson's radar went up. "Like what?"

"You know," Cody said, tap-dancing. "His wallet, keys, phone, documents, anything?"

"You mean does it look like a robbery?"

"Yeah, that's what I mean."

"That's what it looks like. His ID was on him, and we found a cell phone in the alley. Nothing else unusual on him. What kind of documents?"

"Any kind."

Photos, I thought.

"No. His wallet had been cleaned out of cash and dumped. There's no way to know how much was in it."

Thousands, I thought, *to pay off his contact.*

"Denver General, you say?"

"Affirmative. I'm still at the scene, though. We've got the photographer and forensics team going over the alley, then I'll head over to the hospital myself to see if we can get any kind of statement. But from what I saw . . ."

"No witnesses?"

"None that have come forward, which isn't surprising. This is a crappy part of town. People don't tend to talk."

"It happened in an alley," Cody asked. "Any lighting? Any windows that overlook where he was found?"

I could hear Torkleson's voice tense up as he sensed Cody was trying to horn in on his investigation.

"There are overhead lights," he said, "but no lightbulbs. They've all been shot out. And yeah, a couple of windows but no residents in the buildings."

"Sounds like the Zuni Street area," Cody said.

I felt the hair on the back of my neck stand up. Near the Appaloosa Club, then.

"That's where it is," Torkleson said. "Hey, I've got a question for you. Where did you hear about this? I can't see you sitting at home with your girlfriend at four in the morning listening to a scanner."

Cody snorted. "No chance of that."

"So how did you hear about it?"

"The perp called us from Brian's phone."

"*What?*"

"I'll meet you at the hospital, Detective. Make sure you secure that phone you found and get somebody competent to download the call log and the text log. *Do it now!* And I hope to hell you dust that phone for prints, Jason, because whoever stomped Brian held it in his scummy fucking hand."

"Cody, can I ask you something? Aren't you suspended? Should we even be having this conversation?"

Cody deftly swerved to miss a pronghorn antelope on the highway. Melissa said, "My God, that was close."

He didn't miss a beat. He said, "Torkleson, that's my friend you found. We've been friends since grade school in Montana. I want to find out who did this, and you can either work with me or against me. Do you really want me pursuing this as a private citizen? Showing you up?"

"No."

"Then meet me at the hospital with those logs."

WE ARRIVED at Denver General at nine in the morning, after dropping Melissa and Angelina at our house. Not that Melissa didn't want to be there to be with Brian—she wanted to be there desperately—but she didn't think she could take the baby with us after twenty-eight hours in the car. Angelina was crabby and sleep-deprived but had been a good traveler overall.

As Cody and I walked down the humming, antiseptic hallways, I felt as if I were shell-shocked. I was sleep-deprived myself, but the visit with my parents and the news about Brian seemed to knock me sidewise. At the front desk, Cody asked about Brian and was told by a severe black woman the patient was in ICU, and there could be no visitors except immediate relatives.

"Damn it," Cody said, reaching back into his jacket, where he produced a wallet badge and flashed it at her. "We need to see him *now*."

"Go right up," she said, eyes wide. "Seventh floor is ICU. There's one of your policemen up there already."

Cody nodded and pocketed the badge. In the elevator, I said, "I thought they took that away from you."

He nodded. "They took my real badge away. But any cop worth his salt has a couple of spares. You can buy 'em from cop catalogs. No one ever reads the details—they just see the flash."

The officer on the seventh floor wasn't Torkleson but a uniform assigned to Brian. He sat on a metal folding chair outside a pair of entry doors to the Intensive Care Unit signed ICU STAFF ONLY.

"How is he?" Cody asked the uniform, who was young with a crew cut and a wisp of a mustache.

"I haven't heard either way."

"Detective Torkleson assign you here?"

"Yes."

"I'm Detective Hoyt," Cody said, flashing the badge at a distance and pocketing it quickly. He was well practiced, I thought. *He could even fool cops.* Then he spoke with absolute authority. "We need to get in there and talk to the victim. This is Jack McGuane, an intimate of the victim. He's likely the only person he'll talk to."

The uniform shrugged. "From what I understand, he's hamburger. You aren't likely to get anything out of him."

"Let us by, please."

The uniform shrugged and sighed elaborately and called inside on the phone near the door. The door lock buzzed, and we were in.

"Mr. Eastman?" Cody asked the desk nurse.

"Room 738," she said. "Listen, he's scheduled for surgery any minute now. I'm not sure you . . ."

I followed Cody and braced myself. Even so, I wasn't prepared for what I saw when we went into 738.

"*Fuck!*" Cody said beneath his breath.

He was unrecognizable. He was a body beneath a sheet connected to what looked like dozens of chirping and humming machines and hanging bags of fluid. The bundles of tubing that connected his body to the hanging bags looked like exposed tree roots. His face was entirely covered with bandages. Thin gauze covered his nose—two dark spots of blood where his nostrils were—and a fogged-up oxygen mask covered his mouth and nose. His head beneath the wraps was misshapen, crushed in on one side and bulging out on the other. It didn't hit home to me that it was Brian in that bed. No way. This long bag of broken bones and bruised meat could not be him. I half expected the Brian I knew to stroll in from the hallway and say something cryptic or sarcastic.

If it weren't for a sockless ankle not covered by the sheets and a pile of clothing at the foot of the bed I recognized as his, I wouldn't have known it was Brian at all.

I felt something bitter rise in my throat, and I was unable to speak.

Cody approached the bed and fished through the sheets for Brian's hand. He found a ball the size of a mitten.

"They even broke his fingers, those bastards," he said.

He leaned down over the bed. "Brian, can you hear me? It's Cody. Can you hear me in there?"

No reaction of any kind.

"Brian, you'll be all right," Cody lied. "Help me get the people who did this. It was Garrett and his Sur-13 pals, right? Help me get them."

Nothing.

I stepped forward and touched Brian's naked ankle, the only piece of flesh not bandaged that I could see.

"Come on, Brian," I said. "You can do it. Was it Garrett?"

Not even a movement.

Suddenly, the room was filled with orderlies led by a nurse, who was angry we were there. "You two, out of here *now!* He's going straight into surgery, where we've got two trauma docs waiting. How did you get in here, anyway?"

Cody didn't badge her.

I said, "He's our friend."

"The best thing you can do for your friend is step aside," she said, and we did.

Once they were gone, I used Brian's dark bathroom to throw up.

"HE WAS SET UP," Cody said as we paced in the ICU lounge. "Whether Garrett—or his dad—started the communication with Brian about phony photos or came in later I can't say. But he was lured down there, and they jumped him."

"Can we prove it was Garrett?" I asked.

"I don't know," Cody said. "We can try." He stopped pacing and lowered his voice. "Jack, you're square in the middle of a police investigation. You're seeing it from the inside looking out, and it looks pretty fucking confusing, doesn't it? This is what we do when we don't have an eyewitness or a confession. There are rarely black-and-white circumstances. You and I are pretty sure Garrett More-land and his *compadres* did this because you *think* you might have heard him in the background. That and all of this crap that's been going on between you and him. But we can't reveal everything, can we? Like why we were coming back from Montana when the call came in?"

I shook my head, confused. Instead, I said, "When you flashed your badge and lied to those people, it came pretty easy, didn't it?"

Cody glared at me. "What are you saying?"

I swallowed hard. "I'm not so sure lying comes as easily to me."

Cody shook his head. "I'm disappointed in you, Jack. You still don't get it. It's what I was trying to tell you a minute ago. *There are rarely black-and-white circumstances.* We want to get to the absolute truth, but most of the time we fall a little short. I mean, we know what we know—but sometimes we can't prove it to everyone's sat-isfaction because the bar is set too high. A good cop does his best to put the bad guys away. Sometimes we need a little help. Like from our partners"—meaning me in this instance—"or from a judge."

The Aubrey Coates case was obviously still very much on his mind.

He stepped toward me and reached out and grabbed me by the collar and pulled me into him. "As Margaret Thatcher once said, don't go wobbly on me now, Jack. Remember, this is all for you." His eyes shone, and his mouth curled down. I never really felt threatened. We'd fought before in high school, and I cleaned his clock at the time. Of course, that was before he became a cop and learned all kinds of tricks. I said, "I think it was Garrett."

"You think or you know?"

"It was Garrett."

He let me go. "That's what I needed to hear from you—some fucking *truth*."

"But there's so much that just doesn't make sense," I said. "The more I think about it, the less sense it makes. Why does the judge want our little girl? Is he in all of this with his son, or are they operating independently of each other? And how can his wife not even know? How is that possible? Or was she lying to Melissa?"

Cody shook his head and shrugged. "Don't think I haven't thought about all of those things for days since this all started. I know there's a thread that will tie it all together, but right now I come up with nothing."

"Are there even any photos?" I asked. "Will we ever know now?"

"Let's hope to hell Brian recovers," he said. "If he can tell us Garrett was there, it's a slam dunk. Everything changes. Brian testifies, and no judge would place a baby with a gangbanger convicted of trying to stomp an innocent man to death. We won't need any photos—it'll all be over, so think positive. It's amazing what these doctors can do."

Cody leaned in to me. "What's really important is that he comes out of it. Even if he's not sure who did it, can't remember—you know what I mean. If we talk to him first, *suggest* it was Garrett, he's smart enough to know to run with it."

At first I didn't get what he was saying. Then I did. I should have felt something, some physical manifestation of guilt.

"I understand," I said.

"There you go," Cody said, punching me in the arm. "There you go. It's what Brian would want, anyway."

I WAS ON MY CELL WITH MELISSA, telling her Brian was still in surgery and we hadn't heard anything from the doctors yet, when I saw Detective Torkleson in the hallway and heard Cody say, "It's about time!"

Ending the call, I walked over to join them. Torkleson looked tired—rumpled, unshaven. He'd been up for hours—all through the night and halfway into Sunday. He had a thick sheaf of papers in his hand.

"You've got to send a car over to Judge John Moreland's place," Cody told him, "pick up Garrett, and bring him in for questioning. He either participated in the attempted homicide or he was there to cheer it on. He probably lured Brian down there in that alley."

"Whoa, cowboy," Torkleson said. "You've got to give me some-thing to link him to the crime before I send a cruiser. I know you've had this guy in your sights, but he doesn't have to talk. What I want is probable cause. Rock-solid PC. His old man's a judge, don't forget."

As if I could.

"What do you have there?" Cody asked.

Torkleson brandished the sheaf of papers. "Here are the call rec-ords from the victim's phone, as requested. Good thinking on your part." He shook the papers. "Your friend spent *a lot* of time on his cell, I can tell you that. The easy part was printing out the records. Now we've got to spend some quality time on these logs before we start sending out uniforms to pick people up."

"What about prints on Brian's phone?" Cody asked.

Torkleson made a face and held his hands out, palms up. "We're working on that."

"Meaning what?" Cody growled.

"We sort of screwed that up, Cody. The phone was handled by half a different cops and probably the derelicts in the alley who called it in. The prints on it are smudged. At some point someone must have put the phone in their pocket or something. There are no clean prints. I've got our tech guys looking for partials, but it doesn't look promising."

"Shit," Cody said, taking the papers and squinting at the small print. "How far do these go back?"

"That's just the past month," Torkleson said. "Like I said, he spent a lot of time on his cell."

"Jesus, what a talker," Cody said, looking at the most recent page. His finger jabbed the last number. "Melissa's cell number," he said to me. "It'll take days to get through all of this to find how Garrett set him up."

"You're leaping ahead again," Torkleson said. He paused, looked at me, then back to Cody. "And there's something else we need to consider before we put all of our eggs in the Garrett basket. Your friend Brian Eastman was very active in the gay community. I assume you know that fact."

"Of course we know it," Cody said.

Torkleson said, "Well, there are a couple of gay bars down in that district, you know. From what I've found out, he wasn't a stranger at either one. And if you look at a map, this alley we found him in is a natural off-the-street route from one to the other. We've got some officers checking at both bars to see if he was at either one last night, but it's hard to track down the bartenders or patrons on a Sunday morning. We'll do it, but it'll take a few days of good police work.

"But some of the uniforms were talking. They think maybe this was random. Maybe your friend was going from one bar to another when some gangbangers jumped him. He was a pretty good target, you know, the way he was dressed like the ultimate yuppie. Of course, they don't want to float this theory out loud because then it would be a hate crime, and if the mayor heard that, he'd go ballistic."

Cody leveled his gaze on Torkleson. "Most crimes are hate crimes," he said.

"You know what I mean. It could get political . . ."

"Fuck that," Cody said. "It doesn't fit. I'm not saying Brian didn't frequent those bars or know the route—he probably did. But when he called us earlier last night, he said he got a specific call to meet somebody. Maybe the caller picked the spot that would be familiar—I don't know. Or maybe he picked it because it was close enough to the Appaloosa Club that the gangbangers could run back there and clean up. But Brian wasn't out cruising—we know that."

Torkleson was slow on the take. "Hold it—*he* called you? When was that?"

"I don't know. Midnight, I guess."

"And what was he meeting this person for?"

Cody hesitated for a moment. I felt a chill go up my spine. Were we caught?

"Information," Cody said, finally.

"What kind of information?" Torkleson asked, stepping back half a step, distancing himself without realizing he was doing it.

"I don't know," Cody said. "Brian kept it all mysterious. He said he was going to meet someone tonight who was going to give us information that would help us in our case against Garrett and Judge Moreland. That's why he was downtown last night."

I thought, *Cody's high above the crowd on a wire without a net.*

"And that's why you asked me about documents earlier?"

Cody nodded.

"Anything else you've been keeping from me?"

"Not a thing," Cody said.

Torkleson swiveled his head, gave me the dead-eye. "What about you, McGuane?"

I knew I looked guilty. My face was burning up.

"What?" I asked. I tried not to look at Cody.

"You heard me."

I sighed. "The information was supposed to be photos," I said. "Photos with Judge Moreland in them. Something bad enough Moreland would back off."

"Ahhh," Torkleson said, nodding. "You two have been playing a little blackmail game on the side, eh?"

"No blackmail," Cody said. "You can't blackmail anyone if you don't have the photos to blackmail with."

"I see," Torkleson said. "I also think right now I don't want to hear much more. Later, though, I want the whole story."

"Thank you, brother," Cody said, then quickly changed the subject back to the call list. "I'll bet we've got incoming calls from Garrett on here. We've got to check all his numbers—his house, his cell, the Appaloosa Club, his fellow gangbanger's numbers against these."

"That's what I mean," Torkleson said. "We haven't had time to match up any of the incoming or outgoing numbers yet. My shop needs to spend some time on them, figure out who was talking to who."

I realized we were through the gathering storm. I let my breath out slowly.

Cody looked frustrated. "What if Garrett was using a burner?" he asked. "One of those damned Tracfones anyone can buy at Wal-Mart? Then the number doesn't mean anything at all because we can't link the owner to the phone."

Torkleson shrugged. "Unless we can prove Garrett bought it, with a credit-card receipt or something. You know how this works."

My heart dropped. I had thought for a few minutes it would be a matter of hours. Now I wasn't sure they had anything at all.

"You need to send that car," Cody insisted. "Send it *now*, and haul in Garrett's ass for questioning. We know he was there."

Torkleson was puzzled. "How do we know that?"

"Jack heard his voice in the background when they called," Cody said. "Didn't you, Jack?"

"I thought I did."

Torkleson took a moment to study me. "Are you sure?"

"I can't be absolutely positive," I said, "but I thought I heard his voice in the background."

"And you'd testify to that?"

I swallowed hard. "Yes."

"I'm confused," Torkleson said, turning to Cody. "You said you were with some woman named Melissa when you got the call. Now you're telling me this gentleman was there with you and actually took the call?"

Cody waggled his eyebrows, Groucho Marx style. "The three of us were together, if you know what I mean."

Torkleson looked dubious.

"Cody's kidding," I said quickly. "Melissa is my wife. The three of us were together, and Melissa's phone rang. Because it was Brian's phone calling but a voice she didn't recognize, she handed the phone to me. I swear to God."

"Look," Cody said, "if you haul Garrett downtown and start hammering him before he can manufacture a story, you might be able to get him to tell us some lies we can unravel."

"*We?*" Torkleson said. "Are you suggesting you be involved in the interrogation?"

"I can watch him from outside," Cody said, "feed you questions."

"And blow the whole case," Torkleson said. "A suspended cop actively involved in the interrogation. That'll play real well."

210

"Okay," Cody said, "I'll stay completely away. But I'm keeping these call logs. You can download another copy easy enough."

Torkleson wiped his forehead. He was sweating. He jabbed me in the breast. "The *only* reason I have to send a car to the Morelands' to request an interview with that kid is your statement. If it turns out he was in bed the whole evening or playing cards with his good judge daddy, my ass is grass. And so is yours."

"I understand."

He studied me a few more seconds, then looked to Cody.

"Do it," Cody said.

Torkleson stepped away from both of us to use his cell phone. I could have kissed him at that moment. I overheard enough to hear him caution the uniforms to be polite and respectful and to explain clearly that Garrett was being asked to come and talk because of my direct assertion, not because there was any physical evidence. As I heard him, the reason for them going to the Moreland house sounded flimsy even to me.

"You never know what he might say," Cody whispered to me, "once we get him in the box with a tape recorder running. He may give us five things we can disprove later. And if you heard his voice, you heard his voice.

"Good job back there, by the way. You gave him just enough. It sounded plausible. He bought it. Maybe you'd be a good cop."

"No," I said, "I don't think so."

WE SAT in the waiting area for the next hour not reading magazines. All three of us looked up every time a nurse or doctor walked by. Melissa called three times. Each time I had to tell her we hadn't heard anything yet regarding Brian's condition.

Torkleson was dozing when his cell burred. He sat up and patted all of his pockets in an unintentional imitation of Cody before he found his phone in his jacket pocket. He said his name and no more. As he listened, his face got red. The murderous glance he shot at Cody told me things had not gone well.

"Okay, sir," he said, biting his words off, "I'll be down there as soon as I know about our victim. Yes, I'll personally apologize."

He snapped his phone closed with such force I wondered if it would ever work again.

"You burned me," he said to both of us. "I'm in so much fucking trouble."

"What happened?" Cody asked, not affected by Torkleson's vehemence.

"My guys showed up at Judge Moreland's house. The judge was furious. He called the mayor, who called the chief, who just called me. The judge says Garrett was home all night with him, and he refused to send his son to answer questions. He said Mr. McGuane here is harassing him because of a legal matter and that Cody Hoyt is a rogue cop who is completely out of control. The chief asked me why I was even associating with you, Cody."

Cody shrugged.

"Fuck you two," Torkleson said, standing up. "I've got a wife and a little girl and a lot of years ahead of me. I can't let you screw that up."

"I've got a wife and a little girl, too," I said. "This is about trying to keep us together."

He wanted to launch into me, but Cody stood up and put his hand on Torkleson's shoulder.

"Look what this tells us," Cody said. "It tells us a lot. It means the judge is aware of what Garrett is up to. We've been wondering about that—are they working together or apart? Now we know. At last we have some clarity, even though this is about as bad a turn as we could get."

Torkleson shook Cody's arm off, his face still red. I felt sorry for him even as I contemplated what Cody had just said.

"Gentlemen, are you here for Brian Eastman?"

None of us had heard or seen the surgeon approach from the double doors down the hall. He was short and thin, wearing blood-soaked green scrubs.

"I'm sorry," he said, not looking any of us in the eye. "Mr. Eastman has passed."

"He's dead?" Torkleson asked.

"It was probably for the best, in a way," the doctor said. "With that kind of brain damage, he could have never functioned again."

I sat back in the chair and covered my face with my hands.

We'd lost our friend.

We'd lost our advocate.

We'd lost our friend.

Cody's eyes streamed tears. "Man," he said, "I wish I hadn't have been so hard on the guy earlier. He didn't deserve it."

Tuesday, November 20

Five Days to Go

Sixteen

THERE WAS SOMETHING going on at the office. It wasn't a conspiracy of silence, where everyone seems to know what's up except the victim. It was simply that under the circumstances—a closed door meeting in the CEO's office that had started early before the staff arrived and was still going past 9:00 A.M.—some kind of trouble was indicated. The halls, offices, and cubicles were silent. No animated conversations, no laughing. Just tapping on keyboards from every office. I saw Pete Maxfield, the PR guy, walk down the hall to the break room tugging on his collar, as if the heat were turned up. He looked like he felt guilty for *something*. On my way to get coffee, I ducked into Linda Van Gear's office to ask her what was happening. She always knew, but she wasn't at her desk.

I asked Cissy the receptionist when Linda was expected back.

"Oh, she's here," she said. "She's in a meeting with Mr. Jones."

"Who else is in there?" I asked.

"Mr. Doogan from the mayor's office."

My mouth went dry.

BRIAN'S FUNERAL WAS SET for Friday. Because of his promi-
nence in Denver, his murder was front-page news. Mayor Halladay
appeared on the steps of city hall and said he was both mournful
and angry at the same time and that the community had lost a great
man. When a reporter from Channel 9 asked him if it was a hate
crime because of Brian Eastman's well-known sexual orientation,
Halladay exploded, saying if it was, he would personally make
sure the DA charged whoever did it with the maximum penalty under the law. The mayor declared, "Denver will not tolerate hate!"
He was followed by the Denver police chief, who said the department was pursuing every lead, and he was confident there would be
arrests before the week was out. I knew through Cody that Torkleson
and the cops had no more evidence than the day before, but the
chief was assigning several more detectives to the case, and they were
interviewing everyone they could find in LoDo who might have
seen Brian or the assailants that night.

Melissa was in a stunned funk. Brian was her best friend, and he
was simply *gone*. "He gave his life for us," she said through tears. I
didn't know how to respond, so I simply held her. While I did, I
looked at Angelina in her walker, wonderfully oblivious to what was
going on. She'd never see her uncle Brian again, and there was no
way to explain that to her.

Cody was splitting his time between our house and his. The media contingent that had been staking out his block had dispersed,
likely so they could follow the Eastman murder. When I saw him, he
seemed so quiet it was as if he wasn't really there at all. I couldn't tell
whether Brian's murder had knocked him speechless or he was deep
in thought formulating a plan—or both. I do know he was combing
through Brian's call log one number at a time. He used our com-

puter to cross-reference the numbers, and he kept a running list of numbers and names as he found them.

I worried that Jeter Hoyt might just show up since he'd kept the envelope, and was happy to hear that a terrific winter storm had hit Montana and dumped eighteen inches of snow.

CISSY LEANED INTO my office and whispered something I couldn't hear.

"Excuse me?"

"Mr. Jones would like to see you in his office."

I took a deep breath, pulled on my jacket, straightened my tie, and went to get fired.

"HAVE A SEAT, JACK," CEO H. R. "Tab" Jones said. I could tell by the way Linda smiled sadly at me when I entered the office that my assumption had been correct.

"You know Jim Doogan," Jones said, as Cissy stepped out and closed the door.

I nodded. Doogan shook my hand. He seemed almost kind. Despite it all, I still kind of liked him.

"Linda," Jones said, "do you want to tell Jack what we found out this morning?"

Jack, Linda would say, *the police say you've been implicated in the murder of a man named Pablo 'Luis' Cadena. They also say you went to Montana last weekend to hire a thug to intimidate an eighteen-year-old boy.*

Instead, she said, "Malcolm Harris was arrested this morning at Heathrow Airport before he boarded the direct London-to-Denver flight."

"*What?*" That one came out of nowhere.

Linda looked to Doogan to pick up the story.

Doogan said, "Your friend Malcolm Harris is suspected of being a very big fish in an international pedophilia ring. Apparently both Scotland Yard and Interpol have been working on this case for a couple of years, and today they pulled the trigger and made dozens of arrests all across Europe. Harris is considered to be a kingpin of these sickos. They're talking real bad stuff here, Jack. Buying and selling not just kiddie porn but actual children, group sex trips to Asia, about as bad as it can get."

I flashed back to Harris's long foray to the "office" behind the bar in Berlin, how he'd come back flushed. Did Fritz—no doubt a pedophile himself—have photos of children back there on his computer? Or maybe even a child? *Oh, God.* I cringed and felt physically sick.

"Are you okay?" Doogan asked me.

"He did seem a little off to me," I said. "I couldn't quite figure out what it was. And I had this urge to pound the crap out of him that sort of came from nowhere."

"A *little* off?" Jones said, raising his eyebrows.

"Give him a break, Tab," Linda cut in. "I knew Malcolm long before Jack came on board. I always thought he was strange, but I never would have suspected this." She laughed drily. "Lots of people we work with are strange."

I thought, *the way he looked at that picture of Angelina and thought he'd seen her before.* I didn't know what to make of it at the time, but now I figured he'd seen so many photos of little girls that he was simply confused, that bastard.

So many things Harris had said and done that night came flooding back:

"creeping fascism of the politically correct"

"There aren't bureaucrats looking over your shoulder as you live your life, telling you how to speak and think and whom to associate with—taking your freedom away."

"I've seen enough for tonight."

His outright joy in the way the restaurant tenderized the veal . . .

Jones was staring at me.

"Hold it," I said. "You don't think I knew about this in any way, do you?"

"Did you?" Jones asked, again with the eyebrows.

"For God's sake, no!" I was nauseated by the thought. "I have a nine-month-old daughter, Tab." It seemed ridiculous to have to defend myself to a forty-seven-year-old man called "Tab."

"I didn't think you did," Doogan said, "but we have a problem."

I shook my head, not getting it. Linda looked away.

"We—you—have been courting this guy," Doogan said. "The mayor himself has announced this new business coming to town. Channel 9, which is no friend of the administration, as you know, called for a statement. They're all over it. Even though it's unfair, this ain't beanbag we're playing. Imagine a headline that reads: MAYOR HALLADAY AND DENVER CVB COURTED INTERNATIONAL PEDO-PHILE."

"Jack," Jones said, "we're going to restructure the bureau. This international stuff is just too hot right now. The mayor's enemies and the press are always pointing to it as an extravagance we can't afford, and now we've got this. That's what we've been talking about in here. Linda's being moved over to conventions. We've got a position open there, and she's got seniority."

"Meaning I'm out?" I said.

Jones pursed his lips and nodded yes.

Doogan said, "The best way to deal with an issue like this is to get out in front of it. If Channel 9 presses the story, we'll respond by saying we've restructured our efforts and cut staff to avoid embarrassments like this in the future. Your name isn't likely to come up in any way."

"I'm sorry I can't take you with me," Linda said. "Maybe if something opens up down the road."

I sat back. Too much, too fast.

"Sorry it worked out this way," Doogan said.

"You don't know how much I need this job," I said. "You have *no* idea."

"You'll need to get with HR," Jones said. "We'll work out a generous severance package, and I believe you've got vacation and sick time coming."

Looks of strained sympathy all around. Linda, especially.

CISSY WAS SUDDENLY IMMERSED in whatever she was reading on her desk and kept her head down as I opened the door. Pete, who had been loitering in the break room the whole time, tried to thinly disguise his relief.

I went into my office and bent over my desk, my head spinning. How would I tell Melissa?

AS DOOGAN WALKED past my office, I said, "Jim!"

He came in. I said, "You might want to shut the door."

This was the first time I'd ever seen him look ill at ease.

I said, "How much of this has to do with Malcolm Harris and how much has to do with Judge Moreland? He knows I was in on the complaint the other night when the police went to talk to his son about Brian Eastman's murder. I wonder if this Malcolm Harris thing isn't just the excuse he was looking for."

He shrugged unconvincingly.

"You're not talking?"

He looked at my ceiling, my desk, his shoes, everywhere but at me. "Sometimes," he said, "I do things that keep me up at night. I just try and convince myself that running a big city can be messy at times. Sometimes things are done for the greater good, and they aren't necessarily fair or fun."

"I guess that answers my question."

"I've got to go."

"One more thing," I said. "I've got another problem for you, and this one's much bigger than me. I've been thinking about some of the things Malcolm Harris said to me. He's got connections here, Jim. That's why he was going to relocate. In fact, at one point he told me he would be *bulletproof. Bulletproof*. Any idea why he'd say that?"

Doogan looked puzzled. "No idea at all," he said.

"The mayor may have a much bigger problem than me."

Doogan shrugged. "Then we'll deal with it when it happens."

Seventeen

WITH THE PERSONAL ITEMS from my office in a box in the backseat of the Jeep, I roared out of the dark parking garage into a cold but sun-drenched day. I should have been devastated, but I wasn't. Instead, it was as if another burden had been lifted. I was charged up, filled with a full and dangerous kind of energy. I felt manic.

I called Melissa and told her what happened.

"Oh, Jack," she said. "Don't worry, you'll get another job. You're good at what you do."

"Yes," I said sarcastically, "there are openings for international tourism marketers all over town. I just need to snatch one up."

"We'll get by," she said. "I could go back to work after . . ."

"Don't say it," I said, cutting her off.

"Why us, Jack?" There was a catch in her voice.

"I don't know," I said. "It's like we're being tested. And I, for one, am getting damned sick of it."

"So does this mean you'll be home for lunch?"

We both found ourselves laughing at that one, the same kind of uncomfortable laugh one produces to a joke's punch line like, "Other than that, Mrs. Lincoln, how was the play?"

"So does it?" she asked.

"I'm going to go see Judge Moreland first," I said. "We need to have a talk."

She paused. "Is that a good idea?"

"What can it hurt?" I said. "What can happen? The mayor finds out and fires me?"

I FELT GUILTY for not feeling guilty. But in a strange way, my path had been cleared.

I parked on the street in front of the federal courthouse and took the steps two at a time. I would have charged through the lobby except for the guard who told me to slow down, empty my pockets, and walk slowly through the metal detector.

"Write down your name and who you're here to see so I can check you against the preapproved list," he said, handing me a clipboard.

I wrote, "Judge Moreland."

He took it back and asked if the judge was expecting me. "I don't see your name on the approved list."

I said, "Tell him Jack McGuane is here to see him."

I waited impatiently while the guard called upstairs, gave my name. Then shook his head while he listened and hung up. "They say he's not expecting you."

"I need to see him."

The guard narrowed his eyes and looked me over. This was one of those situations where my jacket and tie helped. "Are you a lawyer?"

"No. Judge Moreland is trying to take my child away."

"I'm sorry," he said warily. "You need to leave."

While I was putting my keys and change back into my pocket I looked up to see the man himself, Judge John Moreland, entering the building through a secure entrance accessed by a side street. He wore a suit and carried a briefcase, a long camel-hair coat draped over his arm. A vestibule of thick glass separated us.

"There he is," I said.

Just as the guard reached for his radio to call for help if necessary to get me out of there, Moreland looked up. I startled him. Our eyes locked.

I gestured, pointing to him and back to me. I mouthed, *I need to talk to you.*

Smoothly, oh so smoothly, he turned away and continued on to his private elevator. He stood there with his back to me, waiting for the elevator car to arrive.

"Sir," the guard said, rising to come around the counter. The public elevator on my side of the glass whooshed open and two more uniformed guards stepped out.

The three of them surrounded me.

"I'm going," I said, barely able to talk.

BACK OUTSIDE ON THE STREET, I seethed. As I approached my Jeep I turned and looked back at the courthouse. The three guards watched me from the double doors. And seven stories up, framed by a window, Moreland looked down on me with his hands on his hips. His face was impassive.

I WAS THREE BLOCKS away from the courthouse when I saw an open parking space and took it. My hands were trembling from anger as I opened my phone, got the number for the Alfred A. Arraj U.S. Courthouse from information, and punched the numbers in.

"Judge Moreland's office," a female receptionist said.

"This is Jim Doogan from the mayor's office," I said. "I need to talk with the judge."

"Just a moment."

In less than thirty seconds, I heard Moreland's mellifluous voice. "Hi, Jim."

"Why won't you talk to me?" I said.

It took him a moment, then he chuckled. "Using a ruse to get me on the phone, Mr. McGuane? That's not very sporting. Goodbye, Mr. McGuane . . ."

"Don't hang up! You need to hear what I'm going to say."

He paused.

"You've got three minutes," he said. His voice was all business now. "I need to be in court."

"Your son needs to sign that release," I said. "This can't go on any longer. Enough people have been hurt on both sides."

"I have no idea what you're talking about. Are you referring to having the police come to my house to question my son in regard to that murder? That was a really stupid, desperate play." God, how could he sound so rational?

"Garrett was involved," I said. "I heard him."

"Oh come now. He was at home with Kellie and me."

"I heard his voice. I know it was him. And I know you know it."

"You think you know a lot, Mr. McGuane. Look, I need to be going."

"I lost my job today," I said.

"I'm sorry to hear that, but it's no concern of mine."

"Actually, it is. It means I can fight you full-time."

He chuckled again.

"Why is it your wife doesn't know about Angelina?" I asked. "How can that be? What is your game?"

"Kellie?" He sounded genuinely surprised. "Kellie knows all about our granddaughter. She's been working for a month getting the baby's room ready."

"You're lying again. Melissa ran into her, and your wife didn't know a thing she was talking about."

Moreland sighed. "Mr. McGuane, I know this is tough on you. But it doesn't need to be so tough. My offer still stands. I'm more than willing to help you and your wife adopt another child. I'm surprised you've waited this long, actually. The sooner we can get the proceedings under way the sooner you can have a new baby."

"What is your game?" I said, nearly shouting. "*What is it?*"

"There's no game. I explained everything to you. My son needs to be accountable. Simple as that."

"I think you know everything your son is involved in," I said. "You two have some kind of unholy alliance."

"Oh please." Moreland sounded genuinely ticked off. "I'm beginning to think I made a mistake giving you and your wife so much time. It's given you weeks to martyr yourselves, and you've started to see conspiracies everywhere. I thought you were better than this, frankly."

"*You're trying to steal our daughter!*" I shouted. "Jesus, did you think we'd just *let* you?"

"You mean Garrett's daughter and my granddaughter," Moreland said wearily. "I'm afraid we've had this discussion before."

"Are you going to tell me you don't know your son is involved with Mexican gangs? With Sur-13?"

"I don't have any idea what you're talking about, Mr. McGuane."

"Deny, deny, deny," I said. "Where does the truth fit in all of this, or is that something you don't worry about anymore? Are you so used to handing down judgments that are obeyed that you think you're a god? That whatever you say just *is?*"

"You're embarrassing yourself, Mr. McGuane. And it's a pathetic thing to hear."

I paused. I was shaking. I could tell by his voice that he was going to hang up at any second. I wished I could be more coherent.

"Have your son sign the papers," I said, "so nothing else will happen."

His voice was maddeningly firm and reasonable. "Please think about what you're saying. Are you threatening me? Are you really threatening a sitting federal district court judge? I think we should both just pretend that you didn't just say that, Mr. McGuane, or otherwise you could be charged with a federal crime. Not that I'm threatening you—I'm not. I'm informing you. You don't know what you're saying. We can chalk it up to inexperience and runaway emotion."

"What are you hiding?" I said.

"This conversation is coming to a close, I'm afraid."

"*What is it?*"

"Goodbye, Mr. McGuane."

"Look," I said, "I may just be a rube from Montana who is in over my head. But Melissa is the most wonderful woman I've ever met. She's a fantastic mother, and she loves Angelina like no mother ever loved her child. You can't take our daughter away. I won't let it happen."

"You have five days, Mr. McGuane. Use them wisely. Now if you'll excuse me, I've got to go to work."

"Don't hang up!"

"Goodbye."

I DROVE TO SHELBY'S on 18th—the place Cody had taken me to—and pasted a fifty on the damp bar. "Keep 'em coming," I told the bartender. "Don't stop until this fifty is gone or I am."

CODY FOUND ME at about the time the place was filling up with cops after their eight-to-four shift. He slugged me in the arm hard enough to nearly knock me off my stool.

"Fucking idiot," he said. "Melissa's worried to death. What'd you do, turn off your phone?"

I left it in the car, I tried to say, but the words came out as gibberish.

"I'll give you a ride home," he said. "We can come back and get your Jeep tomorrow." He steered me out of the bar.

"You're a good friend," I said, but it came out "*You a goo fran.*"

"Shut up. We'll grab some coffee on the way home."

"Bourbon."

"No bourbon."

"My head is splitting open." *My hay ish . . .*

We'd only been driving a short time when I gagged and belched.

"Not in my car, knucklehead," Cody said, whipping off the highway onto an exit so I could climb halfway out the window and throw up. It burned like acid coming up. I think I might have hit some of his door.

"I been there," he said, as I got back in and slumped in the seat. "It's our own special corner of hell, ain't it? But if anyone says it isn't fun getting there, I know they're lying because it is fun for a while." Then: "Wipe your mouth."

"I HAD A GOOD DAY," Cody said.

I opened my eyes. It felt like I'd been sleeping for hours, but we were barely out of downtown.

"What?"

"I said I had a good day. A rare good day. With Brian's call log. I think I'm getting somewhere."

It took a moment to register.

"You need to quit feeling sorry for yourself," he said. "You have to be alert and strong for Melissa these next few days. I hope you got this out of your system."

I nodded, afraid to talk and sound stupid.

"I take that as a yes," he said. "Now look, I'm going to have to be gone soon. I may be gone a couple of days, I'm not sure yet. But there's something I need to follow up on, something in the call log. So if you and Melissa can't find me, don't worry. I'll be back."

I tried to talk. Couldn't.

"Yeah, I know we're running out of time," he said.

"SEE YOUR NEW FRIEND?" Cody asked as we drove down my street. I looked out the passenger window and saw three sheriff's cars parked across from our house, each stacked on top of the other. No, not three. As I focused it turned out to be just one.

"They're making sure you and Melissa don't take the baby and try to make a run for it. He's been there all afternoon. Hey, did you do something today to piss off the judge?"

"Yes."

"Thought so. He's calling in his chits with the sheriff."

MELISSA MET ME AT THE DOOR. I would have felt better if she'd scolded me, laid into me right there. Lord knows I deserved it.

She helped me get my clothes off, helped me get into bed. The ceiling spun, and I ran to the bathroom. There was very little left to throw up. I took a shower and cleared my head a little, gargled and outright drank several gulps of the mouthwash.

I was in bed when Melissa brought Angelina in to kiss me good night.

"I'm sorry," I said to both of them. "I'm so sorry."

"Get some sleep," Melissa said, taking Angelina to her bedroom.

THAT NIGHT, I had a dream. It was fused with alcohol. It was cinematic: *A pair of headlights snapped on in a dark garage. The light filled with hundreds of large swirling moths. No, not moths—snowflakes. A* deep-throated engine roared to life and the vehicle, its front grille looking like a mouthful of teeth, blasted out through a two-foot-high snowdrift. Snow exploded as the older-model pickup bucked drift after drift, going fast enough that it wouldn't get bogged down in the heavy and deep blanket of white.

Finally, the pickup swung onto a two-lane ribbon of black highway that was glazed with ice. The full moon lit up the snow in the meadows and sheened the ice on the road, but the pickup didn't slow down. Gradually, as the defroster cleared the windshield, I could see the driver.

He craned forward in his seat, leaning over the wheel. His eyes were dead as stones but there was a half smile on his face. On the seat of his truck was an arsenal of weapons: rifles, shotguns, Taser, bear spray, brass knuckles, leather saps, revolvers, semiautomatics.

The two-lane eventually melded into the interstate, which finally turned south. The ice cleared. The vehicle picked up speed and soon it was rocketing down the interstate, bathed in moonlight. There were no other cars on the road. As the truck hurtled into the night, chunks of ice broke off beneath it and skittered across the highway like comets leaving snow trails.

The heater was blasting, and the radio was up loud, alternating between archaic country western heavy with steel guitars and a Southern preacher who spoke in a mesmerizing cadence while his congregation urged him on. The cab smelled of gasoline, sweat, and gun oil.

At the rate the snow and ice was flying off the pickup, Jeter Hoyt figured it would be clean by time he hit Denver.

Wednesday, November 21

Four Days to Go

Eighteen

IT HAD BEEN A miserable day. I awoke with a monster of a headache and a terrible taste in my mouth. As I brushed my teeth, I stared at myself in the bathroom mirror and didn't like what looked back. My eyes were red coals in dark pools of blue. I looked ten years older than I was, and felt fifty years older. The guilt I hadn't felt the day before hammered me now, made me wonder why I'd drunk away a perfectly good afternoon feeling sorry for myself when I could have been home with my wife and daughter, could have been *doing* something.

By the time I got dressed, it was ten in the morning. After all, there was no place to go.

Melissa was playing with Angelina in the family room, making her giggle. When I saw the two of them there on the floor, I wondered how much I'd missed over the past year being at work. A lot, I knew. This was the place important things were happening, not at the office.

"Da!" Angelina cried happily. I picked her up off the floor and kissed her soft fat cheek. Damn, how babies smelled good. Again, I wondered at what age would they stop smelling so sweet? And I thought, *I may never find out.*

"I thought it best to let you sleep," Melissa said, taking Angelina back. "You were completely out of it."

"I'm sorry," I said.

"Except at one point when you sat up in bed and yelled, 'Here he comes!' That was interesting."

"I was dreaming that Jeter Hoyt was on his way," I said.

Melissa said, "Let's hope you weren't prescient." She shook her head and turned her attention back to Angelina.

I padded to the window and parted the curtain.

"He's still there," Melissa said. And he was: the black-and-white sheriff's vehicle. I vaguely remembered him from the night before. "There's another one around the corner in the alley."

"You're kidding!" I said.

"I wish I was. I saw him this morning when I took the garbage out. He's a nice man named Morales."

"Hmmm."

"I was thinking," she said, "since you're going to be home for a while if I couldn't ask *you* to take out the garbage."

"Sure."

"I may have some other chores as well. I know you're not at your best with time on your hands."

"True."

"And I don't want you just hanging around driving me crazy," she said.

"I've never not had a job. I don't think I know what to do."

"Look for another one, for starters. I left the employment section of the paper out for you. Who knows how quickly you can find something else? And I don't need to tell you it needs to be fast."

"Who knows," I echoed.

"If we need to move, we need to move," she said, bouncing Angelina on her knee, making her chuckle.

I looked at the two of them and felt my eyes mist up. I turned away.

AS I ATE cereal for breakfast, I watched them. I realized Melissa had taken no noticeable steps in preparation to turn our daughter over, even though it was just four days away. She'd packed no boxes, emptied no drawers. She behaved as if by denying the inevitability of it, the exchange wouldn't take place. I conceded I was doing the same thing.

Sheriff's cars in front of the house and down the block in the mouth of the cul-de-sac. There was no way we could slip past them even if we intended to do that. And where would we go anyway? Would we live in our car with the baby, constantly looking over our shoulders?

The obvious places for us to go were my parents' ranch or her parents—her mother's in Seattle or her father's in Phoenix. But because they were obvious, they would be the first places the authorities would look.

There was nowhere else I could think of. If we tried to live on the road, we'd burn through our meager bank account so quickly it would leave skid marks. My severance check and vacation/sick money wouldn't be processed for weeks. By then, if we had run, the sheriff would follow the check to us, wherever we were. Our credit cards would max out fast. We had no other income.

There was no way to sell the house for what little equity we had in it and use the money to escape. In the current Denver housing market, that could take months. I could get a few thousand from the Jeep and a couple thousand for Melissa's car, but what would we run away in?

Every damned option was bad. I felt like driving back to the cop bar and finding that friendly bartender and pasting down another fifty and starting over. I spent the rest of the day organizing the garage and the attic, generally staying out of Melissa's way. I kept my eye out for things we could sell if we had to. I watched a napping Angelina when Melissa went to King Soopers. She reported that she asked the deputy down the street—she described him as a very nice man—if he intended to follow her there and back. He told her no, their orders were to follow only if all three of us were in the vehicle, if it looked like we were attempting to flee our home with Angelina.

"Imagine that," she said, shaking her head.

WHEN THE PHONE RANG after dinner, I grabbed it because Melissa was changing Angelina in the living room.

"It's Jeter. It took me a while today to find that Appaloosa Club."

A rolling tremor went through me from the top of my head and my toes curled in my shoes.

"You're *here?*"

"Got in around noon. Found a place to stay. Took a nap. Now that it's dark out, I want to get to work. Damn—Denver got big on me. Used to be a glorified cow town. I don't hardly know my way around anymore. How many people live here now?"

"Two point four million."

He paused. "That's twice more than all of Montana."

"Yes."

"Where did all these folks come from?"

"All over," I said. "Where are you now?"

"Some fleabag joint on West Colfax. At least this part of town hasn't changed much. There are still hookers around, but I don't think I've seen a white person since I've been here. It's like some damned street in Tijuana."

I didn't know what to say.

"I called Cody, and he didn't pick up, so I'm calling you. I'm going to the club tonight."

"Jeter, please, no."

"What, you worried about my fee now that Brian's dead? Don't. This is a favor to you boys and to that little girl of yours."

"Wait, don't do anything until I get there . . ."

He hung up.

As I got my jacket, Melissa said, "Where are you going, Jack?"

"I don't think you want to know," I said. "That was Jeter Hoyt on the telephone."

Which told her everything, and she turned away. I wondered if she felt as unclean and panicky as I did at that moment.

AS I CLIMBED INTO my Jeep, I heard the motor start in the sheriff's car across the street. For a moment I closed my eyes and stood there with the door open. If he followed me down to Zuni Street . . .

I slammed the door and walked across the street. The deputy was young, fresh-faced, with brown hair and a blunt nose. He watched me approach with a practiced cop dead-eye stare, and I motioned for him to roll down his window. I saw him say something into his mike—probably notifying the cop down the block that I was there—and then his window descended halfway.

"Hello, Deputy."

"That's close enough," he said.

I stopped, put my hands up, and showed my palms to him. "I'm harmless."

He nodded.

"What's your name?"

"Sanders. Billy Sanders."

"And Morales is the name of the deputy down the street? We

might as well get to know you guys and be friends since we're spending so much time together."

He smiled. "Your wife met Gary Morales already."

"Look," I said, "I'm going to go downtown and have a few beers, just like last night. I was wondering if you'd like to go with me?"

"What?"

"Why sit here all night? I'll give you a ride with me, and that way you can keep an eye on me *and* have a couple of beers. I'd like the company because drinking alone is the shits. What do you say?"

He grinned, not unfriendly. "That sounds pretty good, but I'm on duty until my replacement gets here."

"I can be back by then," I offered.

For a second he considered it, then, "Nah, no can do."

"Are you sure? I'm buying."

He shook his head.

"Maybe tomorrow night?"

He laughed. "Maybe."

"I'm going down to a place called Shelby's. You know it?"

"Okay. Thanks for letting me know."

"It's on Eighteenth."

"I know where it is."

"Maybe I'll see you there later, I guess. And if I drink too much, maybe I can bum a ride back from you?"

He laughed. "I haven't done all that much surveillance, but you two are the only people I've ever watched who were so damned nice. You're making me suspicious, to tell you the truth."

"Sorry."

His window slid back up.

I turned and went back to my Jeep and eased out of the driveway. I watched him in my rearview mirror. If he did decide to follow me, I'd just go to Shelby's and read about Jeter in the *Rocky Mountain News* the next morning. In a way, I hoped Sanders *would* follow me. But, as I guessed, the sheriff's car didn't move. He didn't want to be stuck downtown when his shift ended with the possibility of having to give me a ride all the way back, and he knew that without Melissa and Angelina with me, there was no point in following.

Nineteen

ON ZUNI STREET I noticed two things simultaneously: the streetlights were out, and my headlights splashed on Garrett's H3 Hummer as well as a dirty four-by-four pickup with Montana plates.

"There he is," I said aloud.

Because it was so dark, the Appaloosa Club stood out, with its neon beer signs in the barred windows and the fact that it was surrounded by either boarded-up shells of structures or low-rent businesses closed for the night. The lights of the city washed like cream across the sky but didn't reach down into this dark hole not far from it.

Besides the H3 and what I assumed was Jeter's pickup, there were two or three others: classic seventies' Buick and Cadillac boats with gleaming chrome and fuzzy dice hanging from the rearview mirrors. One of the license plates I noticed was "13 13," framed by the green Colorado mountains. The thirteenth number in the alphabet was "M," so "M M," or Mexican Mafia.

I pulled to the curb, punched the light knob in, and the H3 went black.

I sat for a moment in scared silence. He was obviously already inside. I could hear thumping bass from the Appaloosa. My eyes adjusted to the darkness, and the shape of the club emerged. It was small and boxy. The *Pacifico, Corona,* and *Negra Modelo* beer signs seemed to increase in color and intensity. I considered going home.

"No!" I yelled inside the Jeep.

I launched outside in time to see a rectangle of light appear on the front of the club—the door opening—and the inverted "V" shape of Jeter Hoyt and his broad back in a long cowboy duster fill the doorway for a moment before the door closed behind him. He'd been scouting the club from the outside and just gone in.

I always traveled with a winter survival kit in my Jeep. I threw open the hatchback, unzipped the duffel bag in the back, and pulled out a navy watch cap. I thought if I pulled it low over my eyes that possibly—possibly—Garrett wouldn't recognize me. I wanted to follow Jeter inside and get him out before something awful happened. I'd keep my head down and, if necessary, drag him back outside before Garrett noticed him or recognized me.

As I strode toward the club I dug my cell phone out of my pocket and speed-dialed Cody. Not that I planned on a conversation, but I simply wanted to make contact. I didn't expect him to answer. I clutched the phone. I thought if I went inside and all hell broke loose, I wanted him to hear it later as a voice mail so he could get to our house to be with Melissa.

I eased the front door open and slipped inside. The thumping of the music—I didn't recognize the song or the artist but it was crude and raw—hit me in the face and made my heart beat even faster. I took it in quickly: The place was smaller than it looked from outside and both darker and emptier than I had imagined. A couple of morose Latinos in biker gear perched at the truncated front bar. A bald, obese bartender in a wife-beater was behind the bar. His thick arms and shoulders were covered in tattoos, and he had a soul patch under his lip grown long and braided. He was pointing a remote at the crappy single television mounted above the bar in the corner. There was a small cracked linoleum dance floor that was empty and a series of unoccupied booths along the far wall. In the back, beneath a black light, was a round table with five people under a thick halo of smoke.

Jeter was at the bar between the two bikers, trying to get the attention of the bartender with the remote. The duster he was wearing went down to his knees. It sagged beneath his arms. Hardware— and lots of it. He called again to the bartender and was ignored as the fat man rocketed through the channels so quickly it was like a malfunctioning slide show. He blasted through channel after channel until there was a glimpse of female flesh and one of the bikers yelled, "*There!*" and he slowly circumnavigated back to it, something on one of the premium cable channels.

I didn't want to stand next to Jeter and create more of a display than necessary. I took a stool ten feet away from him and kept my head down. I watched him peripherally, noted how agitated he was getting from being dissed. Finally, the bartender placed the remote under an ancient black-and-white movie poster of Anthony Quinn in *Viva, Zapata!* and turned to Jeter with bored contempt. I feared for the bartender.

I didn't turn around and look behind me at the table of five, but tried to see who was there via the filmed-over backbar mirror. Five people, three males and two slutty-looking Anglo females. The smoke they were creating and the dirty mirror distorted the view. There were dozens of empty glasses on the table and an overflowing ashtray. The black light behind them added a garish touch, lighting up dirty fingerprints on the empty glasses, the lipstick on the girls, and the brilliant white of overlarge T-shirts on the two Hispanic males. It was boy-girl-boy-girl-boy at the table. The dark man in the middle was grinning stupidly and bobbing his head to a rhythm while a blond girl next to him stared intently at his ear and rocked up and down and I realized she was giving him a hand job under the table. The other girl, whose hair was jet-black and spiked, fingered a silver ring on her bottom lip and shot glances at the action taking place next to her. Garrett sat on the far left end of the table with a coffee mug in front of him with the string and label of a tea bag hanging over the lip of the mug. For some reason, the bored look on his face and what he was drinking struck me most of all because he had the temerity and confidence to drink hot tea in a place like this. I almost admired him for a second, but only for a second. Again, I wondered what his connection was to these gangsters and why he wanted to be involved with them.

I was heartened by the fact that the five at the table didn't seem to notice Jeter at the bar. They were so self-absorbed that they hadn't even looked up. I knew it would be a matter of seconds, though, before they did. Jeter was hard to miss with that damned big coat.

Getting his attention wasn't easy. I wanted him to look at me so I could signal to him to get the hell out of there. He'd have to see me there, right?

"I'm looking for a shitbird named Garrett Moreland," Jeter asked the bartender loud enough for me to hear. I was shocked by his brazenness. "Is he in here?"

The bartender appeared not to have heard. I glanced into the backbar mirror to assure myself that Garrett hadn't, either.

"*Jeter!*" I hissed. "*Let's go.*"

The biker nearest to me looked up from his drink and scowled at me, but Jeter didn't acknowledge I was there.

"Garrett Moreland, I said," Jeter growled. "Is he in this shit hole?"

The bartender made a point of ignoring him. Instead, he waddled down the length of the bar, asking each biker if he needed anything and going by me as if I didn't exist. As he passed, I marveled at the quantity and misogyny of his tattoos; skulls with spikes driven through them, women impaled on the hood ornaments of late-seventies' Chryslers and daggerlike penises, the American flag dripping blood into the open mouth of a caricature of former VP Dick Cheney.

"*Jeter, goddammit!*" I yelled, trying to shout above the music. "*We need to leave!*"

The biker to my right wanted another beer. The fat bartender ambled back to where he'd started with the biker's empty glass to fill it from the tap. He never even glanced my way. While he filled the glass from the tap right in front of Jeter, I saw the Montanan do a frightening thing: He smiled.

"Either you tell me if Garrett-fucking-Moreland is in the building, you fat greaser," Jeter drawled, "or a particular kind of hell will break out all around you."

There was a beat of silence when the song ended. The bartender filled the glass. When it was full, he nodded almost imperceptibly toward the table in the back.

"Much obliged," Jeter said, turning slowly around while keeping one hand on the bar. I could see him squinting toward the table under the black light.

"Jeter . . ." I said.

Because I was concentrating on Jeter, I almost missed the movements of the bartender, who was fishing around under the counter. And with the deceptively quick movements of a fat man who for years has concentrated solely on the speed of his arms, the bartender stepped back with a black baseball bat and raised it above his head and smashed Jeter's hand with it. I could hear the bones break with the same muffled snapping sounds of dry branches underfoot.

I was frozen where I sat.

Jeter didn't cry out, didn't even pull his hand away. Instead, he turned back toward the bartender with an *I-can't-believe-you-did-that* look.

Surprised that the blow didn't bring this crazy Anglo in the silly coat to his knees, the bartender cocked back and swung again, smashing Jeter's misshapen hand on the bar, presumably breaking every bone that hadn't been broken by the first hit. I'll never forget the sound of contact, like hitting a Ziploc bag filled with pretzels.

I don't know why the bartender did it. I'll never know or understand. All I can guess is that he was reacting to the insult and that he'd done the same thing before in similar situations in order to drive people out of the club. But like my life those past two and a half weeks, what happened next was beyond analysis.

All of us have heard the phrase "He got his head blown off." I'm here to tell you that doesn't actually happen. I know because when Jeter reached into his duster with his right hand and came out with the sawed-off double-barreled ten-gauge shotgun that was once referred to as a coach gun because it was the weapon of choice for stagecoach drivers, and pressed the muzzle into the bartender's forehead with both hammers cocked and fired both barrels, well, the bartender's head was not actually blown off. The top right quarter of it disappeared, and what was left of the mirror behind the bar was spattered with blood, brains, and chunks of bone, skin, and hair. The bartender dropped to the floor as if his puppet strings had been clipped, taking a shelf of beer glasses with him.

The sound was tremendous, and my ears were ringing. The two bikers at the bar dismounted and scrambled and passed me, running toward the door. I watched them from above, detached, as if my own soul and perspective were removed from my body.

Jeter was enraged. He stared at his broken hand for a moment, saying "Why in the hell did he do that?" before recovering and breaking the shotgun open with his undamaged right hand. The two huge, spent, and smoking shells hurtled back over his shoulders on either side of his head. He transferred the weapon under his left arm and dug into his duster pocket for two fresh shells. He reloaded and he snapped the shotgun closed with an upward jerk, turning toward the back table while he cocked both barrels. His broken left hand hung uselessly by his side.

"WHICH ONE OF YOU SHITBIRDS IS GARRETT MORELAND?"

I realized that the high-pitched noise in my ears was one of the girls shrieking.

The gangster on the right end of the table farthest from Garrett pushed back so hard in his chair that he sent it flying behind him. He stood up next to the table. The dark boy in the middle, who had been getting serviced, stared openmouthed while he inexplicably felt the sudden need to button himself back up. The blond girl next to him screamed while holding her hands to the sides of her face. Garrett still had both of his hands on the table wrapped around his mug, his bearing remarkably calm, his eyes taking in the man with the shotgun, who was approaching him, as if trying to place him, trying to figure out why he'd called out his name.

"You the shitbird Garrett?" Jeter asked him.

Jeter didn't notice that the man who had stood up was bent slightly forward now, his arm behind his back digging for something in his pants.

Jeter pointed the shotgun with one hand, said again, "You Garrett Moreland?"

And the gangster pulled his weapon, a semiautomatic, and fired four quick rounds—*pop-pop-pop-pop*—with the weapon held sidewise out in front of him. Jeter's coat danced, and he stumbled back a step, then swung the shotgun over and it exploded again and kicked higher than Jeter's head. A great bloom of red spattered across the chest of the gangster, who fell back over the chair he'd previously sent skittering across the floor.

Patiently, Jeter slid the shotgun back into its sling inside his duster and came out with a stainless-steel .45 semiauto. He shot the dark boy in the middle point-blank in the neck before the gangster could rack the slide on the pistol he'd been fumbling for. The gangster's gun skittered across the table and fell to the dirty carpet.

"Run away, girls," Jeter said. "I've got business here with young Mr. Moreland."

The blonde kept screaming as she ran, her hands still pressed to the sides of her head. There was a moment when our eyes locked as she ran toward the door, and I wondered if she'd be able to identify me later.

Jeter stepped aside for the female with the spiked hair, not expecting her to stop, turn, pause, and shove a pistol into his armpit and pull the trigger three times with muffled *bangs*. He cried out with a yelping sound, the hand with the pistol dropped to his side, and he staggered several steps to his left before collapsing on the dance floor in a heap.

"*Goddammit!*" he bellowed, sounding more angry with himself than with the girl. He writhed on the floor, making himself a moving target for the girl with the spiked hair, who clumsily tried to aim at him. He rolled to his belly and came up with the .45 and took her down with three rapid shots.

Like a bear cub, Jeter rose to all fours and, with a grunt, he was back on his feet. The second gangster he'd shot was still sitting upright at the table, his hand clamped to his neck. Arterial blood squirted out between his fingers. Jeter staggered over to him and put the muzzle of his .45 to the man's forehead.

"*Sign your stupid name on them papers,*" Jeter said in his ridiculous Mexican accent, "*or you die, senõr!*"

I walked stunned through the acrid hanging gun smoke and put my hand on Jeter's shoulder. Shotgun shells and spent casings littered the floor.

"That's not him," I said.

"*Your signature or your brains, senõr!*" Jeter said, pressing hard with the gun.

"Jeter, that's not him!" I shouted. "Garrett ran out the back while you were on the floor!" I was fairly certain Garrett never saw me.

Jeter paused, letting that sink in. I could hear the rapid patter of blood on the floor from the wounds inside Jeter's coat.

"They all look alike to me," he said with a harsh laugh, and pulled the trigger. The gangster flopped backward, his eyes wide-open, a smoking hole in his forehead.

JETER STOOD UNSTEADILY and holstered the .45. His face was drawn and white, his eyes sallow.

"Man," he said, "I really fucked this one up."

I nodded.

"I shoulda played that different," he said. "I never would of thought that girl would have a gun. This is a rough damned place."

I didn't know what to do. Try to get him to the Jeep? Take him to a hospital? Leave him there? Wait for the police to show up? I didn't hear sirens yet.

"I don't want to die here," Jeter said. "I want to die in Montana. Not in Denver. Not in this shit hole with these shitbirds."

He tried to take a step toward the door, but he couldn't seem to get his legs to obey. Blood streamed from the hem of his coat and pooled on the floor.

"I'm really shot up," he said weakly. "It's like everything warm is pouring out of me. I'm gettin' real cold. Help me, Jack."

"Where do you want to go?"

That grin. "Montana."

"We can't go to . . ."

"I can hear Cody talking to me in my head," Jeter said suddenly. "I just can't hear what he's saying."

"Cody?"

"Yeah, I hear him."

And I remembered I was still clutching my cell phone. I looked at it, saw the call I'd placed had connected five minutes ago.

I lifted it to my mouth. "Cody?"

"Jack, are you all right? Jesus—all I could hear were gunshots."

"I'm okay, but your uncle Jeter . . ."

"I heard. I'm on my way. Hang tight for five more minutes." He clicked off.

Jeter chinned toward the bar. "See if you can find some different music on that stereo, Jack. Find some good old country I can die to. Hank Snow, Little Jimmy Dickens, Hank Williams, Bob Wills—something good. I can't stand the crap they play in this place."

With that, he pitched forward like a felled tree. His head hit the dance floor so hard, the fall alone might have killed him.

I WAS LEANING against the bar when Cody came in. I'd unplugged the beer signs in the windows and turned off all but the black light over the table so the Appaloosa Club looked closed from outside, and no patrons would come in. I was having an out-of-body experience again, thinking I wasn't really there.

Cody pulled on a pair of rubber gloves.

"Help me get him into my trunk," Cody said. "If we leave him here, the cops will eventually trace him to me."

"Where are you going to take him?"

Cody shook his head. "Up in the mountains. I've got a place in mind."

"He wanted to go to Montana," I said dumbly.

"I'll get him up there one of these days," Cody said, grasping Jeter's collar and dragging him toward the door.

Cody said, "Jesus, how much hardware does he have under that coat?"

"I've never seen anything like this before," I said, walking behind. "It was terrible, Cody. It was a slaughterhouse in here. The bartender broke Jeter's hand with a baseball bat, and Jeter started blasting. Garrett got away."

"I heard. You called me, remember?"

"We're going to go to prison," I said.

"I don't know," Cody said, looking around the club. "Looks gang-related to me. It looks like maybe a big fight over meth-distribution territory."

"Do you really think that's how the police will see it?"

Cody paused and looked up angry. "Are you going to help me, or what?"

"DON'T RACE OUT OF HERE," Cody said, after we'd lifted Jeter's body into his plastic-lined trunk and slammed the lid. "Take it slow and easy. The last thing you want is to be pulled over for speeding. Judging by that look in your eye, you'd confess."

I nodded.

"Go home," Cody said. "I'll catch up with you later."

He gave me a brotherly punch in the shoulder. "We probably should have kept Uncle Jeter out of this. He was past his prime and over his head. And he was too much of a bigot to think straight."

"You should have seen him in there," I said. "I'll have nightmares for the rest of my life."

Cody looked around. The street was dark and lifeless. "Let's get out of here, Jack."

I turned toward my Jeep.

"Jack," Cody called after me. I looked over my shoulder. "Until tonight, it's been another really good day."

I DROVE WEST TOWARD home on I-70 with the radio on KOA for sound but not hearing a word. I checked my rearview mirror every few minutes, expecting to see a squad car with wigwag lights flashing. My speed varied from forty to eighty, I couldn't concentrate. I set the cruise control at sixty-five so at least I wouldn't need to worry about *that*.

I felt dead inside, and my head was in a fog. Only then did I wonder what Cody meant when he said he'd had another good day. Had he meant with Brian's call log?

The scene at the Appaloosa replayed over and over like a loop of tape.

Did Garrett see me? Did he know why Jeter was there? Would he go to the police to tell them what he'd seen, or would he play it like he did with Luis—with silence?

Could the blonde ID my face? What about the two bikers? Did they get a good enough look? Would Cody get pulled over driving up to the mountains with his dead uncle in his trunk?

God.

I found myself drifting off the highway and nearly overcorrected into a pickup in the next lane. I tried to concentrate.

I didn't hear the first part of the report on the radio, maybe because I'd learned over the years to tune out much of what was on the radio. I caught it midway through. . . . *The police spokesman says there was a quadruple homicide tonight at a Zuni Street tavern . . . gang-related . . .*

Gang-related.

I WAVED at the new deputy in his black-and-white across the street from our house, and he waved back.

Inside, Melissa came down the stairs in her nightgown.

"Why didn't you call?"

I shook my head.

"Honey, are you okay?"

"No," I said. "No, I'm not."

"Did Garrett sign the papers?"

Thursday, November 22

Three Days to Go

Twenty

I FINALLY DRIFTED INTO an unforgiving sleep around four in the morning and when I woke up Melissa was standing over me with tears in her eyes. I expected her to say, "The police are here."

Instead, she said, "It's Thanksgiving Day, Jack. I *forgot*. Can you believe that?"

"I can," I said, rubbing sleep from my eyes, "because I forgot, too."

"How can a person forget it's Thanksgiving?" she said, and burst out crying.

I stood and held her. She seemed to dissolve into my arms, and I could feel her hot tears on my shoulder. I knew she wasn't truly crying about forgetting Thanksgiving.

IT WAS COLD and overcast. The mountains had no tops, and milky tendrils extended down into the valleys like cold fingers.

Winter had won again and was reclaiming lost territory, I thought. It was snowing hard in the high country. I thought of Cody having to drive up there somewhere, and hoped he'd made it back okay. I blew in my hands as I walked across the street to the sheriff's department black-and-white. Billy Sanders was back. His motor was running so he'd have heat. This time, he didn't caution me to keep my distance.

He lowered his window, and I bent over into it. I could feel a breath of warm air come out as well as the fake-cheese smell of Doritos. The bag was on his lap, and I could see several crumpled soft-drink cans on the floor. The morning *Denver Post* was beside him on the passenger seat. The headline shouted MASSACRE IN NORTH DENVER.

Man, oh man.

"Are you okay?" Sanders asked me. "You don't look so good." He closed one eye in puzzlement. "My replacement said you weren't out all *that* late."

"I wasn't," I said, and changed the subject. "So you have to work on a holiday, huh?"

Sanders nodded. There was a line of orange powder from the Doritos on his upper lip, and his fingertips were orange. "Yeah, kind of a bummer but that's part of the deal."

"I'm going to King Soopers to get groceries," I said. "My wife suggested we invite you in for a Thanksgiving meal. We won't have turkey and all the trimmings because we both forgot what day it was, but we'll have plenty of something else. I was thinking I'd bring back some roasted chickens and I need to know how many will be at the table. What do you say?"

He looked at me with suspicion for a moment. "Your wife really wants to invite me in?"

"She sent me out here to ask."

Melissa had surprised me with the suggestion. She'd said, "Thanksgiving isn't Thanksgiving unless we can share it with others. Since all our family is out-of-state, well, let's invite our watchers."

Sanders said, "What about Morales?"

"Melissa is out back talking to him now."

He shook his head and looked genuinely touched. "Man, that would be great. I was thinking I'd be sitting here all day feeling sorry for myself, and I guess technically we'd still be on the job since we'll be keeping an eye on you. Maybe we can even forget about those rules about drinking on duty just this once. Can we pitch in on dinner?"

"Sure, if you want. Why don't you call Morales, and the three of us can go to the store together?"

He laughed and reached for his mike. After talking to his partner, he called dispatch and asked for another car to watch our house while he and Morales "followed the suspect." After receiving a confirmation, he looked up at me, and said, "Sorry; we can't risk your wife taking off on us with that little girl while we're gone."

THE TWO DEPUTIES and I cruised the aisles of the grocery store like giddy teenage boys planning a camping trip. I pushed the cart, and they dropped items in it—canned cranberries, sweet potatoes, packaged mashed potatoes, jars of cream and brown gravy, a jar of CheezWhiz (Sanders!), two six-packs of beer, a couple *more* six-packs of beer. The aisles were empty except for a few desperate shoppers getting last-minute items. But no one was as desperate as the three of us because none of us had planned or shopped for a last-minute Thanksgiving meal before. There were four roasted chickens in the deli section. I didn't ask when they'd been roasted, and I bought them all.

"Better to get too much than not enough," I said.

"This is great." Billy Sanders laughed. "What about these dinner rolls? They look pretty good."

"Throw 'em in," I said.

"You are really nice people," Morales said, as we rung up.

261

"I've never had my surveillance targets invite me in for dinner before."

I thought, *We used to be good, too.*

THE DEPUTIES WERE AS inept in the kitchen as I was, so the three of us let Melissa shoo us out so we could drink beer and watch football. "Just one," Morales said, and so did Sanders. Just one turned into a lot more. Melissa didn't seem to mind doing everything herself. I heard her as she cooked and hummed happily. The smells coming from the kitchen were delicious. Angelina crawled between the three of us, offering up toys that we'd take and pretend to hide. She was once again a charmer and had both deputies giggling and mugging for her.

As I sat and watched them, the events of the evening before came rushing back, and I tried hard to steer them away. I jumped when my cell phone rang. Cody.

"Excuse me," I said to the deputies, who paid no attention to me. I took the phone into the kitchen and surprised Melissa, who quickly shoved something behind the microwave.

"Hey," I said into the phone.

His voice was grim. "Are you all right?"

"As much as I can be," I said.

"I mean now. I'm just down the street, and I can see two cruisers at your house."

"Oh that," I said. "We invited the deputies in for Thanksgiving. Why don't you come, too?"

I knew Cody had no place to go except his cop bar, where they put on a spread for single, divorced, and on-duty officers.

"Are you kidding?" he said.

"No. Come on—we've got plenty of food." I looked to Melissa, mouthed "Cody," and she nodded emphatically. She seemed to be enjoying this. She took a long drink from a glass of what looked like orange juice.

"Can I bring somebody?" Cody asked sheepishly.

"Of course you can. Who is she?"

"If only," he said. "I'm supposed to meet Torkleson. Can I bring him along? I guess his wife and daughter are in California."

"The more the merrier," I said. "Melissa loves cooking for a herd of cops, don't you, honey?"

"Oh yes," she said loudly enough Cody would hear.

Cody said, "Give me a half an hour."

I closed the phone and walked over to the stove to look inside some of the pots. "Smells good," I said to Melissa.

"Considering the eclectic mix of stuff you guys brought home, it's the best we can do," she said.

I reached behind the microwave and pulled out a half-full bottle of vodka.

"Since when do we keep this on hand?" I asked. Melissa had always been a "glass of wine with dinner" kind of woman. The last time I'd seen her with a drink was back in college, and even then she didn't appear to really like it.

She looked stricken that I'd found the bottle.

"It's okay," I said. "I'm just a little surprised you felt the need to hide it."

"You must be joking," she said. "I wouldn't leave it out in the open. What would everybody think?"

"They'd think we've had a really wicked month," I said.

"When you go to bed I sometimes come down here in the kitchen," she said. "I have a drink or two and try to figure out what we did to deserve this. Sometimes I take my drink upstairs and just sit by Angelina's crib and look at her and cry. Sometimes I come in and look at you, too. The only thing I can come up with is that we're cursed."

"No," I said, "we're being tested."

"Then I guess I'm flunking the test."

"Not at all," I said, brushing her cheek with the back of my fingers.

She asked me, "Are we disintegrating?"

I didn't know how to answer that.

I PAUSED for a moment before going back into the family room and looked through the angled slats on the kitchen door at Sanders and Morales. Both had their backs to me and were preoccupied with Angelina and the football game.

I thought: *I could knock them out from behind, and we could gather up our daughter and get in the Jeep and go.*

The kitchen was filled with heavy objects I could use—cast-iron skillets and pots, a rolling pin somewhere, that damned big mixer. For a few seconds my heart raced as I envisioned the scenario. I'd hit Sanders first because he was the closest, then go after Morales before he could stand and draw his gun. But knocking them out? I winced. That only happened on television and in the movies. What if the blows just opened up gashes, and one or both cops remained conscious?

No, I thought, the only way to ensure our escape would be to take them out. I glanced over my shoulder at the block of knives. That Santoku knife was sharp, substantial, and seven inches long. I could slit Sanders's throat and go for Morales's neck to cut it open or, if necessary, plunge the blade into his temple or heart. That might be possible, I thought. But could I do it in front of Angelina? Would she scream and be forever scarred?

That's when Sanders gathered Angelina up and sat her on his lap. And Melissa said, "Jack, could you go get the leaf for the table?"

CODY SHOWED UP with Torkleson, a baked ham, and a case of beer.

In the kitchen I whispered to Melissa, "What safer place for an

accessory to a quadruple homicide to be than at a dining table surrounded by policemen?"

She said, "I don't find that funny."

MELISSA THREW HERSELF INTO preparing the meal. The
glass of vodka and orange juice that always seemed to be full explained at least a measure of her vivacity. She clucked at me again
for our odd choices of canned food and the fact that we had enough
beer to serve a battalion. Cody and Torkleson seemed to get along
well with the two deputies, and the four of them talked shop, their
voices getting louder as they drank more and more beer. I felt
ashamed for my murderous thoughts, and for a while had trouble
looking Sanders and Morales in the eye.

Finally, Melissa announced to all of us that dinner was ready,
and we shambled in and took our places at the table. Melissa said
a prayer, and I glanced up to see all four men with their heads
bowed.

As for me, I wasn't on very good terms with God just then.

THE TALK AT THE table turned inevitably toward the multiple
homicides at the Appaloosa Club last night. I could feel my heart start
to beat harder, but I feigned uninformed interest and kept my head
down. The one time I looked up, Cody and I exchanged a fleeting
glance.

Torkleson said, "If I hadn't traded shifts with McCoy and
Scruggs, it would have been my case. Those poor guys. The mayor is
all over us because of the Eastman murder, and now this. Man, the
heat those guys are under."

"Any ideas who did it?" Morales asked.

Torkleson shrugged. "Some blond chick says she was there. She told the Scruggs it was a single shooter—a huge hairy guy with a beard and a long coat."

Meaning Garrett Moreland had not talked to the police, just like before. Either he was scared, or he had something serious to hide. I recalled how calmly he had sat there at the table cradling the mug in his hands when Jeter approached him and called out his name.

"Bullshit," Sanders said, then acknowledged Angelina in her high chair. "Sorry," he said to Melissa.

Torkleson agreed. "Yeah, I know what you mean. One guy doing all that? It's hard to believe. I don't know if the blonde is credible at all. She says the big hairy guy just pulled a shotgun out of his coat and started blasting."

Morales said, "She says this big hairy guy just let her leave? Her and nobody else? Come on . . ."

Torkleson said, "She claims she thought her friend was right behind her out the door, but it turns out her friend was one of the victims. Shot three times in the chest."

"A big hairy guy?" Sanders said. "Sounds like she's been watching too many movies. This thing has 'gang' written all over it."

Cody nodded. "You've got that right."

Torkleson said, "That's what we're thinking, too. Two of the victims were local leaders of Sur-13. It's like somebody was trying to cut the head off that beast, probably the 32 Crips or Varios. Maybe the Crenshaw Mafia, who are gangster Bloods—we've heard they're moving in from Southern California. No way this was random. It was a power play. And get this: One of the shooters used a ten-gauge shotgun. That's serious hardware. I thought those guys stuck to nines and the occasional AK-47."

But they didn't get Garrett, I thought. I wondered just how deep Garrett was involved with the gangsters. Then I thought: *He could be a leader, too. It could have been a meeting.* That made me think differently about Garrett.

"A ten-gauge. Jeez." Morales said. "I bet that made a mess."

Torkleson said, "From the photos I saw, well . . ." He glanced over at Melissa, who was rapt but very pale. I'd not told her any of the details of what had happened in the Appaloosa Club, only that things had gone horribly wrong, and Garrett got away. She looked at me, trying to read me.

". . . Let's just say there was a lot of blood," Torkleson continued.

"I'm sorry," Sanders said, "but I can't get all weepy about hearing that some big boys from *Sureños* 13 got hit."

Morales agreed.

"Two of the victims were bystanders, though," Torkleson said. "The friend of the blonde had a couple of priors, but nothing of note. The bartender was an ex-con and probably a member of Sur-13, but I'm sure he wasn't a prime target—he was just there."

"Nobody saw or heard anything?" Cody asked innocently.

Torkleson shook his head. "Nobody but the blond girl so far. You know the neighborhood—it's deserted at night, and not a lot of cops go by there even though they're supposed to. And from what I understand, gunshots at night aren't at all rare in that neighborhood."

"So who called it in?" Cody asked.

"A citizen," Torkleson said. "Some guy said he went to the bar for a drink, but the place looked closed, which was unusual. He looked in a window and saw the bodies."

"Anything else?" Cody bored in. I hoped he wasn't being too obvious, but I recognized the fact that he was just being Cody the relentless cop.

"One thing, and it's not much," Torkleson said. "A warehouse delivery driver called in and said he sometimes uses that street to get to his shop. He said he saw a light-colored Jeep parked in front of the place at about the time we figure it all went down, but that's all we've got."

"Hey," Morales said, gesturing toward me with a spoon, "Mr. McGuane here's got a light-colored Jeep. He was gone last night for a few hours."

"That's right," Sanders said.

I felt my insides clutch up. Melissa was dabbing at some sweet potatoes on Angelina's face, and I saw her freeze.

Sanders said, "Maybe on the way to the bar, you stopped at the Appaloosa Club and shot four people."

"Maybe," I said.

"Looks like we've solved the case," Morales said, digging into the mashed potatoes.

Sanders said, "Now we can get a commendation and a raise and be on TV standing next to the mayor. Excuse me, can you pass me the ham?"

I began to breathe again. When I looked over at Cody, he winked at me.

Melissa stood up unsteadily, but I assumed I was the only one who noticed. "Who wants dessert?" she asked. I could tell she wanted to top off her glass again when she went over to the counter.

WE WERE IN THE LIVING ROOM, and it had gotten dark outside. Tiny little hard balls of snow pinpricked the west windows and melted on impact and slimed down the glass, leaving snail tracks. The second Thanksgiving Day game was in the first minutes of the fourth quarter, with Dallas ahead by twenty and John Madden extolling the virtues of Turducken and eight-legged turkeys. I was frankly surprised the deputies and Torkleson had stayed so long. And they seemed in no hurry to leave. There was still plenty of beer, and Cody had cracked open the Jim Beam Black. I wondered if they'd stay until the end of the game or until the alcohol ran out, and I was pretty sure it would be the alcohol. Angelina was charged up by the company although she was starting to get wild since she'd refused to take her nap. Why nap when there were four men doting on her? Melissa was in the kitchen cleaning up and, I assumed, working a little on the bottle of vodka. I couldn't get the image of her sitting bedside with her glass, watching our daughter and me while we slept, out of my mind.

I loved Melissa, and now I knew the depths of her feelings were unfathomable. When—*if*—we turned Angelina over, I couldn't imagine Melissa not melting down, and me with her. She said we were disintegrating, and the loss of our daughter would no doubt push her over the edge. I wasn't even sure I'd know her anymore, just as I was starting to wonder what would happen to me, what I'd become with the loss. I could think of no scenario that wasn't terrifying.

I'd read where the loss of a child was the most devastating thing that could possibly happen to parents. I believed that. But presumably the loss in question was due to death or accident. No one had studied what it was like to hand over a child because of a legal anomaly. And to hand the child over to people who might just be monsters.

"THAT ENGLISH PERVERT," Torkleson said to Cody and the deputies. "Did you hear the latest about *him?*"

Of course that pulled me out of my reverie.

"What was that asshole's name?" Torkleson asked. "You know, the one who was going to move here? He was on 9 News."

"Malcolm Harris," I said.

Torkleson was obviously drunk. His words slurred, and he was talking too loudly. As were Sanders and Morales. They'd been practically shouting at each other for a half hour, telling cop stories, comparing cop notes. Cops, like ranchers and outfitters of my youth, were generally suspicious and taciturn men, except when they were around their own. Then the yapping began, and it was endless. I had only half listened, spending most of my time worrying about my wife and trying to keep Angelina from acting out. I was hoping Melissa would be done soon in the kitchen so she could take our daughter upstairs and calm her down and get her to bed. But when Malcolm Harris's name came up, I leaned forward in my chair.

"What about him?" Cody asked. Strangely, Cody seemed to be the most sober of them all. I'd noted that although he was drinking, he wasn't pounding them down like usual—or like the others were. I could only attribute his restraint to the "good days" he'd been having. Cody only drank when he was bored, which was most of the time. When he was wrapped up in a case or a project, he restrained himself.

"Who is he talking about?" Sanders asked Morales.

"That guy," Morales said. "Don't you watch the news or read the memos?"

"Fuck no," Sanders said before noting Angelina in my lap, and saying, "Sorry again."

I was thankful that at that moment Melissa came into the family room and scooped up Angelina. She said good night to everyone and was lavished with "thank-yous" and overdone praise. Her eyes misted as they thanked her—she cried so easily and quickly now—and she took our daughter to bed. I was grateful she didn't seem wobbly or lit up, and I made a note to check the level of the vodka bottle behind the microwave.

"You know that guy," Morales said. "The English guy. He was on his way here to move his company or something. I got a call to go to the airport just in case he was on the plane. If he landed, we were supposed to arrest him, but they got him before he boarded, I guess. He was some big-time pervert pedophile."

Sanders shook his head. "I never heard of him."

"Anyway," Torkleson said, as tired as I was of the deputy interplay, "it turns out he had a connection to somebody here."

That got Cody's attention, and mine.

"Aubrey Coates," Torkleson said. "Coates's e-mail address and phone number were all over his records. Scotland Yard thinks our man was part of this pervert's child porn and trafficking network. Can you believe that?"

"I wish he would have made it here," Sanders said, "so somebody could shoot the bastard. I hate those scumbags."

"I woulda shot him," Morales said, and I believed him.

"Hold it," I said, my head spinning. "Malcolm Harris had a connection to Aubrey Coates?"

I recalled Harris and the conversation:

My friends in Colorado say that compared to what I'm used to, I'll be bulletproof! That's the term they use, bulletproof. I love that.

Really? Who says that? I asked.

Oh no, he said coyly, I won't reveal my sources.

So his source was Aubrey Coates? What was Coates talking about? How was Coates bulletproof?

I looked to Cody for some kind of clarification, but Cody looked as mystified as I was.

Torkleson said, "But I heard the fucking U.S. Attorney won't go after Coates again. Not after Coates beat the rap the first time . . ." Torkleson lurched to a stop, realizing what he was saying and who he was saying it to. He looked over at Cody. "Sorry, man."

Cody glared at him with murderous eyes.

"What?" Sanders said. "What the fuck?"

Morales leaned back on the couch and beheld Cody and Torkleson. "Let's be cool, men," he said.

"What?" Sanders said again, completely confused.

"I wasn't thinking," Torkleson said to Cody. "My mouth was running away with me."

Cody said, "It sure fucking was."

"Be cool, brothers," Morales, the peacemaker said, standing up so he was between them. "Everything's cool here. We got women and babies in the house."

Sanders stomped a foot. "Would somebody please tell me what the fuck is going on here?"

Morales spun on his partner, said, "What's going on is Thanksgiving dinner is over. Our replacements will be here in twenty minutes, and it's time to go."

Melissa—thank God for Melissa—broke the tension by bringing

Angelina down the stairs. Our daughter was in her footie pajamas, and despite the fact that she was exhausted, she beamed at the cops, who were on the verge of going after each other.

"Angelina wants to say good night," Melissa said.

Sanders, Torkleson, and Morales stood up. They thanked Melissa once again and shook Angelina's chubby little hand. She rewarded them with a squeal each, which made them laugh.

"She's so tired, she's goofy," Melissa said. "So are you guys."

"What a darling," Morales said.

I kissed my daughter good night, but she was preoccupied with the men in the room whom she'd charmed to death.

"See you in a few minutes," I said to Melissa.

As she carried Angelina up the stairs, our daughter squirmed her way up over Melissa's shoulders so she could wave and laugh at the cops in the family room. Morales was smitten, as were Torkleson and Sanders.

Sanders, aware of why they were assigned to watching our house, said, "It just ain't right what's happening."

Morales shook his head, said, "No it isn't."

Torkleson quickly shook hands with me and thanked me for dinner, and was out the door into the snowstorm. Cody bored holes into Torkleson's back the whole way.

Sanders and Morales followed him. All I could think of was what in the hell Coates had told Harris—and why.

"THAT ASSHOLE," Cody said, seething, "showing me up like that.

"He wasn't thinking," I said, "he was just talking."

"Which is the problem with the whole fucking department. They don't think."

"Do you want a nightcap?" I asked.

Cody shook his head. "I'm done."

"The connection between Malcolm Harris and Aubrey Coates," I said. "There's something going on here I can't figure out. Something big and awful."

"Sometimes," Cody said, looking over my head, "I wish I had a license to just kill people. I'd kill a lot of them and make the world a better place. I'd start with Aubrey Coates and Malcolm Harris, and move to Garrett and John Moreland. There's about fifty others on the list I can think of."

"Cody . . ."

"Don't 'Cody' me," he said.

"Brian's funeral is tomorrow," I said. "Do you want to go with us?"

"It's tomorrow?"

"Yes."

"Jesus. I still can't believe he's gone. It hasn't sunk in yet."

"I know what you mean."

He looked at me. "No, I won't be there."

That troubled me.

"It has nothing to do with Brian," Cody said. He lifted his hand and pinched his thumb and index finger together. "I'm *this* close to cracking this thing."

I inadvertently took a step back. "You're kidding."

Cody's eyes blazed. "Nope. I think I've got it. I just needed to have the time to go through those call logs and do the police work. I think I've just about cracked it."

"Tell me," I said.

He smiled. His smile resembled—unfortunately—his Uncle Jeter's. "I'll tell you when I've got it," he said. "I can't put you two through any more false hopes or bad plans."

Cody grabbed his coat from where it was thrown over the couch. He gestured upstairs. "That Sanders guy is a doofus. But he's right when he says this ain't right, and it ain't."

He paused at the front door. Snow shot in. "Coates is a dead man walking, he just doesn't know it yet. But yes, I agree with you that there's more to it than what we know. This Malcolm Harris thing throws me for a loop, but somehow I think it all connects. I just don't know how yet."

"When will I see you?" I asked. "There's only three more days."

"Not soon," he said. "I'm going to New Mexico."

"Why?"

"Later," he said, waving me off. "Keep Melissa off the booze," he said. "I'm worried about her."

Friday, November 23

Two Days to Go

Twenty-one

THE FUNERAL FOR BRIAN took place in Capitol Hill at the largest chapel I'd ever been in, and the place was packed with mourners we didn't know. The décor was airy and sterile, all light pine and clean lines. Oh, and a small stylized cross hanging from a chain in a corner toward the front, as if placed there as an after-thought.

"A church designed by IKEA," I mumbled to Melissa, trying to make her smile. Didn't work.

If Brian were in charge of his own funeral—which in some ways he likely was—I thought it would look like this. It was larger-than-life, heavy on the hubris. An alt-rock band played contempo-rary dirges while a PowerPoint slide show presented shots of Brian skiing, swimming, speaking at a podium, clowning around, dancing, and costumed as both John Elway and Spider-Man at various par-ties. His remains were in a squarish marble urn on a velvet-covered riser at the front of the church. Brian's partner, Barry, spoke about Brian's loyalty, creativity, affection, and "ability to light up a room." Barry seemed like a calm counterpoint to Brian, and I could see how the two fit as a couple.

Barry was followed by Mayor Halladay, who gave not only a moving speech and tribute to Brian but vowed to those in attendance that he'd make sure the killer was caught and brought to justice. There was a swell of clapping when the mayor said Denver was no place for hate crimes, and that Brian's death would forever be remembered as the incident that ushered in a "hate-crime free zone." The mayor's assumption that Brian's murder was the result of his cruising downtown bars revealed where Mayor Halladay's head was. It also spoke to the lack of progress in the investigation.

I found myself looking around at the mourners as the mayor spoke. Many of the faces I'd seen in the society section of the *Denver Post* and *Rocky Mountain News,* and a few on television news. Brian always claimed he knew everybody who was anybody in town, and the outpouring at his funeral proved it. I was proud of him for making such an impact on this city while still remaining our small-town friend.

We sat near the back simply because there were so many people already there when we arrived. Sanders and Morales, of course, were with us but, thankfully, in street clothes. The two of them sat directly behind us at the service. I heard Sanders whisper, "World-class fruits and nuts in this place," to Morales.

Melissa whispered into my ear, "What bothers me is it's as if I didn't know Brian at all. Who are all of these people? The only one he'd ever mentioned was Barry. It seems like Brian had a secret life."

"We were his secret life," I said. "This room was his real life."

The mayor finally stepped aside. The band, somewhat inexplicably, played a cover version of REM's "Losing My Religion."

"Goodness," Melissa said. "Don't they know they're in a *church?*"

Although Cody said he wouldn't be there, I kept an eye out for him nevertheless. He'd left me with a strand of hope, and that strand was all I had.

When the band was through, a hip pastor with long hair and a stylish half beard and open shirt told us that we weren't there to mourn a death but to celebrate the life of an "awesome" human being. He began telling anecdotes about Brian—all from Denver, where he became public, none from Montana—that apparently had been gathered up by Barry and Barry and Brian's friends. Some were quite funny, but they were striking to Melissa and me because they were stories we'd never heard before about a friend we knew in a totally different context, and Melissa was soon both laughing and crying hard, which in turn made Angelina cry.

"I'll take her outside," I said, and Melissa willingly let me. Sanders followed.

The mountains were still shrouded in snow clouds. The ski resorts, from what I'd heard on the radio, were getting hammered. Marketing and PR spokesmen tried to outdo each other on the amount of "champagne powder" that had accumulated over the night. I knew most of the spokespeople personally from my work in tourism and knew they really weren't as breathless about falling snow as they sounded on the radio.

Angelina preferred being outside to inside, as she usually did. She pushed away from me as soon as we were outside, wanting to get down. I held her as she tried to push away. I couldn't let her down because Melissa had dressed her in a velvet dress, pink tights, and a heavy coat. As I struggled with her I found myself directly in front of Jim Doogan, who leaned against the trunk of a leafless tree and smoked a cigarette.

Doogan leveled his gaze at Sanders, who was a few steps behind me. He didn't say who he was but apparently he didn't need to.

"Give us a few minutes, will you?"

Sanders turned and walked back to the church and sprawled out on a bench.

"Is the mayor done in there?" Doogan asked.

"I think so."

"Was he good?"

I shrugged. "Good enough. He didn't say any bad things about Brian."

He laughed. "That Eastman guy caused us a lot of headaches. He used to drive the mayor out of his mind because he knew how to work the system and work the mayor. I always thought it was sort of personal."

"Brian was tough," I said.

"He was. And there's something I want to say to you. This is between us, okay?" Doogan said.

"Sure. I always confide with the guy who fires me. Not a problem."

Doogan snorted a small laugh. "You know I'm no more than the messenger boy, right? The mayor and the judge are close. The judge's wife is a major contributor, so the mayor has some obligations, if you catch my drift."

"I do." I fumbled with Angelina, held her tight to me. "But this is bigger than that."

"What do you mean?"

"Remember when we talked about Malcolm Harris?"

Doogan nodded.

"Do you know who his connection was here in Colorado?"

He shook his head.

"Aubrey Coates, the Monster of Desolation Canyon."

Doogan was lifting the cigarette to his mouth, but he froze.

I said, "Like I told you the other day, the mayor may have a bigger problem on his hands than he realized. If it turns out a major international pedophilia ring is headquartered in this city right under his nose, that won't help out his political ambitions, plus his pal the judge may be blamed for letting Coates walk. How will that one play on 9 News?"

280

Doogan said, "No, no. That wasn't the judge. That was lousy police work. No way that could be linked back to the mayor in any way. You're just throwing crap out there."

I *was* just throwing crap out there, but some of it stuck. I could tell his head was spinning a little. He was thinking how to mitigate the situation.

Said Doogan, "You're grasping at straws—anything to get back at that judge."

I didn't respond.

"I heard you tried to force your way in to see him the other day," Doogan said. "And when you couldn't get in, you called him, using my name with what could be construed to be vague threats. The mayor asked me to look into it, but I haven't gotten around to it yet."

"Thank you."

"I'd suggest not making a habit of that."

He turned his attention to Angelina, who was still struggling and had knocked my hat screwy on my head. "This is your little girl, eh?"

"This is her."

"She's the one . . ."

"*Yes.*"

He shook his head and looked away. He seemed genuinely moved.

I said, "Yes, she's the one the mayor's good friend Judge Moreland plans to take away from us Sunday."

Doogan took a long pull from his cigarette and blew the smoke out in an endless stream. "Judge Moreland, he's something else. He's a type, Jack, a rare type. I see his kind all the time, but he's a rare specimen."

I let him go on.

"You're looking at things the wrong way. You're making wrong assumptions. In my line of work, the politicos who are really going somewhere are never about the here and now. The good ones—and Moreland is a good one—think long-term. They *fixate* on the prize. Because they do, sometimes it isn't easy to figure out the moves they're making right in front of your eyes. You've gotta think long-term if you want to figure 'em out, and you haven't been thinking long-term."

I said, "What's he fixated on?"

Doogan said, "The Supreme Court."

I shook my head. "How can taking our little girl possibly help him get on the Supreme Court?"

"I don't know, Jack. You need to figure that one out. But I know that's what he wants."

I LEFT DOOGAN there by his tree. Sanders was a few feet behind again. As we approached the parking lot, I heard a powerful burbling engine fire up, and I instantly recognized it. The sound was like a straight razor to my throat.

Garrett's yellow H3 backed out away from us. I couldn't see inside well because of the dark-tinted windows, but I thought I saw two profiles—Garrett and his father.

"What, do you know who that is?" Sanders asked, noting my reaction.

So Garrett had come to the funeral of the man he'd stomped to death to what, gloat? And why would Judge Moreland have come? To see what?

Angelina squirmed in my arms and pointed toward a squirrel scrambling down a tree. She said, "Cat!"

I started to laugh when something hit me so hard my knees nearly buckled. I looked from my little girl to the departing H3 and back to my little girl. I thought, *He came hoping to see* her.

Which went back to the beginning, the simple unanswered question: Why did they want her?

And everything seemed to make sudden and terrible sense.

Bulletproof. What could be more bulletproof than a pedophile being a partner in crime with a judge? The judge in whose courtroom the Monster of Desolation Canyon—another participant in the international ring—had gone free?

Angelina cried out, and I realized I was squeezing her too hard. I eased up and looked at her. She was beautiful by all accounts, with her dark flashing eyes, her smile, her manner, and not just proud-parent beautiful.

I felt like I'd had the breath punched out of me.

I carried her toward the back parking lot of the chapel where I'd seen a couple of black-and-whites and Torkleson's nondescript Crown Victoria. The cops were there, no doubt, to see who came to the funeral because the case was still wide-open. Torkleson leaned against his Crown Vic talking with another detective—they stood out as cops even at a funeral where there were more suits and ties than usual—and a couple of uniforms.

Torkleson must have seen something in my face as I approached because he excused himself from his colleagues and met me on the sidewalk.

"Hello, Jack," Torkleson said.

"You said Malcolm Harris was connected with Aubrey Coates," I said. "How did you find that out?"

Torkleson shrugged. "Phone records, e-mails, uploads, downloads. A lot of technical evidence concerning ISPs and proxy servers and other stuff I really don't understand, but from what I was told, Coates transmitted big files and images overseas from that trailer of his. The Brits traced it back from Harris's computer. Unfortunately, we don't have the original files anymore, as you know." He shot a look over my shoulder to see if Cody was lurking anywhere and could attack.

"I don't know where Cody is," I said. "Don't worry about him."

"Why are you asking me this?" he said.

I said, "Because I'm pretty sure if you dug into the evidence for the charges, you'll find communication between Harris and Coates and someone else here in this city."

Torkleson looked at me closely. "We've got a team assigned to that," he said. "They're working with the Brits and Interpol. Perverts are getting arrested one by one all over the world. Are you talking about someone in particular?"

"Judge Moreland or his son Garrett," I said. "Or both."

Torkleson closed his eyes and took a deep breath and moaned. "Not again," he said. "You know what happened when I sent officers to his house based on your so-called tip."

"This is different," I said. "Of all the places he could relocate, Malcolm Harris chose Denver. He said he was coming here because he would be *bulletproof*. Somebody assured him it would be fine for him. And what better proof of it than when a child pornographer and molester like Aubrey Coates gets set free in Judge Moreland's own courtroom?"

Torkleson started to argue, but stopped. I could see wheels turning, things falling into place for him as they did for me.

"How do you know Harris?" Torkleson asked.

"I met with him on behalf of the CVB," I said. "Before we knew what he was."

"Jesus Christ," he whispered.

"Do you have access to the evidence against Harris?"

He nodded. "I'd have to get with one of our tech guys to interpret it," he said. "But I think we have all the supporting documentation that's been compiled. It's just a matter of cross-referencing phone calls, e-mail addresses, IP stuff—I *think*."

"Can you try?" I asked.

Torkleson looked over his shoulder to assure himself we hadn't been overheard by his colleagues. "I'll try," he said softly.

"Thank you," I said, wanting to kiss him.

"But I don't think it will pan out," he said, putting his hand on my shoulder. "If there are electronic trails from Coates and Harris to Moreland or his son, I think we'd already know it. This case has been in the works for a hell of a long time."

"I understand," I said. "But won't it be easier if you're specifically looking at a particular target—Moreland's or Garrett's computers or phones—than cross-referencing a whole city?"

"Maybe," he said. "I don't know."

By then Angelina had lost all patience and worked her arms free and was swinging at me, her little fists thumping against my topcoat lapels. "Down! *Down!*"

"*Angelina, no.*" The tone of my voice silenced her. She began to cry, and I was sorry I had snapped at her.

THAT NIGHT I ROLLED over in bed and opened my eyes and caught Melissa sitting there in the dark staring at me, a drink in her hand. No doubt wondering why she'd married a man who couldn't keep her family together.

Saturday, November 24

One Day to Go

Twenty-two

WHEN THE TELEPHONE RANG at seven thirty in the morning, I rolled over and grabbed it, rubbing my eyes and hoping it was Torkleson or Cody with news. After waking to find Melissa watching me the night before, I hadn't slept for hours and had just fallen asleep.

"Is everything ready for tomorrow?" Judge John Moreland asked.

I didn't respond.

Moreland said, "I know this has got to be tough. Please don't make it any tougher on either one of us than it needs to be."

I said, "I'm on to you."

There was a beat of silence. He said, "What?"

"You heard me. You'll be in prison, where you can never touch a little girl again. And you know what happens to your kind in prison."

When he spoke again he sounded angry and impatient. "I have no earthly idea what you're talking about." I had hoped he would act guilty and reveal himself. He was a good actor.

"Really?" I said.

"You've gone off the deep end. I hate to say it, but getting the baby out of that . . . environment can't be soon enough."

"You'll be wearing a jumpsuit and shoes without laces, and you'll spend all your time looking over your shoulder for the next attack," I said.

A heavy sigh. "I've done everything I can to be compassionate," Moreland said. "I never needed to give you the time, but I did. I've offered to help you and your wife with another placement, but you've spurned that offer. All I get from you is threats and paranoid rants. You accuse my son of murder and me of something I can't even say out loud. I would have hoped this entire painful thing could have been accomplished with some kind of maturity for the sake of the child, but I see that's just not the case."

Man, he *almost* convinced me with that one. He was damned good, I'll give him that.

"I'm on to you," I said again.

"Oh, for heaven's sake . . ."

I punched off and looked up to see Melissa in the doorway, holding Angelina in her arms.

"Was that him?" she asked.

"Yes."

"What did he want?"

"He wanted to make sure we were ready."

"Kind of him," she said, with a kind of hopeless sarcasm. She closed her eyes. I stood up in case I needed to steady her. Angelina reached out for me, cried, "Da!"

I COULDN'T EVEN EAT the toast I'd made and stuck to cup after cup of coffee. With the mug in hand, I wandered through the rooms in our house as if seeing them for the first time in a while. White winter light filtered through the blinds and curtains. It was a different quality of light than fall or summer, a more dispassionate hue. It was obviously cold outside because the heater clicked on and forced warm air through the registers with regularity. I thought, *Maybe this happens all the time, and I've just never noticed it before.* I tried to remember the last time I'd checked our furnace in the basement and couldn't recall when I'd done it.

Sanders and Morales were in their usual places. Wisps of exhaust from their running engines dissipated into the air.

I'd not told Melissa of my suspicion regarding Judge Moreland or my conversation with Detective Torkleson. Maybe I should have, but I was banking on the fact that Torkleson would call confirming the judge's links to the ring, and it would all be over.

MELISSA DECIDED the house was missing something and decided to bake bread. Soon, the smells of baking bread filled the place, taking the edge off the day. *Good call,* I thought.

In Angelina's room, there were boxes stacked up in the corner and marked SUMMER CLOTHES, WINTER CLOTHES, and TOYS AND GIFTS.

It was really happening.

For the fourth time that day, I pulled out my cell phone and speed-dialed Cody's number and heard, "The number you are calling is out of the service area at this time. Please leave a message . . ."

THERE WERE SEVERAL more phone calls throughout the day, none of them Torkleson or Cody. Melissa's mom and dad called from different places and she talked to each of them longer than I could remember her ever doing. Her face flushed as she talked to her father, and I could tell she was getting angry.

"We *had* a lawyer," she said, heatedly. "It's not like we didn't have a lawyer, Dad. It's that there wasn't anything he could do."

She scowled as he went on, and when she saw me watching, she rolled her eyes.

"Gee, Dad," she said, "it's really great you are suddenly so concerned and seem to have all of the answers. But where were you three weeks ago when we could have used some of your wisdom?"

My parents called shortly after, before Melissa had cooled off. She talked to them and told them the situation hadn't changed. After a while, she handed the phone to me.

My dad said, "Your mom is too busted up to talk anymore, sorry."

"I understand."

"I guess this is the kind of thing that can happen when we turn everything over to the government and to the lawyers," he said. "When a whole society abrogates personal responsibility, these kinds of situations come up." I'd heard his theory many times before that everything was better back in the pioneer days, when people dealt with each other fair and square, their word backed up personally by their reputations or their guns—without the involvement of third parties like lawyers or politicians.

"Dad, I can't sit on the front porch with a shotgun on my lap and keep them away."

"I know you can't," he said. "And it's a damned shame."

I thought of my grandfather's Colt .45 upstairs in the closet, and said, "Yes, it is."

Dad said, "I was joking to your mother that we ought to send somebody like Jeter Hoyt down there to straighten things out. That'd give those big-city types a dose of frontier justice, wouldn't it?"

I smiled bitterly to myself. *Frontier justice hadn't matched up real well with Sur-13.*

"Too bad we can't do that," he said.

I PACED. I called Cody's cell phone again and again, getting angrier with him each time. Same with Torkleson, who wouldn't answer his cell, either. I called the detective division, and the receptionist said Torkleson was out and she didn't know when he'd be back. She asked if there was anyone else who could help me, and I said no, I needed to talk to Torkleson.

I stayed away from both Melissa and Angelina because I didn't want my building anger and fear to effect them. I went upstairs and checked the loads in the .45, and went downstairs and looked at my furnace and wondered how in the hell it worked.

For once, what my father said made some sense. Why couldn't I sit outside on my porch with a shotgun across my knees and keep the world away from my family?

I couldn't stay home, but I couldn't leave Melissa and Angelina, either, so I threw on my parka and went outside. As I approached Sanders, he slid his window down and held out his hand, palm out.

"That's far enough, Jack."

"Why?"

"The sheriff didn't like our Thanksgiving dinner together. He told both of us to stop fraternizing with you and your family. You know what's happening tomorrow."

"And what would that be?" I said, angry.

"Jack, just stay back."

I turned around and stomped back to the house. As I did I whipped out my cell phone and called Cody.

Out of service range.

I called detective division again, and the receptionist said she'd put my message on his desk on top of the pile of my other messages.

DURING ANGELINA'S AFTERNOON NAP, I went into the kitchen as Melissa pulled more loaves of bread from the oven and put them on the counter to cool. I couldn't even count the number of loaves she'd baked during the day—maybe twenty-five, maybe more. The kitchen was overwhelmed with the smell of yeast and flour and golden crust. There was more dough on the table, and it was obvious she was going to keep baking bread until she ran out of ingredients. I took a cursory look around the hiding places in the kitchen and didn't see the bottle.

"You don't have to keep looking," she said. "I'm not drinking."

"JACK, IT'S DETECTIVE TORKLESON," Melissa said, shaking me awake. I'd fallen asleep in my chair in the living room out of exhaustion, and it took me a second to register what she'd said. When it did, my heart revved like a race-car motor, and I grabbed the phone and bounded up the stairs into our bedroom and shut the door.

He said, "I've been up all night since we talked. I hijacked our best tech gal and made her stay up all night with me in the basement of the building with her computers. We've been going over all of the evidence Scotland Yard and Interpol sent over . . ."

I tried to swallow, but my mouth was dry.

"Jack, we can't make any links at all between either Harris and Moreland or Coates and Moreland. We've got nothing to connect them."

I nearly blacked out and had to reach for the headboard to steady my legs.

"Can you keep looking?" I said. My voice was weak. I'd staked everything on this. "Maybe Garrett has a secret computer? Maybe they know how to mask their telephone numbers and IP addresses somehow? Hell, I don't know. All I know is that there has to be a connection."

Torkleson sighed. "Jack, I'm not saying there isn't a remote possibility. I'm not saying that. But the electronic trail between Coates and Harris is like a freeway. There's nothing like that with the judge—not even an old cow trail, if you know what I'm saying. There are some IP addresses my tech gal can't isolate, but nothing substantial, and nothing we could go to the DA with. It's a dry hole, Jack."

"It's got to be there," I said.

"Look, we've done all we could. It's an interesting theory you had that plays into your situation, but nothing we can pursue in any way, shape, or form. Maybe somewhere down the line Harris will say the judge is a known associate, or give up his name up for leniency. There's always that."

"It will be too late," I said.

"I know," Torkleson said.

I found myself looking out the window at Sanders's cruiser. It was dusk and getting colder. Exhaust puffed from his tailpipe.

I said, "When you lose all hope, what have you got left?"

"I can't answer that, Jack."

"Neither can I," I said, before thanking him and hanging up.

"HAVE WE DONE IT all wrong, honey?" I asked later that afternoon, as the sun dropped behind the mountains.

She stopped and looked at me, her eyes blinking oddly. "What do you mean?"

I shook my head. "Maybe we played it all wrong, because look where we are. Tomorrow they're coming to take her. Maybe we should have hired a new lawyer, tried to take the judge to court to stall this at least. I know everyone said we'd lose in the end, but at least we'd have had more time. Instead, we tried to get Garrett to sign the papers, and he never signed them." I didn't even want to mention all that had happened, all that had gone wrong.

I said, "We could have done that or we could have hit the road right away and decided to go out with guns blazing. Maybe we could have created a media spectacle, gotten the press and the public on our side. Maybe that would have scared the judge and Garrett away."

She took in a deep breath. "I've thought of those things. Believe me, Jack, I've never once stopped thinking of what we could do. Neither would have worked. I think you know that."

I wasn't so sure. "At least we could have tried."

"We *did* try," she said, her eyes tearing up. "We tried with the help of our best friends, and we did everything we could do. And I want you to stop speculating right now. All I've got in the world is the knowledge that we did all we could."

I sat down heavily at the table. She came over and put her hands on my shoulders, leaving flour handprints.

"And we still don't know why they really want her," I said.

But I had an inkling, a thought so dark I still couldn't share it, despite what Torkleson had said. And when I looked up at my wife, I could see by the emptiness in her eyes and expression that it had crossed her mind as well.

Sunday, November 25

The Day

Twenty-three

AND IT WAS OVER.

Even now the events of that morning are wispy and sharply painful and disconnected in my mind. I remember everything, but I have trouble putting the events in order. Even now, as I recall them, my heart palpitates and my breathing gets shallow and irregular and I find myself reaching out to steady myself.

It was early in the morning when the doorbell rang, I remember that clearly. The sun hadn't yet percolated through the clouds and, with an inch or two of fresh snow on the ground, it seemed ice blue outside. I remember my eyes shooting open and being instantly awake and thinking: *It's them.*

A BLAST OF WINTER as I opened the front door to find Sanders, Morales, the sheriff with his big gut and gunfighter's mustache, plus a female deputy I hadn't seen before. All of them crowded on my front porch wearing identical sheriff's department dark coats, condensation like smoke from their mouths haloing around their heads as they stood there like a small black army from hell. They stamped snow from their boots as they came into the living room.

Outside, parked in my driveway with the motor running, were Judge Moreland and Garrett. Waiting.

Behind me, Melissa came down the stairs holding Angelina. When she saw the cops she said, "Oh my God."

The female deputy was introducing herself, talking in I'm sure what she thought as competent and soothing tones. I didn't hear a word she said.

I can't recall if I lost it as she held out her arms for our daughter or when the sheriff said the Morelands "just want the child. They aren't interested in the boxes."

Something white-hot exploded behind my eyes and I was on them—punching, kicking, gouging, trying to get through them to the door so I could get outside and pull Moreland and Garrett from their car into the snow and kill them with my bare hands. Sanders went down with a surprised look on his face, and his fall took down the sheriff. The female deputy shouted while she unclipped her pepper spray and threatened me with it. Either Sanders or the sheriff clipped me hard in the jaw with a frozen fist and my teeth snapped together and my head snapped back and for a second I was staring at the ceiling. Then my arms were pinned to my sides and my feet left the ground as Morales picked me up in a bear hug and slammed me face-first into the couch. I saw spangles and little else for a moment. There was a knee in my spine and my arms were wrenched back. I heard the *zip* sound of flexcuffs being pulled tight around my wrists.

Through a fog, Melissa said, "I just can't hand her over to you. *I can't perform that act.*"

The female deputy said, "That's all right, I understand. Just put her in that swing, and I'll take her out. You don't have to hand her to me that way."

"I can't. I can't."

"Please, ma'am. We don't want to have to restrain you to take the child. Think of the girl, think of the girl in your arms. We don't want to risk hurting anyone."

Melissa did it.

I heard an animal roar that turned out to be me.

Deputies cried, looked away.

The female deputy wrapped Angelina in blankets she'd brought along and backed toward the door, flanked by Morales and Sanders.

Directly in front of me, inches away, was the hem of the sheriff's coat as he directed them. I could feel the cold emanating from it.

Angelina realized that she was being taken away and she screamed and her chubby hands shot out from beneath the blanket toward Melissa. The deputy quickly covered them back up.

Melissa shrieked and dropped to her knees.

The front door closed as the female deputy went outside with Angelina.

The sheriff said to Sanders, "Call the EMTs."

To me, "Can I trust you to help your wife if I cut you loose?"

"Yes," I said.

Melissa climbed back to her feet with the help of Morales, who was openly blubbering.

The sheriff watched the exchange outside through the front window, then said with grim finality, "It's done."

My cuffs were released, and I rolled off the couch to the floor, scrambling to all fours. Melissa was clutching herself, her eyes wild, her face bone white. I rushed to her.

She collapsed in my arms, but I held her body tight against mine so she wouldn't slide to the floor. I duckwalked with her that way to the couch.

They say that when a person dies, the body suddenly becomes lighter as the soul leaves, that it's been measured. Melissa didn't die, but I remember thinking that her soul had left her because she felt featherlight in my arms.

As I picked up her legs and put them on the couch, I heard the tires of Moreland's car crunch snow as it backed up and left.

A few moments later an EMT van, lights flashing, swung up into the driveway. The EMTs had no doubt been on call just down the street in case they'd be needed. Suddenly, there were more dark-clothed people in our house. They helped Melissa up the stairs into bed. I stood on the landing shell-shocked, my eyes burning. My jaw hurt.

There was a heated discussion as Morales and Sanders told the sheriff they refused to arrest me for assault, and if he insisted on it, he could do it himself, and they'd walk off the job. I heard him say, "Jesus, okay, *okay*. You guys are too damned close to this situation, that's for sure." While he talked, he sucked on a bloody front tooth that had been dislodged during the scuffle.

Sanders said, "You bet your ass we are."

I went upstairs.

Melissa was sedated. Her eyelids fluttered and her grip on my hand relaxed to nothing and her hand dropped away. I looked up at the EMTs and insisted I didn't need anything, didn't want anything.

When I went back downstairs, the sheriff had left. Morales and Sanders stood there with their heads down, staring at their boots.

Sanders said, "I hate my job."

Morales said to me, "Can we leave you? You won't do anything, will you? You won't hurt yourself or anyone else, will you?"

I shook my head no. Which meant *yes*.

And it was over.

THAT EVENING, as the sun set and suspended snow and ice crystals lit up with the cold fire of it and the temperature dropped to minus ten, I checked on Melissa in our dark bedroom. Still sleeping. The EMTs said she would likely be out all night. Nevertheless, I left her a note on the night table in a scrawl I didn't recognize. I wrote:

I'M GOING TO GO GET ANGELINA.
IF I DON'T COME BACK I WANT YOU TO KNOW I
    LOVE YOU WITH ALL OF MY HEART.
LOVE, JACK

I slipped the Colt .45 into the front right pocket of my parka. It was heavy. To balance out the load, I emptied the box of cartridges in the left.

THE COLD SLAPPED ME right in the face. When I breathed in, I could feel ice crystals form in my nose. The snow squeaked beneath my boots. That sound made me grit my teeth, and the hairs on the back of my neck stood up.

I'd forgotten gloves, and the metal of the door handle of my Jeep stung my fingers.

"Where do you think you're going, Jack?"

I froze. Cody.

I turned stiffly. He was walking across my lawn. His car was parked in front of the house, and I hadn't even noticed it.

"I'm going to kill Judge Moreland."

"So it's over? They took her?"

"Where were you? I've been trying to reach you for days."

"I broke my stupid phone on a guy's head."

"I need to go."

"He probably does need killing," Cody said. "But not now. Not by you."

"Stay out of my way, Cody."

He reached out and grabbed my coat sleeve. I wanted nothing

to do with him, had no desire to hear his words. He wasn't there when we needed him, and I had to do this myself.

Cody said, "What I'm saying is that you don't need to go over there right now. You won't get close anyway—the sheriff's got cars in front of Moreland's house just in case you thought of trying something like this. All this will do is land you in jail."

"I don't care."

"You should," said Cody. "Because I've fucking cracked this thing. We're going to be able to get that son of a bitch Moreland *and* get your daughter back."

I blinked.

"That's right," he said.

"How?"

"I've got somebody with me you'll want to meet."

I looked at Cody's car again. There was no one in it. But I noticed something I hadn't seen before. The car was trembling a bit, rocking slightly side to side.

"He's in the trunk," Cody said. "Let's go get him and have a little talk inside."

Twenty-four

INTRODUCE YOURSELF TO MR. MCGUANE," Cody said to the disheveled little man he shoved roughly through my front door.

He mumbled something in a tight-lipped way that sounded like "My-wott."

"Where's Melissa?" Cody asked me.

I chinned upstairs. "Sedated."

Cody shook his head. "Bastards. Is she okay?"

"How could she be?"

"*Bastards.*"

"They came this morning. The sheriff and three deputies. The judge and Garrett stayed out in their car and didn't even come in."

My-wott stood there, watching us go back and forth as if he were observing a tennis match. By his blank expression I could tell he had no idea what we were talking about.

"Sit," Cody said to My-wott, indicating the couch. The little man shuffled over to it stiff-legged and sat down. I could see now why he couldn't talk and could barely move: He was freezing. His skin was sallow. His teeth were chattering so hard it sounded like popcorn popping. My-wott was thin, stooped, mousy. I guessed his build at five-four, 130. He had badly cut brown hair, thick horn-rimmed glasses, no chin but a prominent Adam's apple, and his face was a moonscape of old acne scars. He had furtive, darting eyes and a manner to him that was weak and annoying. I felt sorry for him but wanted to hit him at the same time. He wore a red-checked plaid shirt, baggy jeans, and Crocs shoes. His arms shot out when he sat down, and I noted a massive gold Rolex on his wrist that just didn't go with the rest of him. It looked like it weighed two pounds.

My-wott had a nasty-looking bruise right in the middle of a small bald spot on the back of his head. Cody saw me looking at it, and said, "That's how I broke my damn phone."

Cody dragged two chairs from the kitchen and placed them in front of him. He spun his around and straddled it, placing his arms on the top of the backrest. His eyes were gleaming, and his mouth was set in a sarcastic snarl. "I said, introduce yourself to Mr. McGuane." To me: "Jack, have a seat."

The little man looked down at his Crocs. His legs shook violently.

"Speak the fuck up," Cody said, and slapped him sharply on his face. I glared at Cody, who ignored me.

"Wyatt," the man said.

"Wyatt what?" Cody barked.

"Wyatt Henkel."

"And where are you from, Wyatt Henkel?"

"You mean now, or where I was born?"

Cody slapped him again.

"Jesus, Cody," I said.

Cody looked at me. "When you hear what he's going to say, you're going to want to do more than slap him."

"Still," I said.

"I was born in Greeley, Colorado," Henkel said, forcing the

words out through his chattering teeth. "I live now in Las Cruces, New Mexico."

"Good," Cody said. "Now tell Mr. McGuane why you're here. Why your telephone number was on Brian Eastman's call log from his cell phone."

Henkel looked away from Cody and stared at our gas fireplace, which I'd turned off a few minutes before as I left the house.

"I'm freezing to death," Henkel said, turning to me. "I've been in that trunk for eight hours."

"Seven hours, tops," Cody said. "Quit whining."

I got up and walked over to the fireplace to turn it on.

Cody said, "No—keep it off."

"Look at him," I said.

"Fuck him," Cody said. "We'll turn on the fireplace once he starts talking." To Henkel, Cody said, "*Fuck you.* Got that?"

Henkel avoided meeting his eyes.

To me, Cody said, "I noticed some weight in your coat pockets. Are you carrying?"

"Yes."

"Good. Get that gun out of your pocket. This is your grandpa's Colt .45 Peacemaker, right?"

I drew it out. It was heavy and cold, and it looked like a blunt instrument in my hand.

Cody said, "Cock it and put the muzzle against Wyatt Henkel's forehead. If he tells a lie, I'll ask you to pull the trigger. Don't worry about his brains splashing all over the wall because I don't think he has any. And don't worry about the body afterward, either. I'll just take it up to where I buried Uncle Jeter. It's a perfect place nobody will ever look. Maybe the coyotes will dig up their bones in 2025, but by then who gives a shit?"

Cody defused my look of horror with a barely perceptible wink that Henkel couldn't see because his head was still down. *Okay,* I nodded. *Now I get it.*

Henkel's head came up slowly. He was terrified.

I cocked the hammer and the cylinder rotated and I put the muzzle above his eyebrow.

Cody shifted in his chair and pulled his departmental .40 Glock semiauto. He held it loosely in his hand. "In case he misses," Cody said to Henkel.

"Let's start again," Cody said to Henkel. "State your occupation."

Henkel's voice was high and reedy. "I'm a janitor at Las Cruces High School."

"A janitor, eh?"

"Yes, sir."

"Yes, I like that. Call me 'sir.' And call Mr. McGuane here 'sir' as well. Now tell me how long you've had your job."

"Seven years."

"What is your salary?"

"I make $26,000. It's considered part-time."

"Interesting," Cody said. "You pull down 26K, but you live on five acres and you have two new vehicles. Is that correct?"

Henkel tried to swallow, and his Adam's apple bobbed up and down. "Yes," he said.

"And you have that big piece of gold on your wrist. Is it a fake? One of those Taiwanese knockoffs?"

"It's real," he said.

"And that Escalade you drive—was it stolen?"

"No, sir."

"You live well for a part-time janitor, don't you, Wyatt?"

"Not as well as some, but I do all right." His voice had gained some confidence. He was warming up both literally and figuratively. Which angered Cody.

"Shoot him," he said.

I pushed the gun harder into Henkel's brow.

"No!" he cried, his eyes round.

"Then answer me straight," Cody said. Cody even scared me.

"Okay," said Henkel.

"You weren't always a janitor, where you?"

"No."

"What other jobs have you held?"

"A lot of 'em. I'm not very smart, I guess." Although Cody was asking the questions, Henkel was answering them to me. Probably because despite my gun, Cody scared him more. "I do my best, but people just don't like me. No one's ever really liked me."

Said Cody, "I can see why. Again, what jobs have you had in your life?"

Henkel's eyes rolled up as if trying to remember. "Retail, mostly. Wal-Mart, Target, Pier One. I moved around a lot between New Mexico and Colorado."

"You didn't mention that one-hour photo place you used to work at," Cody said. "You know, that one in Canon City, Colorado."

"Oh, that one," Henkel said, his face getting even whiter. Cody'd struck a nerve.

"Tell Mr. McGuane when you worked there."

He thought for a second. "It was 2001."

"Before everybody went digital," Cody said. "Back at the end of the film-and-print days."

"Yes. I don't think that shop is even there anymore."

"Royal Gorge is outside of Canon City, right?"

"Yes."

"That's quite a spectacular place, isn't it?" Cody asked. "Lots of tourists go there to see it and walk across the footbridge and look down at the Arkansas River. There's even a state park there, right?"

I tried not to look at Cody to ask him where the hell this was going.

Henkel paused, then said, "Yes."

"In 2001, the caretaker of the state park brought in some film to have developed at your shop. Do you remember that?"

Henkel tried to swallow again but couldn't.

"Could I have a glass of water?" he asked me.

"You can have a bullet in your head," Cody said. "Again, do you remember when the caretaker of the state park brought some film in to you?"

"Yes."

"He brought in lots of film to be developed, didn't he?"

"Yes."

"You're not supposed to look at the prints that you develop, are you? And the way the equipment worked, there was no reason even to see them. The processor was automatic, right? The only time you even touched the prints was when you put them in the envelope for the customer, right?"

"That was the policy."

"But in this case you looked, didn't you, Wyatt?"

His voice was a croak. "I looked." As he said it his eyes darted to Cody and back to me.

"What was on the prints, Wyatt?"

"Nature stuff, mostly. But there were a lot of pictures of children with their families. The families were camping or hiking."

"Were photos of children pretty much all the customer took?"

"Yes."

Cody shot me a look. I still didn't know what the point was.

"And why did you run a second set of prints to keep for yourself?"

Henkel briefly closed his eyes.

"Wyatt?"

"There were four pictures I wanted to keep," he said.

Cody leaned back and reached into his coat with his free hand and brought out a manila envelope. "Are these the four photos you kept, Wyatt?"

"You know they are."

Cody handed the envelope to me.

Cody said, "Who has the originals and the negatives?"

"The customer."

Cody smiled sarcastically. "And who is the customer, Wyatt?"

"Aubrey Coates. He was the park caretaker at the time."

I felt an electric bolt shoot through my chest, and I almost pulled the trigger accidentally. Suddenly, it was as if all around me, for three weeks, there were dozens of sheets of clear plastic, each with a brush of color and several errant squiggles. Individually, none of the sheets made sense. But when they were placed one upon the other, a whole image emerged. It was as if everything we had learned and done over the last three weeks made horrifying sense.

I lowered the pistol and opened the envelope, knowing what I would find.

Brian was right. There *were* photos.

The first was of a young family of three hiking along a narrow trail. There was a rock wall behind them so it was obviously in a canyon—Royal Gorge Canyon. The photo was grainy, and there was a pine twig in the bottom corner of it, indicating to me that the shot was taken at a great distance, and the photographer was hiding in a stand of trees. The woman—plain, heavy, obviously pregnant—was in the lead. A boy of twelve or thirteen was last. It took me a moment to recognize him as a young Garrett. The man in the middle was John Moreland.

The second photo was slightly blurred, but it was obvious that Moreland was tugging on his wife's arm, and she was reaching out wildly to steady herself. Garrett stood in sharp focus, looking on with what looked like intense interest.

In the third photo, Dorrie Pence Moreland, the ultradevout Catholic homely homebody who was a drag on her husband's social and political climb and who was bringing another child into the world to compete with her monomaniacal and psychopathic firstborn son, could be seen cartwheeling through the sky, her long black hair flying behind her like flames.

311

In the fourth, Garrett prepared to deliver the *coup de grace* with the large rock he held over his head to the broken body of his mother while his father looked on approvingly.

I went through the photos a second time, then a third.

"My God," I said. "So Coates owns the judge."

"That would be correct," Cody said.

"Which is why he was bulletproof."

"Bingo."

"So he's been blackmailing him all these years?"

Cody nodded his head and raised his Glock, pointing it at Wyatt Henkel's head. "Sort of. Tell him, Wyatt."

If possible, Henkel suddenly looked even smaller and more pathetic.

"It was me who blackmailed the judge," Henkel said. "I told him I had the pictures. I put them on a copy machine and sent a copy to him to prove it. So for years he's been paying up."

Cody said, "Hence the vehicles, the large spread, the Rolex. But you lied to the judge, didn't you, Wyatt? You told him you had the negatives."

Henkel nodded.

Cody said, "So when Brian Eastman started putting word out among all of his acquaintances that he was searching the country for someone who had some kind of photos on Judge Moreland, you contacted the judge again, right?"

"Yes."

"To tell him the price would be going up or you'd sell the photos to Brian, right?"

"Right."

Strangely, Henkel was warming to the revelations. It was obvious he was proud of himself. I really did want to shoot him, but not before I'd heard everything.

Cody said to me, "I'm speculating now, but it's speculation based on Henkel's role in this. When I was investigating Coates, I always

312

wondered why Coates quit working at state parks five years ago and switched exclusively to campgrounds on federal land. It was just one of those little things that stuck out and didn't make sense to me. Now it makes sense. Coates's job switch corresponds with when Moreland was named to the federal bench. Henkel here had the photos and wanted money from the judge—and got it. Coates didn't want money—he needed security. Coates knew someday he'd get caught so he contacted Moreland and told him about his hole card. He wanted to make sure he was tried in a federal courtroom because he knew who the judge would be. Another thing: There are *nine* district court judges. Coates must have somehow made it known to Moreland that someday he might show up in his court-room and that he'd need a favor. So how did Moreland make sure he'd be the presiding judge if this unknown blackmailer got hauled before him? He worked the system from the inside, and made sure he'd be the judge for serious crimes committed on federal land. Moreland wanted to be in control of the situation for his own sake in case the second blackmailer ever needed that favor. That's why Coates was bulletproof."

"Son of a bitch," I said. Then: "Hold it. Why would Coates risk taking his film to Henkel? Wouldn't Coates be worried that Henkel or somebody would see the shots of the murder?"

"I can answer that," Henkel said. "I don't think at the time he realized what he had. Those photos are blown up, that's why they're so grainy. In the originals, the people look like ants against that wall. I think he may have gotten a shot of her falling, but I don't think he knew that the judge pushed her. I don't think he knew what he had until he got home and looked closely at the prints."

"And he never came after you?" I asked, skeptical.

He smiled for the first time. Rotten yellow stubs for teeth. "I was long gone if he ever did. I took those blowups and kept them with me when I moved from place to place, job to job. I think he tried to find me a couple of times. Once a man showed up at my store in Salida asking about me. I heard it from the other room and walked out the side door and never looked back. Another time I came home after work in Durango and saw some kids who looked like Mexican gangsters parked in front of my apartment building. I just drove right by and all the way to New Mexico."

Cody nodded, as if another piece of the puzzle had just fit into place. "So when you left the message about Brian Eastman, did the judge call you back?"

"No. It was the judge's son, Garrett. He's the boy in the pictures—the one with the rock."

"Right. And what did Garrett say?"

"You're going to kill me, aren't you?" Henkel asked us.

Cody screwed up his face. "I'm at ninety percent yes. But there's ten percent to play with, Wyatt. You need to convince me you're worth that ten percent by telling me the truth."

I could see Henkel thinking, running through the arguments. Finally, he said, "Garrett said they'd pay more but only if I called Eastman and told him I had the photos. I talked to him, and he agreed to meet me here in Denver. Garrett gave me the directions to give to Eastman, but he told me not to go. I guess Garrett met him instead."

I shot him.

The explosion was deafening. I don't know how Melissa slept through it, but she did. And Henkel was writhing on my couch, clutching his shoulder where the bullet hit, smearing bright red blood all over the fabric.

Cody wrenched the .45 out of my hand before I could cock it and finish Henkel off.

"For Christ's sake, Jack!" Cody yelled. "We're not done with him yet!"

"I am," I said, but what I'd just done shocked me.

Henkel grunted and moaned.

Cody grabbed him by the hair and sat him back up.

"Talk fast," Cody said, "and maybe you'll get to live."

"It hurts," Henkel said through bared teeth.

"It's gonna hurt a lot more!"

"I'm going to bleed to death."

"Maybe."

Cody leaned over him, his face inches away.

"As far as you knew, Coates never contacted the judge again until recently, correct?"

"As far as I know," Henkel said.

Cody looked to me, nodding. "When Coates found out I was closing in on him, he must have contacted the judge and reminded him what he had all these years. Imagine Moreland's surprise when he found out that one of the two people who knew about Dorrie's murder was the very pedophile we were closing in on. Moreland had the search and arrest warrants on his desk, of course, so he tipped Coates we were coming. That's how Coates knew to destroy everything ahead of time. And he made sure Coates walked."

A million thoughts were going through my mind. I tried to put them into some kind of order.

"But Cody," I said, "Coates walked because of what *you* did."

I instantly regretted saying it, and Cody's eyes flashed with pure rage.

"I'm sorry," I said. "But . . ."

Cody said, "Up until tonight there has always been one thing about that trial I couldn't figure out, and that was how Ludik knew everything there was to know about my movements after we arrested Coates. I mean, Ludik's smart, but he's not *that* smart. Somebody tipped him, and I think it was Moreland. He didn't do it with a phone call or anything that obvious, I'm sure. He probably told some court gossip something like, 'I just hope this is a solid case because there seems to be some real chain-of-evidence problems with it'—something like that. He probably heard about me through the DA or some blabbermouth cop. So Moreland put it out there so Ludik would hear it thirdhand and investigate. I'm not saying I didn't fuck up, Jack—I did. But Moreland set the whole clusterfuck in motion—from tipping Coates to the search warrant to suggesting to the defense they take a second look at the chain-of-evidence list."

It made sense.

Cody turned from me and shoved his Glock into Henkel's nose. His voice was flat. "When I came to your house in New Mexico, you were packing up your car. Where were you planning to go?"

Henkel said, "We were going to do the exchange."

"What are you talking about?"

"There was going to be an exchange. A big meeting, where everybody got what they wanted."

Cody slapped him again, and Henkel winced. The cushions were getting dark with lost blood. I could smell it, and it was sharp and metallic and it made me want to gag.

Henkel was fading. His eyelids were starting to drop.

"WHAT EXCHANGE?" Cody screamed.

"The judge was going to get all the photos and the negatives from Coates and me once and for all," Henkel said. "I was going to get my big payoff from the judge. We were going to meet at Coates's place up in the mountains tomorrow morning."

Cody said, "What was Coates going to get?"

Henkel coughed and nearly passed out. He said, "What he said he always wanted—his own little girl."

And at that moment I realized who had sent the photo of Angelina to his associate Malcolm Harris in London—Aubrey Coates. I recalled Moreland taking that photo the morning they came to visit when he went upstairs with Melissa. It was the reason he was so insistent that he see her, and the reason he asked Melissa to turn her over for a better look.

Monday, November 26

The Day After

Twenty-five

THERE WAS SNOW FALLING on I-70 that night as we drove to Desolation Canyon. It had started snowing around midnight and gotten progressively worse. The only vehicles our four-car caravan encountered on the two-hour drive from Denver were snowplows with yellow wigwag lights flashing and the occasional four-wheel-drive pickup. My nerves were shot, and I had trouble keeping coffee down. Cody had made three calls after dropping Henkel in a heap outside the emergency-room doors of Denver General: Sanders, Morales, and Torkleson. Torkleson had responded with a crime scene tech and a team of four SWAT officers in heavy black clothing. Morales and Sanders showed up in Morales's jacked-up four-wheel-drive pickup. Morales brought his wife along to watch over Melissa. Torkleson drove the lead vehicle, with Cody in the passenger seat and me in the backseat.

A panicked thought hit me. "What if they won't do the exchange without Henkel?" *Jesus,* I thought again, *I never should have shot him.*

"Good thinking," Torkleson said, and plucked his mike from the cradle on the dashboard. "I'm switching over to a nonpublic channel," he said as he called the state highway patrol. Locating a trooper he knew, Torkleson persuaded the man to put out a false report about a fiery head-on collision near the New Mexico border, and to identify one of the fatalities as a man named Wyatt Henkel. When the trooper agreed, Torkleson said to Cody and me, "We know Coates listens to police scanners, and if he hears that report, I'm sure he'll relay the info to the judge. That'll explain why he isn't there."

"You're the man," Cody said to Torkleson. "Both Coates and the judge will be happy to hear that Henkel—and his photos—are cooked."

I TRIED to sort out what we'd learned as we drove. Cody seemed to be doing the same thing.

I asked, "How did Coates learn about Angelina in order to pressure the judge for her?"

"I'd wondered that myself," Cody said. "Until I checked on the federal jail roster before the trial and found out that Coates shared a cell for two weeks with a slimeball named José Medina, who was in for trafficking. Medina is a big-shot Sur-13 gangster and a known associate of Garrett's. Garrett probably mentioned to Medina he had this adoption agency hounding him—bragged about it, most likely— and Coates overheard Medina talking about it. That's the kind of thing Coates would pick up on, especially since he had his deal going with the judge already. So he doubled down on his demands of the judge because Moreland had nothing to bargain with: the negatives and photos *and* a little girl of his own in exchange for an acquital."

"It makes me sick," I said.

"No shit," Cody said. "What makes me even sicker is that the judge would go along. Or appear to go along."

"So why did Moreland and Garrett kill Dorrie?" I asked, guessing the answer.

"We'll probably never get a confession out of either of them," Cody said. "But I'm thinking Dorrie couldn't live with her guilt any longer for providing an alibi for John on the night John's parents were run off the road. The more she got to know him, the more she was *convinced* he'd done it—well, it was eating her up inside. She was going to church more, right? Pouring her heart out to God that she was married to a man who'd killed his own parents, and she'd provided the alibi. Maybe she asked John outright if he did it, or maybe he just guessed she wanted to tell somebody. Either way, John knew he had to get rid of her. Plus, he was probably already putting the hardwood to Kellie. So, if you're John Moreland, you have a heavy guilt-ridden wallflower who can bring you down on the one hand and a blond knockout with money on the other. Easy choice for John."

"But why did Garrett finish her off?"

"Because Garrett is a sick, twisted, evil little fuck," Cody said. "Your instincts were right about him. Plus, by helping his dad with the crime, Garrett knew he'd always have a bargaining chip and something to hold over his dad's head. In a way, killing Dorrie set Garrett free."

"And John knew what Garrett was from an early age," I said. "Imagine knowing your son is like that? And just living with it and covering up for him whenever possible. And the judge had to cover up for his son, or Garrett might confess what the both of them had done."

I said, "Jim Doogan told me something at Brian's funeral about men like Moreland. He said once a man likes that gets his eyes on a prize—in this case the U.S. Supreme Court—every move he makes is in preparation for it. I didn't realize what Doogan was saying at the time, and I don't think he did, either. But if you're John Moreland, and you want to be a Supreme, how can you even consider the possibility if your only son is a gangster?"

"Good question," Cody said. "How?"

"You mitigate the situation," I said. "You take in your bad son's illegitimate child and raise her as your own. You show the world that even though your bad-seed son has no responsibility, you do. You clean up the best you can for your son's indiscretion. You turn a negative into a positive. You also know that it's only a matter of time before your crazy-ass son goes down, and you don't have to worry about him anymore. It could have easily happened at the Appaloosa Club the other night. And when it does, you breathe a sigh of relief and go on."

Cody turned and smiled. I could see his teeth in the dark. "You might make a good detective after all, Jack. But there's something wrong with your theory."

"What?"

"Why would John hand over the child to a known pedophile? Aren't people going to find out?"

I thought about that for a while. Then it hit me hard. "Moreland is clever," I said. "Clever enough to figure out a way for Angelina to *disappear* after a short while, maybe even to stage a disappearance or a kidnapping. I could see him making a tearful plea on television to the kidnappers, turning Angelina into a new Lindbergh baby *who is never found.* He'd be a hell of a sympathetic figure. And someday, if a member of the Senate Judiciary Committee has the gall to question him about taking the child from our home all those years ago, he says he felt horrible about it and did all he could to help the young couple adopt another child, but not nearly as horrible as he feels about her fate at the hand of kidnappers and what an outrageous thing to ask! He comes off looking like a tragic saint."

Torkleson whistled, and said, "For the love of Pete."

"Now you're thinking like a Moreland, Jack," Cody said. "Ten steps ahead."

CODY KNEW THE LAYOUT and geography of the canyon because he had planned the raid on Coates months before, but he complained that it looked different in the dark and covered by snow. There was plenty of bitching when he said the only way to move in on the trailer was from behind it on foot because there was only one road into the campground, and we didn't want Coates to see us coming. So we parked on the shoulder of a gravel road on the other side of the mountain from the campground and plunged into the forest to climb. The snow was fluffy and knee deep. There was no wind at all, so the pine boughs sported three or four inches of snow looking like foam on the top of a beer mug. It was impossible to climb through the thick trees without hitting boughs and dumping snow down our necks. We all wore high-topped winter boots. The beams from our headlamps flew around in the trees as we climbed, and it was hallucinogenic, so I tried to keep my head down and concentrate on the trail in front of me. The SWAT guys carried automatic weapons with scopes, and Morales and Sanders had brought their hunting rifles. The .45 was in my parka pocket.

I was sweating hard by the time we reached the top, but my thoughts of Angelina and Melissa and Coates and Moreland propelled me. I finally stopped throwing up when there was nothing left in my stomach.

As we grunted and cursed our way down the other side of the mountain toward Desolation Canyon Campground, the eastern sky started to lighten into a dull, creamy gray. I doubted we would see the sun itself.

CODY GATHERED EVERYONE when it got light enough to see without headlamps. From where I stood, I could see a big opening below me and ahead of me: the empty campground. There were picnic tables stacked high with snow, and steel cooking grates mounted on metal posts. The roads to and from the individual campsites were untracked except from mule deer, as was the access road from the highway. Sheer canyon walls rose on either side, which made it darker than it should be at seven in the morning.

We all stood in the trees breathing hard, flushed from the climb and the descent. Billows of condensation rose from our labored breathing. One good thing about the falling snow was it muffled sounds.

Cody bent over and pointed out Coates's trailer. We could barely see the top of it through the trees a quarter of a mile away. As I'd heard about in the courtroom that day, the aluminum roof bristled with antennae and both satellite television and Internet-access dishes.

Cody and Torkleson debated the approach, and they decided to flank the park with two SWAT officers on each side of the trailer. Torkleson told his men to stay in the trees with clear shooting lanes. Cody reminded them the trailer had a back door as well.

Sanders and Morales agreed to split up, each going with two SWAT officers. Torkleson, Cody, the tech guy with his video camera, and I would move straight down the middle of the trees toward the back of the trailer, where Torkleson would establish a command post to direct traffic.

"Turn your radios down and put your earpieces in," Torkleson told his men. "*Communicate*. Report what you see so we all know. This exchange is supposed to happen at nine, so we have an hour and a half to wait."

"To freeze to death," one of the officers said sourly.

"To save a little girl and put three monsters away," Cody said.

As the men checked their weapons and equipment before splitting off into teams, I thanked each one of them for coming and I shook their hands. I hugged Morales and Sanders, and they hugged me back.

"We're glad we could make it," Sanders said. "We've got to square this thing."

"We'll get her back," Morales said, fire in his eyes.

WE FOUND a small clearing 150 yards from Coates's trailer and stamped the snow down with our boots. It gave us something to do, and the work kept me warm. We were on a steep hillside and could see out over the top of the trailer and the park and the access road. There was a thick U of four-foot-high juniper between us and the trailer to hide behind. Every few minutes Cody would raise his binoculars and study the trailer, watching for movement.

To me, Cody whispered, "I wish we could just go down there and cap the guy, believe me. But we have to do it this way, Jack." He looked up to make sure Torkleson was far enough away that he couldn't hear, and said, "You and I are dirty. We've got to get all these guys involved and let them make the arrest and the case. My name's got to be out of it, and so does yours. Henkel will make the case for them when he testifies. I wish you hadn't have shot him."

"Me too," I whispered back. "Something snapped inside."

"It happens." Cody grinned. I noted the frost on his eyebrows and three-day length of beard.

AT 8:45 we saw headlights coming down the access road into the park.

I couldn't hear what the SWAT team was saying to Torkleson through his earpiece, but Torkleson said, "Yes, we see it. Can anyone get the make?"

He listened, nodded, and turned to us. "A yellow H3 Hummer."

"Garrett's car," I said.

"Showtime," said Cody.

THE H3 WAS MOVING very slowly. It wasn't the snow that was holding it up but caution by the driver. I borrowed Cody's binoculars and tried to see who was inside. The smoked glass made it difficult, but I thought I saw the silhouettes of two heads.

"I still don't get Garrett," I whispered to Cody. "What is it with him? I can't figure him out."

"Psychopath," Cody said. "We may never understand. The kid crushed his mother's head in with a rock while his dad looked on. This is one gene pool that needs to be drained for good."

Realizing the implication of that statement, he said, "Jack, I'm sorry. I didn't mean Angelina, for Christ's sake."

I shook my head. "She's *our* daughter, Cody. She has nothing to do with Garrett."

But I can't lie and say what Cody suggested didn't shake me to my core.

GARRETT'S SUV SLOWED to a stop in front of the trailer. It was close enough I could hear the ratcheting sound of the emergency brake being pulled. I still couldn't see who was inside. They kept it running, and the headlights were still on. If Coates was inside he would have to know they had arrived.

The passenger door opened, and the dome light inside the H3 went on. I raised the binoculars. Garrett driving, the judge in the passenger seat. And between them, covered in blankets in the backseat in a car seat, was Angelina.

My heart filled my mouth. "Screw this! *We've got to go get her.*"

Cody reached out and put a gloved hand on my arm. "Not yet, Jack. At this point they might be able to come up with some kind of lie that explains why they're here. Remember who we're dealing with, Jack. We've got a judge with connections and a known pedophile who has never been to prison. They both know how to work the system. We've got to let this play out so we can get them *cold.*"

The crime-scene tech had set up a tripod and leaned into his camera eyepiece.

"Got 'em?" Torkleson asked.

"Perfect," the tech said.

Torkleson bent his head to the side, listening to his earpiece.

"Coates just opened the front door," he whispered.

The judge climbed out of the vehicle.

"He's having a stare-down with the judge," Torkleson reported. We couldn't see Coates yet because his trailer blocked our view, but I could follow his movements by watching the judge's eyes through my binoculars. Finally, the judge motioned toward the trailer and pointed at his car.

We couldn't see Coates until he approached the H3. He was lightly dressed in some kind of dark one-piece overall suit, and he wore a fur cap. When he bent over to look into the backseat, I could see him rub his hands together and hear him squeal with delight—an inhuman sound that made a shiver rocket up my spine and lodge at the base of my skull. He started to move closer to the car when Moreland blocked him.

"Kill them," I said.

"Wait," Cody cautioned again. "They still haven't done anything yet."

"Cody," my voice rose, "that's my *daughter* down there."

Torkleson looked away, concentrating on what he was hearing through his earpiece. "They're arguing about terms," he said. "The judge doesn't want to hand over the baby before he gets the photos and the negatives."

I could see the judge gesturing at Coates, and Coates crossing his arms and shaking his head. The words got heated, and I could hear shouting but couldn't make out what was being said.

At last, the judge nodded and turned to the car and barked something at Garrett, who was still behind the wheel. Garrett's door flew open, and the boy jumped out into the snow. He walked around the back of the H3 and opened the rear door and leaned in to unbuckle the car seat.

"Don't fucking touch her," I said.

"I can't believe he brought her," Cody mumbled.

Garrett freed the seat and swung the carry handle up. With one hand, he carried the seat away from the car and placed it in the snow between the judge and Coates. I raised the binoculars to my eyes so hard the eyepieces hit me in the forehead. I focused in on the car seat. She was covered in the same blanket the deputy had brought with her to our house. I couldn't see her face. I imagined that her dark eyes glistened and her mouth was screwed up and she would begin to cry, not knowing where she was.

"Behold, the exchange," Cody said, as Coates reached into his clothing and withdrew an envelope. He squatted and stuck it into the snow near the car seat.

"Hold it," I said, my panic rising. "*There's something screwy here. It's the wrong kind of seat*," I said, and felt Cody and Torkleson look at me, puzzled. "I've helped her in and out of car seats so many times I know for a fact that Angelina outgrew an infant seat like that months ago."

I swung the binoculars over to Garrett. He had walked back to his car and was leaning against the grille, watching both men, smiling at how childish they looked negotiating terms.

The judge grabbed the envelope and tore it open. He rifled through what was inside several times. When Coates made a move to reach for the car seat, the judge warned him off until he was through. Apparently satisfied after a few moments, he nodded to Coates, who took a step forward to pick her up. I saw the judge mouth "no" and lift it himself to hand it over.

Then the judge raised the seat with one hand, using the other to tuck the blankets around Angelina. As Coates reached for the seat with a leer on his face, the judge seemed to shove it at him, one hand on the handle and the other in the blankets. Suddenly, the back of the seat blew open and there was a sharp *pop* and the snow from a thousand pine boughs across the face of the mountain dropped to the earth in a smoky white cascade.

Coates fell back, his arms outstretched.

Ripping out his earpiece, Torkleson screamed into his handheld, "Who the fuck did that?"

"Not me," Morales shouted. "It wasn't one of us, I don't think."

Cody and I flew through the brush we'd been hiding behind toward the trailer. A pine branch slapped me in the face and took my hat, and we were scrambling down the hillside in the deep snow. I could see two officers emerging from the trees on the right side of the trailer, hollering to Garrett and the judge to freeze.

Running, falling, a mouthful of snow and pine needles, back on my feet, Cody in front of me with his gun drawn.

Shouting from everywhere.

We ran around from the back of the trailer to where the judge and Garrett stood. The cops from both sides of the canyon were out of the trees now; so were Sanders and Morales, with their hunting rifles. The H3 and the father and son were surrounded.

Judge Moreland saw cops on both sides of him and raised the car seat in front of him so if anyone took a shot at him it would need to pass through it to hit him. His expression wasn't scared, or angry, but calculating.

"Thank God you got here, Officers," the judge said in the tone he used from the bench. "My son and I have a permit and we were up here trying to find a good Christmas tree, but we got lost. I realized we'd stumbled on Aubrey Coates . . ." And then he noticed Cody and me and he lost his train of thought and his ridiculous words tailed off.

I drew the .45, cocked it, and said, "Hand over that car seat and the gun in it or I'll kill you a thousand times."

I could see in his face that he was considering keeping it, using the seat as a shield.

"Drop the seat and the gun and hand over the negatives, Judge," Cody said, his weapon down along his thigh. "We've got Wyatt Henkel singing like a bird, and we've got the exchange on tape. You're fucked, so cooperate or die."

"Maybe you didn't hear me," the judge said, glaring at Cody and me with the righteousness of a true liar, "my son and I were going to cut down a Christmas tree . . ."

Cody laughed at him. "You don't understand, Judge. The camera's off. What happens now is your word against eight officers of the law and the father of the child you took."

That's when Coates moaned and thrashed in the snow.

"Son of a bitch," Cody said, wheeling. "I thought he was dead." And he raised the Glock and fired four times point-blank into Coates, who went still. That froze everyone. Cody dug into his parka and pulled out a nondescript revolver and flipped it at the body.

"This is why I always carry a throw-down," he said to Moreland.

The judge looked to Torkleson, who huffed and puffed his way from around the back of the trailer. "Aren't you going to arrest him? Didn't you all just see what he did?"

No one said a word. The judge lowered the smoking car seat into the snow. The blankets fell away to reveal a life-size baby doll. The large-caliber revolver lay across the doll's thighs.

Cody squared off, facing the judge. "Who's next? You," he said, then nodding toward Garrett, "or the fruit of your loins?"

Out of the corner of my eye I saw Garrett bolt for his father's gun. Before any of the cops could tackle him, I raised the .45 and shot him. I tried for his chest, but I hit him in the stomach, and he doubled over and sat back in the snow, holding his belly.

"Freeze," I said.

"You're supposed to do that the other way around," Cody said.

"I'm not a cop."

Garrett burned two holes in me with hate-filled eyes. "Aw, you don't really want her," he said. "She comes from me and him, don't forget. She's missing the same part I am. You'll see."

I shot him in the head, and he flopped back, his blood steaming and stinking and staining the snow. In my mind I severed the con-nection between Garrett Moreland and Angelina. Forever.

Torkleson stepped between the judge and me, and said, "That'll be enough, gentlemen." He gently took the gun out of my hand and slipped it into his jacket pocket. From the other pocket he drew a nickel-plated semiauto and tossed it at Garrett's body. To the judge, Torkleson said, "Too bad. He had such promise. He could have been a great gangster."

To his men and Deputies Sanders and Morales, he said, "We all saw the same thing, right, Officers? Both Coates and the boy here pulled weapons and were killed. And we'll all testify to that, my brothers?"

One by one everyone agreed. Morales wept with joy and dropped to his knees. Sanders stepped over and put a gloved hand on his part-ner's shoulder.

"But that's not true," Moreland cried. "I killed a known pe-dophile in self-defense! You all saw that, right?"

"Ha," Cody said, picking up the revolver from the car seat and sticking it into his belt. "I was wondering where my lost piece was. Now I've found it."

Canon City,
Colorado

Tuesday, November 18

A Year After

Twenty-six

I WAS CONVICTED OF AGGRAVATED Assault with a Deadly Weapon for shooting Wyatt Henkel and was sentenced to one to three years in the Colorado State Penitentiary in, of all places, Canon City. The original charge had been for a class two felony, which could have been eight to twenty-four years, but the DA was sympathetic and knocked it down to a class five. The judge, also sympathetic, had no problem with that. When he sentenced me I said, "Thank you, Your Honor," but not because of the reduction. I said thank you because I deserved to go to prison, and I wouldn't have been able to live with myself for the things I'd done unless I did. I was also thankful that the worst of my actions were never discovered by the DA.

The judge said he'd write a letter to the parole board urging early release, but he said I should be prepared to serve a year. How does one prepare for that?

———

SO NOW I WEAR an orange jumpsuit and laceless boat shoes and every article of clothing I have is stenciled with CDOC—COLORADO DEPARTMENT OF CORRECTIONS.

The food is tolerable, but the scenery outside—when I can see it—is pretty nice. My Rocky Mountains are still there, although they're the southern Colorado version, and they aren't snowcapped. But they're with me, always, to the west, framing my days and nights and stretching all the way to Montana.

I'm in the general population. The guards protect me because they, like the judge and DA, are sympathetic. I've never asked them for favors, but they give them. I have my own cell with a bed, a washstand and a toilet, books, and this laptop computer. There are books in the library and decent medical care. I'm pleasant but not friendly with all the rest of the population. The only time I see the truly dangerous inmates is across the room at mealtimes.

YES, I'VE SEEN JOHN Moreland. Five times, to be exact. He saw me too, even though he pretended he didn't. Moreland wears a white jumpsuit, meaning he's on death row. All of us avoid the guys in white, and the corrections officers segregate them from us.

The judge was convicted in the trial some of you followed on truTV and the cable channels. Despite his investment in household names like Bertram Ludik as his defense attorneys and his earnest testimony—where he claimed both Aubrey Coates and his son Garrett were murdered in cold blood during a botched raid on the pedophile's residence that he mistakenly blundered into while looking for a perfect Christmas tree—the jury convicted him for murder in the first degree for killing Dorrie. Those four photos I first saw in my living room are among the most recognized images in America among those who follow murder trials, I've read. They were even printed in *People* magazine. Despite the photos and Henkel's testimony, John

Moreland has never admitted to either the murder of his parents or of his wife. He claims he was railroaded by rogue cops. He also insists it was he who shot Aubrey Coates, not the police.

During the trial, all of the officers who were there in Desolation Canyon that morning contradicted his allegation. One by one they told a version of events different from Moreland's. Why?

Because Cody, perhaps inspired by the judge himself, was thinking ahead. He knew that in prison, the lowest of the low was a child molester—considered even worse than a snitch. It was open season on child molesters, and even the guards looked the other way. In this case, the inmate was a judge who tried to aid a molester by letting him walk. Moreland is an ADSEG—Administrative Segregation. Despite that designation, I've heard he's been attacked several times, beaten, raped, and stabbed. I wonder if Dorrie's ghost approves. Maybe she has enough faith to forgive him. But I don't.

I sent him a note, via the guards. It read: I'M GETTING OUT IN A YEAR. HOW ABOUT YOU? MELISSA SENDS HER RE-GARDS.

There was no reply.

KELLIE MORELAND WAS INVESTIGATED and quickly cleared of being an accessory to her husband and her evil stepson's crimes. She claimed she was shocked and angry when John showed up that Sunday with a nine-month-old and announced she was now a part of their family. Kellie told police she accused him of ruining her life and in a quote compared to Butterfly McQueen in *Gone with the Wind,* said, "I know nothing about toddlers. Nothing." She said she fed Angelina grapes and toast and cried. When the police showed up the next morning with Melissa, she opened the door with Angelina in her arms and enthusiastically handed the baby to her mother.

———

MELISSA AND ANGELINA come to see me every Saturday. Angelina is a chatterbox. She's still beautiful and charismatic. I must admit that each time I see her, I look for anything in her behavior or demeanor that would suggest what Garrett said or Cody inadvertently hinted about her was true. I've never told Melissa what either said, and I never will. But when I look at Angelina and play with her, I find a bright, loving, busy little girl. I see nothing that suggests Garrett was right. Nothing.

I've come to realize something that for three weeks of my life I'd begun to doubt: There are good people in the world. Good people, kind people. I think of Cody, Brian, Torkleson, Sanders, Morales, the SWAT team, my lawyers, the guards, the judge who sentenced me. They all could have chosen to be cold, cruel, indifferent. That would have been easy. Brutality, I think, comes naturally to human beings. But they chose to be good, even if what they did could be questioned within the strict confines of the law. I am not cynical.

But I am pragmatic. I know anyone is capable of anything, including me. It's a fine line between good and evil and, given the situation, the line moves. Oh, how it moves. It moved for me, but I still managed to cross it—repeatedly. And I've learned that once you cross it, bad acts become more effortless to commit because the moral restraints have loosened, and justifications cushion the implications of the crime. It becomes effortless to set things in motion, then stand by and let them happen, which is what I did. Effortless.

Which is why I'm here and why I should be.

And this is what I'll teach my daughter.

MELISSA IS WORKING FOR the Adam's Mark Hotel as general manager. They live in a condo on the fringe of downtown Denver because we had to sell the house without my income. Melissa insists the condo is perfect and she's shown me photos of it and it looks nice. The only thing she regrets, she insists, is that I'm in here and Angelina is in day care every day.

I guess we both have our keepers.

MY PARENTS DROVE all the way down from Montana to see me. I could tell by the way they entered the room they were as embarrassed as hell. I was embarrassed for them because I knew the security procedures probably set them back. I don't think my dad has ever walked a step in his life without his Leatherman tool, and my mother had to confess she had wire in her bra. As they sat at the table in the gen-pop visiting room, they held hands—the first time I'd ever seen them do that. I became fixated on their hands because they were so rough and knobby—the hands of hard workers—in a place where the supposedly tough guys had soft and smooth hands. My dad joked that he always thought I'd wind up in a place like this once I left the ranch, and my mom scolded him for saying that but didn't disagree.

"That was nice when you stopped by," she said. "I hope you'll do that more often."

"For Christ's sake," Dad said to her. "He's in prison!"

"But he won't always be," she said, turning red.

I promised to come visit. I told them it wouldn't be that long.

My dad said, "Good, I got fence to fix."

My mom said, "And I've got pies!"

CODY IS BACK in Montana, splitting his time between working as a detective in the Helena Police Department and helping my dad out on the ranch. He says he's happy, and I believe him. He has a steady girl and says he wants to bring her to Colorado to meet us. He's come to see me a few times when he drives south to visit his son, Justin. He urges me to move back to Montana when I'm released. I'm considering it, although there are no Adam's Mark Hotels in Montana.

Obviously, I've a lot of time on my hands to think about everything that happened during those three weeks. Some things became clearer in retrospect. I confirmed them during a conversation with Cody when he visited.

"You never really told Jeter to back off when we were in Montana, did you?" I asked.

He hesitated, looked around, struck a match to light a cigarette under a sign that read ABSOLUTELY NO SMOKING. "No."

"Why did you mislead us?"

"Had to. You and Melissa got cold feet, Jack. You couldn't pull the trigger because you've got scruples. I don't have that problem. I knew we needed Jeter to force the issue and maybe take out Garrett. So when I went back into Jeter's, I asked him if I could use the bathroom and wished him good luck in Denver."

"That's why you were on the scene so fast after the incident in the Appaloosa," I said.

He nodded. "I was down the street. I wished I could have prevented you from following Jeter into that place. I had no idea you'd be that stupid."

Then he winked.

OH, AND ONE MORE thing. An amazing thing, a miracle. Melissa is seven months pregnant. The night of conception was our last night together before I went to prison. For once, I guess I had a live round in the chamber.

When I get out, we will have a daughter and a son. I wonder what our son will be like. I can't wait to find out. We've already decided his name, a long one. Cody Brian Torkleson Sanders Morales McGuane. After his uncles.